Granite Grit

By
Lee Cooper

To Elizabeth

from The fighter writer

Dedicated to
My Mother, Grandmother, and friend Leigh
Henderson.

Parents are not to be put to death for their children, nor children put to death for their parents; each will die for their own sin.

Deuteronomy 24:16

Only a man who knows what it is like
to be defeated
Can reach down to the bottom of his soul
And come up with the extra ounce
of power it takes to win
when the match is even.

Muhammad Ali.

Chapter 1

The Beginning of the End:

Standing in this run-down, retired shipyard building on the banks of the Clyde, a desolate part of Glasgow, staring down at the palms of my shaking hands wondering what my fists had turned me into. Wondering how I let things escalate this far.

Across from me was a beast, a monster like no other I had seen, a modern day Barbarian only interested in seeing me defeated, lying in a puddle of my own blood and piss. A man that had no mercy and had destroyed everyone he had faced. He earned his reputation as the hardest man with two fists in the country.

The nonchalant look as he stared me down across the circle of thugs and gangsters was one I had never seen, no signs of weakness. Instead, a burning fire of hatred for life, hidden beneath intense, intimidating eyes. The doubts were racing around my head like never before, where will I be after this is all over? Will I get through this?

But this was no time to reflect. I had to stay focused on the task at hand, or I'd be lifted off this cold concrete floor in a body bag.

It was the money, or so I kept telling myself, but to be truthful, I was hooked on the game. The buzz of the crowd, the feeling of tearing your opponent apart, the pure adrenaline you get when you swap punches, and of course the sight of your foe lying on the floor partially paralysed. The cash handed to you after victory was secondary to the real reason I stood in this building.

The countdown was on. Five minutes to go.

There was going to be a duel between two warriors that no one in this crowd of peasants had seen before and a battle no one in this room will forget. My hands began to feel clammy with sweat and my legs started to shake with fear. All this was hidden on the inside, but on the outside, the only feeling that was projected from my face and pumped-up frame, was the need to see The Reaper broken down, in pain, bloodied, bruised and begging for his life.

I was the main man. The top dog. Not him. He was just some cunt in the way of me becoming the hardest in the country. I had come too far, gave up everything. Lost the love of my life and my two kids, to let this degenerate Liverpool faggot beat me.

Time was ticking and I could smell his blood, I could picture me smashing his head off the concrete floor. He gave another stare from across the room. He looked as pumped as I did, standing a few inches taller than me and every bit of his body ripped with muscle. His arms were bulging, his stomach, body and back were all ripped, with a set of traps on him that made seeing his neck difficult.

His physique and the look of hatred in his eyes made him spine-chillingly evil to face. His two sidekicks looked as if they were giving him his last pep talk. That wasn't going to help him, no pep talk was going to stop me fucking him up and sending him in a taxi to the morgue.

I took my eyes off his, turned my back and gave myself a final word, as the memory of my murdered mate ran through my head.

Things went unusually dead in the room, as if the crowd were awaiting the start of a hundred metre race. Everybody knew what they were about to witness, they knew history in the underworld was about to happen. I briefly felt a shiver up my spine and the strangest feeling I had been here before, or maybe this was my destiny?

A shout of a minute to go came. This was it. The time had come to dethrone this cunt and separate his head from his body. My heart beating like a mad man, the adrenaline kicked into overdrive and my blood pumped through my veins with fear, my breath heavy in anger and anticipation of the first exchange of fists.

Tim, one of a few friends I had left that didn't fear me, turned and fixed his stare into my eyes, nodding his head. "You fucking ready for this, Joe?"

"Born ready, my friend."

"Last-man-standing, no fucking mercy, or you'll be a dead man."

"There will be none!" I answered, no sign of remorse for what I had to do. Or, what he might do to me.

"No guts! No glory!" Tim grunted from the depths of his throat.

"Let's get the show on the road." The so-called ref in the middle of me and The Reaper shouted.

Tim took a step back, still looking me with overwhelming uncertainty and anxiety written over his face, as if this could be the last time we exchange words.

I turned around, stepped towards The Reaper, leaving all doubt behind, ready to fight for my right to exist. As The Reaper did the same, our eyes locked, glaring at each other like a couple of battle-hardened warriors.

We met in the middle…

Chapter 2

Stuck in a Rut, 2014:

Living in a prosperous town in the North East of Scotland called Inverurie, with a population of roughly eleven thousand, my life was like any typical family man. A clique wee place where rumours grew legs and limbs, making their way from one side of town to the other.

The place had the usual scuffles outside the pubs during the weekends, the usual alkies every town acquires, propping up the bars in their local boozers. Tearaway youths and twenty somethings binging on coke and illegal highs like MCAT, going wild at the weekends.

Having a football team in the Highland League, Inverurie Loco Works, gave the families of the town something to cheer at the weekends. An excellent school system and plenty for the kids to keep them occupied.

Overall, a better place to bring up a family than Tilly.

Things were tough at the time. I was skint, the family was skint. It wasn't always like this though. Only in the recent months after losing my job at the Paper Mill in January, that things started to go downhill.

The Mill went bust resulting in three hundred and twelve workers losing their livelihoods. The company called us to a meeting out of the blue, and that was it, the Mill had to close. I didn't know the ins and outs of the finance part of the shutdown but I know this, it left us with nothing. Everyone was in the same boat, devastated.

Sacked without any kind of redundancy because the company went bankrupt. A lot of empty pockets hovered around town at that time, leaving the town in a big hole. The Mill was the main source of income for the many of families in the area. I'd been there since leaving school and it left me with nothing.

All the years of breaking my back, keeping up with my jobs and taking orders from arrogant arseholes that thought they were big dicks because they'd been placed into a supervisor's role, was all for nothing in my eyes. My loyalty to the place was not to be rewarded.

I was content with the routine, job and life in general. It paid me to raise a wonderful family and keep a house. But that all changed rapidly in the next two years. We had savings, but it was never going to last long with the cost of living getting higher and higher. Where was I going to get another job? I didn't have any skills or any kind of trade.

I missed out on getting involved in the oil industry that thrived around Aberdeen and the surrounding areas and the money that went with it. It would cost an arm and a leg to get survival and medical certificates now, and I didn't have that cash.

Making it even more challenging to get a job was the fact I didn't drive. There wasn't any need growing up and I didn't need a car to get back and forth to work when I stayed in Aberdeen, catching a lift from a workmate that shared the same shift. Then living in Inverurie, I cycled to work. A driver's licence was a waste of money to me. The cash it would take to get a car on the road nowadays was outrageous. We would never be able to afford that.

For the next six months after losing my job, I sank further into the normal life of an unemployed man, picking up the role of house-husband which definitely didn't suit. I made every effort to pick up another job here, but with three hundred people all chasing new employment at the same time, it made it almost impossible.

There was a recycling plant nearby, three positions were advertised. I applied but so did countless others. It was just luck of the draw that would claim you a job. Forty people got interviews with three chosen, probably because they knew the right person in the right place.

It's who you know rather than what you know.

After three months, the savings started to dry up and the bills started to pile up. May, my wife of eight years, had been hassling me since getting paid-off to apply for welfare, but being as stubborn as shit, I wouldn't do it. A man that has to sign on to support his family wasn't something to be proud of. But running out of options, I had no choice in the end eventually, signing on and receiving my entitlement of £155 a week.

May had a part - time job in the local corner shop. Worked twenty hours a week paying next to minimum wage, £135. The combination of these two things were never going to pay the mortgage and mounting bills every month, plus keep food on the table and clothes on the kids back. But, as little as it paid, we were very thankful that May had this job.

The constant hunt for work was frustrating, getting pessimistic and passive about my situation.

When you're out of work for a while, stuck in a rut, it can drain your desire and enthusiasm for life, which had a knock on effect. Most days I was left to handle the kids and tackle the household chores.

When there wasn't anything else to do, lazing around watching the pish daytime TV was routine. When I could be bothered, weights or hitting the boxing bag would keep me busy.

Working in the Mill since I left school at the age of sixteen was almost all I knew, well I say almost because…

Chapter 3

Boxing as a Teen:

I was a fighter at heart.

My entire life, fighting in some form or other, followed me around like an unwelcome shadow. Witnessing punches being thrown in anger, right back to my first memories. My old man introduced me to violence from an early age along with boxing at the age of fourteen to 'toughen me up.' It soon became obvious I held a talent for it.

By the time I reached eighteen, I had developed into a five foot ten beast of a man. I was battle hardened and living under my father's reputation. Having all I needed at my feet to become a well-known face in the boxing world. Dedicated, hardworking, with a head like granite, broad shouldered, good tempered, muscles ripped and hardened with the constant years of hard training, never showing an ounce of fat, fighting around eighty-five/seven kilos in the cruiserweight category.

As a teen, I had sun-streaked, curled blonde hair, flowing down past my ears and into my eyes. At times I couldn't be arsed getting a cut, but always kept a smooth chin, carrying a smashed-up nose that came from countless breaks. Bright blue-green eyes that came from being fit and healthy, although quite often had shades of black and purple surrounding them. I kept myself well-dressed outside the gym as there was never a money shortage growing up.

The other kids were quite jealous of the labels I wore. Tilly wasn't exactly the catwalk of fashion.

I quit boxing at twenty-three because I made the classic mistake that any good coach would tell you not to do. 'Don't fall in love, or your career will go down the shitter.'

I'd had my fair share of amateur fights by that time, guessing around fifty. I never kept a good log of them. To be honest, once Junior, our first kid was on the way, that signaled the end of my boxing career, didn't want him growing up around any kind of violence after my own childhood of horror.

Guys in the boxing game used to say I had a promising future, could've had it all, but I wasn't interested.

Now thirty-two, patches of frosty-grey growing through my clean cut hair and lazy-cut stubble, I had developed a slight overhang in the belly department, and I was getting older and slower, my enthusiasm for life also getting grey.

Being a lot heavier too, maybe around the hundred kilo mark, I couldn't tell to be exact as after the boxing finished, the scales were the first thing to go. They were your enemy as a fighter, going through the constant battle to hit target weight. Once retired, they were the first thing I binned.

I never wanted to stop boxing, but a violence-free life for my kids is what I yearned for. If I was to get any kind of crazy injuries that could put me on the sick from work, I wouldn't be able to afford to look after my wife and kids the way they deserved.

My sole important thing in life was to keep a roof over their heads, clothes on their back, grub on the table and love in their hearts. Protect them, idolize them, and be with them through heartache and hardship. Strangely, that is exactly the reason I travelled down the wrong path, to keep money coming in again. I'd been employed for the last sixteen years and it got me nowhere. I didn't take the piss at work, only ever took my due breaks, was never late and never took a sick day. The only time I had taken off was the days my children were born, the short time I required off to look after May in her time of need and the ten week spell after my poor mother committed suicide.

A model employee as they say, but look at me now, totally skint, not able to provide for my family. Not able to buy any luxuries for May or the kids. Not able to take the kids on holiday or even go out to enjoy a meal.

The whole situation really started to piss me off and it had to change.

Chapter 4

Strange Turn:

Things took a strange turn one late Indian summer's night around eight o'clock. The sun beaming down over the red cloud-line and the air fresh. Taking advantage of the fine night, I went out jogging, the streets quiet enough at this time for some solitude. Jogging the odd night was a great way to get out of the house to clear my head of all the stress and worries hounding me from the ever increasing bill stack in the top drawer.

Quite a long run, around four and a half miles, which would take me about forty-five minutes. A good amount of time to be out the house, the longer the better. The fresh air and time on my own was therapeutic.

I worried so much, not knowing how we would be able to pay the mortgage and bills in the coming months. The £155 welfare went into the bank each week along with May's £135, but it just wasn't enough for us. The savings now gone. Our pot was empty.

My jog took me round the outskirts of Inverurie via the dual carriageway, returning over the river Don bridge heading back into town and toward my house. This bridge was the main road in and out of the place towards Aberdeen. Passing the bridge and listening to Oasis 'Morning Glory' blasting in my ears, I vaguely made out somebody shouting at me.

"Joe! Wait! JOE!"

I stopped on the pavement, removed my earphones and turned around looking to see who the Hell was shouting. A silver Mercedes was doing a U-turn in the middle of the road, redirecting straight towards me, as I stood silent on the pavement. As the car approached, I still couldn't figure out who it was with the low sun blinding me. The car pulled up beside me, the window rolled down, and I then instantly knew exactly who it was. My old boxing pal Tim! I started to grin, happy to see my old friend again after all these years.

"Well, well, if it isn't the famous Joe Marks!"

"Jesus Christ. Is that really you, Tim?" Taken totally by surprise. I hadn't seen this guy for years.

"The one and only! How's tricks?"

"Just grand, mate. How's life treating you?"

"Aye fine, lad."

"Still boxing?" Curious to know what he was up to nowadays.

"No, not fighting any more. Just doing the coaching side of things at the Kilgour Club. What about you? When's the last time you threw some leather?"

"Ooh, Jesus. It's been about 8 or 9 years since I've been in a gym. Kilgour club?"

"Aye, in Tilly. It belongs to a pal of mine now."

"My old gym! What happened to Stevenson?"

"Aye, that's right. No idea about Tommy, retired, moved on, I suppose."

"Jesus, that brings back some old memories. What you doing through these parts on a Wednesday night?" I asked.

"Visiting my Gran, she's in the Garioch care home." Tim replied with a sigh.

"Where you staying now? Manor Avenue in Aberdeen still?"

"Na. Got myself out of there when the wife started to show a bump. Didn't want my kids growing up in a place like that. I've got a place in Kingswells now, just outside town. It's a lot quieter there."

"Aye, you're right, mate. That's why we moved out here from Tilly, get away from the kind of life I had there."

"Hey, how about coming to the gym one night, have a little work-out, then we'll get a proper catch up? Judging by the size of your gut, you need it." Said Tim with a smirk.

"I'd love to, but I don't have any way of getting there and back."

"I'll take you! I'll visit my Gran beforehand, then I'll pick you up afterwards. There's a guy I know at the gym who could give you a lift home. He stays around here somewhere."

"Give me your number 'en, and I'll give you a shout. I'll have to clear it with the wife first, you know what women are like, eh? Could be doing with something to do like, been out of work for a while and bored out my tits."

Tim wrote his number on a receipt and handed it over. "You're still wi' that gorgeous May, are you?"

"Of course mate, married wi' a couple sprogs. Have you just the one?"

"I wish. Twin boys and they're a fuckin' handful."

"Bet they are. Tim, it's been great to chat but I'd better finish this run before the old legs seize up. I'll call you, alright?"

"Sure, no worries Joe, nice to see you. Catch you later."

Tim rolled up his window and sped away in his flashy silver Mercedes C63 AMG, with the twin exhaust roaring through the big engine.
I hadn't seen him since ending my boxing career nine years ago.

He was a tall gangly guy around six foot two, wide, bony shoulders, gnarly fingers on the end of long snarly arms, with more muscle in his elbow than his bicep. His face hadn't changed, thin and gaunt with high cheekbones, a bony jaw usually coated in stubble and a ruffled head of shabby hair that hadn't seen the use of a comb in years.

He slogged around slowly but not sloth-like, never appeared to have a worry in the world as he scraped his knuckles across the deck like an orang-utan.

Nothing would phase Tim, wise beyond his years and had been since we were young tearaways. Back in the day we did a lot of training together, competing at the same weight, but fortunately we never had to fight each other, only spar. We didn't want to fight, we were too close.

He was in an awkward category of boxer, limber with long arms, feet moving quicker than his hands and brains. He's the kind that would drive me insane inside the ropes. The constant game of chase was similar to trying to catch the Roadrunner, once you thought you had the clever cunt stuck in the corner or up against the ropes, he would slip away like a mongoose slips a snake. Just as your brain registered where he had slipped to, that's when he would lay his counter-attack, leaving you weary and confused.

19

We knew each other too well, in and out of the ring. When sparring, we knew what each other had planned almost before we knew ourselves. Sharing countless rounds together, we were like two lost brothers brought together over the love of throwing leather.

Our two coaches constantly got us together for sparring and training sessions when we had upcoming bouts. He fought for a club in the centre of town called Aberdeen City Boxing Club and I fought for the Drones Club, now renamed to Kilgours. It was good to see the guy after all these years.

Finishing my jog, the memories flowed back, giving a much needed spring to my steps.

Chapter 5

The House and Home:

Our house was located on the outskirts of Inverurie in a fairly new scheme, the perfect place to bring up kids, with the only traffic being from residents.

The houses were freshly up ten years ago, the area kept clean and still looked in great nick. The neighbours were OK, noisy bastards at times, but the whole town was and of course everyone wanted to know your business. I had learned that from working at the Mill all those years. My only advantage in the early years, I stayed in Aberdeen away from all the gossip.

Lots of families lived around the cul-de-sac and our two young ones were always playing with the neighbour's kids, out in the gardens or in their homes. We had a three-bedroom detached house at the end of the street, painted a creamy colour, with a short drive and a garage.

I arrived home a bit later than normal after the chance meeting with Tim. I kicked the muck off my trainers before heading in. Entering our house, the natural wood-look staircase was on the right, the striped brown and grey papered hall led to the kitchen, with the entrance to the living room on the left through the glossy varnished doors.

As soon I got through the door, my youngest, Jess, ran to me, gripping my leg with a cuddle. She was four and attending pre-school. A total cutie with bright, shiny, loose blonde hair flowing down her shoulders and bottle-green eyes she inherited from me. The rest of her flawless looks inherited from her mother, making her a little darling.

"Daddy, was you out running again?" She asked in a squeaky high pitch, looking up at me with her dreamy eyes.

"Yes, hon. Daddy was running again. Have you had your supper yet?"

"No, not yet. Mummy's making spaghetti."

"Ooh, great. Be a good girl, get yourself cleaned up and tell your brother, wherever he is, to do the same."

She paused and thought about it, trying to weigh up if playing with her doll was more important.
"OK daddy, I'll go wash my hands and tell Junior." She climbed up the stairs, using her hands for support, shouting "Junior! Supper! Get ready!" Right bossy little madam she was.

They were both great kids, but Jess in particular was so well behaved.

I wandered through to the kitchen where May was setting the table, looking gorgeous as usual. A perfect, slender figure, even after two kids and at the age of thirty two, and five foot five. Wavy black hair curved at the base of her neck, dreamy chestnut eyes, and olive skin, darker than the usual Scottish woman. The woman of any man's dreams. The only word I could use to describe her was majestic. I counted myself blessed every day I woke in her arms. She could make any man turn his head to take a second look. I was lucky to have her, considering I wasn't that much of a looker with my smashed up nose and scruffy appearance. Somehow, May must have seen the good in me.

"Hi, good looking, what's cooking?" I asked, smiling.

"Spaghetti and meatballs. Hungry?"

"Bet your ass am hungry, after that run. I'll get these sweaty clothes off, and grab a quick shower."

Showering, I prepared myself to ask the question, but the truth was I intended on going to Kilgours with Tim, with or without her permission.

We all sat down at the solid wood dining-table in the middle of the kitchen, a compact room once everyone was seated. May insisted we have supper every night at the table to generate the 'family feeling' as she put it. Her cooking was equal to her beauty. Everything she made I ate with enjoyment over the past 13 years.

With the kids sat down, we all started to eat. The kids were always well behaved at the dinner table, or anywhere really. That was down to May's natural mothering, so patient. I had never heard her raise her voice to them, and she didn't need to.

I sat carefully priming myself to ask the question on my mind and failing a couple of times, already knowing she hated the word boxing.

I decided I'd get the kids out the way first. At the end of our meal, I asked my seven year-old, Junior, to clean up.

Just as well behaved as Jess, but as he was getting older, a little bit of cheek was setting in. His chestnut eyes inherited from his mother were beginning to glint smugly, a know-it-all, the same smarty-pants every kid is at that age, but we were all young once. Being slightly taller than the average kid his age, I thought he would probably grow into a big strapping lad like his old man. Quite a looker, he was already attracting the attention of the girls in the playground. He would break some hearts in the future. And, he was gifted at getting his own way, especially with his mother.

"Son, could you clean up the dishes when we're done, please?"

"But Dad, I've never had to do that before!"

"I know, but as you get older you have to help your parents out around the house like I had to when I was younger." Actually I meant parent.

"Can I get ice-cream if I do?" Asking in a 'You help me and I'll help you' kind of way. He wasn't stupid this one, learning the same old manipulating routine we all did.

"Just do it son, and don't argue. Arguing is for spoiled people and if you want ice-cream, ask your mother." I said and slid the decision over the table to May.

"Well, if you do a good job with the dishes, I guess I could let you have some. And Jess, too." May tilted her head at Jess, lovingly.

"Mummy, am not going to say no to ice-cream, silly." She squealed in that cute little way of talking that would melt the hardest hearts. We all chuckled around the table. She was a little diamond, she was.

With the kids sitting at the table, murdering their plates of Mackie's ice-cream, I turned my attention to May, leading her through to the living room, sitting her down on the sofa and cuddled into her. The room toasty, with the free-standing gas fire burning for the past hour.

"May, I have something to ask you?" Saying slowly, with a hint of dread in my voice.

"I don't like the sound of this, Joseph." Joseph, only said when she didn't care for my manner. It wasn't even my real name, she just did it to let me know she was pissed-off.

"No, it's nothing bad. I bumped into Tim the night when I was out jogging. You remember him?"

"The guy you trained with all the time?" She said, pretending to be stupid, but May knew exactly who he was.

"Aye, that's the one. We had a good chat at the side of the road, and he asked if I fancied going back to boxing, and I do May. Am so fuckin' sick of this house-husband shit. It's making me depressed."

"Joe, we're skint. How the Hell can we afford that? And I never liked that Tim guy. He always seemed a bit dodgy to me."

"Look, it won't cost anything, May. Tim's picking me up and as he's coaching now, he won't charge me anything, am sure. And I know he doesn't exactly stay on the right side of the law, but he was just trying to make a few quid, like all of us. Besides he's got a family now, so he's probably a changed man." I kept my speech polite, trying to butter her up.

"Well, I know, not working and sitting around the house all day is getting you down, so I'm not going to stop you. Besides, I know you, Joe. You'll go anyway with or without my permission." May spoke proper for the area, she was brought up that way.

"Thanks. Sometimes I wonder what I've done to deserve you."

"It's probably something to do with your big heart." She placed the palm of her hand on my heart and looked lovingly into my eyes. "You always do right by us and you know, there's a tiny piece of me that loves you." She muttered, sarcastic but affectionate.

"Haha, cheeky. I love you, too."

I moved in and gave her a slow kiss, gazing back into those eyes and said "Thanks, you're the best, babe."

As soon as the conversation finished, I grabbed my phone, gave Tim a call, and asked him to pick me up. He would be coming back into town next Tuesday to visit his Gran, and would pick me up around 6.30pm.

Jesus it was only Wednesday! I'd have to wait a whole week. Like a young excited schoolboy, it was sure to drag, but for the first time in ages, I had something to look forward to.

The coming week, I carried on doing my usual daily routine of waking the kids for pre and primary school, getting them dressed, fed, and then walking them to school. Always letting May sleep in a little in the morning, because her part-time job didn't start until 11 in the corner shop not far from us.

Right around the time she got pregnant, May had a horrifying, life-changing experience working in A&E in Aberdeen Royal. Her best friend Amanda, someone she'd shared countless memories with since primary school, was in a horrific car crash on the A90, colliding head-on into the back of an articulated lorry. The impact smashed her rib cage, causing a massive lung puncture. It was at nine o'clock, Saturday night, an hour into May's shift. The ambulance got stuck in the traffic caused by the accident, as it tried to race its way to the hospital. Amanda's left lung needed surgery. The medics only just managed to keep her alive. Arriving at the hospital, Amanda was rushed into the operating theatre, May by her side. Then, her second lung collapsed and along with internal bleeding from her injuries, she died within minutes, holding May's hand.

Earlier that day, the pair were shopping in town, laughing and enjoying life. Amanda was so pleased to hear the news of May's pregnancy. We were so happy before Amanda's accident, and her death affected May's mental state for years. Emotionally she couldn't function, sinking into a deep depression, worried she'd never be the same person again.

She wasn't, and neither was Amanda's family.

I was there for May every minute possible, like she was there for me in my time of grief. With the money worries we had, she talked about returning to nursing. I couldn't have that. The emotional trauma that would cause, would tear her apart.

My job situation showed no signs of change. This lifestyle was draining me. Don't get me wrong, I loved spending so much time with my kids. More than my father did for me when I was young, but that's another story. But, this situation was not for me. Making some kind of money was a must...

Chapter 6

Butterflies:

Time gradually ticked away for the next six days, finally taking it to a rainy, dull Thursday evening. I grabbed the old kit-bag, but smelling like a dead cat, it was binned. Borrowing one of Junior's rucksacks, I filled it with my old gear that also hadn't seen fresh-air for years. An overused pair of black gloves, a wrinkled, cut-up blue head guard, my old gum-shield, wraps, spare t-shirt and a bottle of tap water. Dumped it at the front door and impatiently waited for Tim.

I'd been in the garage a couple of afternoons, banging away at my rock-hard boxing bag, trying to get rid of the rust collected on my now overweight, sluggish body. Putting on a little weight over the years as you do when you get older, slowed me down a bit.

Getting tired in the shed having workouts, some of my punches felt as if bricks were hanging from my wrists and logs were tied to my feet, but being heavier had one advantage. I packed more power. Dishing out a few KO's back in the day, I knew I had a bit of power. However, others thought I was too much of a softy, sometimes letting opponents off the hook, when I should have done a number on them, finishing them off.

I put that down to my youth, walking around battered and scared out of my wits most of the time. Especially the fights I had after Mom passed. Maybe I had some unfinished business deep down in my subconscious. My Father always said "Ye' could be the best, boy, but yer' too weak."

Keeping reasonably fit over the years with my running and spending a couple hours in the shed a week, but I wasn't in near good condition as I once was. The limits my Father used to push me to made me the fittest man in the gym, and on most occasions, the fittest man inside the ropes.

Feeling that nervous tension about returning to the gym, I wondered if there would be anyone I knew? Would anyone remember me?

I used to be a big name in and around Aberdeen gyms and fed off my Dad's reputation, but at the same time, having no interest in becoming anything like that vicious bastard.

Tommy Stevenson, my old coach, used to keep me in tip-top condition, technique and sharpness wise. He passed on a lot of knowledge. I wonder what happened to the guy and how the gym looked now.

The doorbell rang and I knew it was Tim. I immediately jumped up, said goodbye to everyone, grabbed my bag and bolted out the door.

"Alright, Joe? Jump in. You ready for this the night? I bet you've missed it."

"Aye, fuckin' right I have."

"You're in no' too bad a shape there, except for this gut!" He jabbed his finger into my belly, grinning. I was in fair shape around my shoulders and chest, but my belly sagged.

"I've kept a little fit over the years but not anything like the man I used to be!"

Driving to the gym, we reminisced about old times that seemed like a lifetime ago now, and how much blood, sweat and tears we shared over the years. We had a laugh talking about all the guys that we fought and the amount of times we had had our noses broken. Any boxer worth his salt had his nose broken at some point in his career. Boxing was like going for a swim, you couldn't go into the water without getting wet.

Tim was always a straight to the point kind of guy and didn't pull any punches telling you something you didn't want to hear. That's what I liked about him, his honesty. Especially when he used to tell me that I didn't have the killer-instinct in some of my fights.

The conversation soon turned to our families. "So, you've twin boys, 'en? Hope they get their looks from their mother." I joked, even though I had no idea who she was.

"Aye, and it's a good job. I didn't want 'em having this long face." He joked back.

"What you doing for work?" I asked, fishing.

"Am a bit o' a scrap dealer really, plus I've got a few things on the side that earns me a few quid."

"On the side, eh? I remember you havin' plenty on the side when we were young."

"Aye mate, don't judge. I'm just the middleman."

Wasn't going to ask what the stuff on the side was, I knew. Like May said, he was a bit of a dodgy cunt when we were younger, and obviously still roams in the same circles. Always selling goods to people on a 'Don't ask, don't tell' basis from the back of his car.

You didn't have to ask where the stuff came from. It was obviously hot. But always cheaper than any shop around. I bought things like CD'S, DVD'S, even a TV for my Mom once, after Dad smashed it one Sunday afternoon, arriving home legless from the pub.

If you needed anything, Tim was the man you went to see, the local Del Boy. Selling anything from a kitchen spoon to a Ford Escort exhaust.

Right before we got to the gym, the old butterflies swirled in my guts, which was welcomed, because it showed I still had the fear. You needed to have the fear.

Chapter 7

Tillydrone-The name is a corruption of the Scottish Gaelic 'Tulach Droighne' meaning a knoll with thorn trees growing on it.

Kilgours:

As we headed closer to Kilgours gym in Tillydrone, I had honestly forgotten what a uniquely raw place it was. More so in the late eighties and early nighties, when an eerie silence from the cold streets gripped your insides. The high-rise, worn-out seventies built flats, ground surrounded by plain patches of muddy grass, with a couple of trees shadowed by terraced tenement flats. Bits of wooden ply as windows. Rubbish blowing around the area without a chance of seeing a bin, until the local council man turned up once a week to have a small tidy. The graffiti layered onto the local shop and Chinese takeaway was just left, owners probably tired of the continued chore of scrubbing it off. Tilly may have been described as a poor area of Aberdeen, but the characters I grew up with there, were far from poor. Hanging out with Sketchy Bob and Leroy Brown, gallivanting around the area, causing havoc and getting pished, was all the entertainment for young people in the area. It went hand-in-hand with the surroundings. That and chasing down the local pie, starting fights, or ending your pal's scraps. Sketchy Bob was one who bore the brunt end of a fist now and again.

Nicknamed because he always looked suspicious and stoned. His deal spot was at the end of Muggers Bridge, beside Hayton road dishing out scores and ounces to his list of clientele in between chases from uniformed police and panda cars. Smoked joints like fags from morning to night, and had the odd dealer scouting him for overdue weed debts. Turning eighteen, he ended up doing a seven-year stint at Shotts prison. Riots outside the Broadsword were common at weekends. Three of us were regular underage drinkers and the older punters didn't exactly take a shine to us, especially Leroy 'Gigolo' Brown. A ladies man who had a black book as thick as a granite brick. Seventeen at the time, he wasn't a stranger to the single mums in the area, visiting while their men were at work, on the piss or out on the rob. He was useless at defending himself, always said he was 'A lover, not a fighter' and that was true, going by the amount of times I had to step in and defuse a situation, knocking-out any cunt in my way, then getting my Dad's fist for kicking in one of his mates. Other than that, the lad's club flooded with bodies, beer cans, sexual capers and organized street scraps. Despite the in-house squabbles, people were loyal. Fight meetings like the ones held on Castlegate Terrace seen Tilly gather in numbers, carrying tools like iron-bars and knuckle-dusters, as common as pulling your socks up, ending the feuds in graphic fashion. Even Leroy and Sketchy Bob would get involved. These were great memories from my youth, unlike others I unwelcomely carried around

On the way to Kilgours, we passed a couple of rusted, burnt-out cars on different streets. This was also a common occurrence, usually a district feud or an insurance scam. This was the reason I did a bolt out of here when me and the wife decided to bring up a family. It was no place to bring up a child. Couldn't let your kids out to play on their own, it was just too dangerous, they could easily bump into a junkie, or be picked up by some paedo roaming around.

During the day it was a sombre place, all the kids at school or skiving out of the area, so their parents didn't catch them standing in a corner puffing a joint or downing a can. Most of the adults were recovering from the night before, or the single moms struggling with life, many bringing up their kids from the inside rather than the outside.

As we approached the gym, I saw that it too had seen some rough years. The outside, once so fresh, was now covered in weeds, with crap dumped all around. The walls of the stone-built gym, covered in graffiti, the windows and doors now with steel-shutters, protecting them from the hooligans and thieves. The cladding panels on the roof rattling loosely in the night wind, and the walls soaked with water streaming down from the broken guttering, the building badly needed repair.

Tommy wouldn't have been happy knowing his old place had turned into this.

I followed Tim to the door and cautiously walked behind him, not knowing what to expect. Just inside the door, there was a compact changing-room on the left. The interior walls in my memory were brilliant white with hanging posters of famous boxers. Wooden, shining paneled flooring, a vending-machine for sugar snacks and cold drinks, bins for the rubbish. Now…it was dank, grey and stank badly with stale sweat and mould. No more shiny floor, but ruined with black rubber scuff marks from trainers and littered with empty water bottles.

We nipped into the small changing-room and changed in the chilliness of the night. The room as damp, cold and sour as the rest of the building.

"Just come through when you're ready lad, and grab a rope." Tim said, then quickly stomped off to the left and through to the gym room where I heard a few people skipping.

The skipping was soon drowned out by someone turning the volume up on the stereo, blasting out some hard-core dance beat.

The walk through to the main gym was down a small corridor with more litter strewn on the floor and kicked out of the way. That old aroma of stale sweat hit me like a ton of bricks, as soon as I entered the gym and with that, a bucket-load of memories raced through my head. I had missed this odour, as crazy as that sounds.

The gym hadn't seen much maintenance over the years. The four bags hanging in a square shape from blue painted steel beams had tears, rips and duct-tape wrapped round them to hide the holes. The mirrors around the room were hanging squint on the worn-out, once white, painted walls. Mouldy torn mats on the floor and the lights hanging from the roof with galvanised jack-chains badly in need of replacing. A real classy place this had turned into.

Focusing my eyes on the hung ropes located at the front of the room to my right, I walked over and grabbed a rubbery plastic one, six men skipping and peering at me. They took a good fix at the fresh meat. It was the usual intimidating stare you get walking into a new gym for the first time, sizing you up wondering 'Who the fuck is this?'

You couldn't help get the feeling you were a stranger walking into a Western saloon with your spurs spinning round.

I took my place and started skipping at the front with my back to them. A cracked mirror in front of me, so I took the opportunity to glance at the men skipping behind me.

A couple of real, big-muscled heavies were right at the back, but the rest of the men appeared in good shape, even the couple who were nursing black eyes. Their eyes had that focused look in them, as they warmed up their bodies. I got the impression that they weren't the chatty kind you'd share a cup of coffee with.

The ring was still in the same place, an offset area of the gym to the left. Tim was talking to a couple of suspicious characters, deep in conversation. He paid particular attention to the older, pale, big-bellied one, who looked in his mid-forties maybe early fifties.

Towering around the six three height, about a couple of inches taller than Tim, dressed in a longish leather coat and pair of scabby jeans with white trainers. Looking around a hundred and fifteen kilos, with his belly shaped like a bowling ball. He leaned arrogantly against the wall with his hands in his hip pockets. His patchy fair hair combed to the side to hide his receding hairline.

The other character, the shorter of the two, was heavy-set, absorbing the conversation. Skin clay-coloured, almost Maori-like, gold hooped earring and heavily greased hair. As wide as he was tall.

He stood barrel chested and arms out wide. Casually dressed in a badly matched tracksuit.

While they spoke, everyone carried on skipping to a timer sounding every three minutes, with one-minute intervals.

Tim finished talking, picked up a stopwatch from beside the stereo, switched off the automatic timer and hung the stopwatch round his long neck. "Right, another round, then we'll get stuck into the circuit."

The circuit, I knew it well. Forty minutes of Hell. Move around the room, station-to-station in three minute rounds between thirty second breaks. Move between the four boxing bags, the speed ball, floor-to-ceiling ball, sit-up station, pull-up station and shadow boxing. This got the sweat up and wore you out. It was going to exhaust me being the first night back.

No pain, no gain.

"Right, have a break, five minutes before we get started. Wrap up!" Tim shouted from the front, standing beside the two suspicious characters as they both sat squashed on a weight bench, looking onto the room.

I got my wraps and gloves out my bag, resting while wrapping my hands in front of one of the bags, still not breaking radio-silence with the rest of the boxers.

Tim approached me. "How you coping, lad?"

"Aye, am alright, like."

"Well, don't go burning yourself out on the circuit, you're no spring chicken now. You do remember what the circuit is?" Tim took a real professional approach to his job as trainer inside the gym. Pushing the men hard, giving them the motivation they needed. Not teaching any kind of technique, but really good at egging them on.

"Of course I remember, you cheeky cunt." Tim walked away, back to work.

"OK chumps, circuits start on my shout. OK, on ye go!" He said, pushing the start button on his stopwatch.

Beginning on the bag, I took it from there to move around the room from station-to-station, getting more exhausted with every round that passed, and was soon breathing out my arse.

The sweat ran down through my hair and forehead like rainwater. That was only after twenty minutes. Tim was right, no spring chicken now.

The other boxers in the room banged away like men possessed and didn't look like putting the brakes on. Grunting and growling at every fist thrown at the bag. Thrashing the speed-ball and getting encouraging shouts from Tim and the big character that decided to join in on the coaching.

He had a mean and arrogant attitude, yelling straight into a couple of guy's faces as if it was as normal as the day was long. The circuit was surely coming to an end, I hoped. I needed a timeout.

A couple of rounds later, shadow boxing around the middle of the floor, Tim finally calls out. "Time, boys. Roy and Chris, you two in the ring." He nodded his head toward two guys.

"Alright, boss." One of them answered.

Roy was a big man, the biggest of the boxers here. Six foot two, wearing a loose bodybuilder's vest exposing his hairy chest, making his bald head look even larger than it was. Around thirty something and a body shaped like a Coke can. Looked more like a retired bodybuilder than a boxer if you ask me, but looks mean nothing in this game and judging how he hammered the bag, I think he knew his stuff.

Chris on the other hand had a smaller frame, probably just under six foot but not nearly as chunky as Roy. In his late-twenties with a full head of black hair, toned muscles bursting through his light grey t-shirt. His calves, for fuck sake, were massive. Like Popeye's arms, they were.

They geared up, entered the ring, taking a corner each. Tim had the stopwatch, leaning over the top rope, waiting to start the clock.

"Alright boys, you two ready?" Tim said as he gave them both a customary look like a referee would in a bout, and both replied with a grunt. "OK, I'll start the clock, three minutes."

The two men came squaring up to each other in the centre of the ring, without the traditional headgear on for sparring. They started a raw-looking spar, throwing bombs to and fro as if it was a fight. It looked brutal from the start, no feeling-out process. It was straight to the point of trying to hurt one another.

Roy stood his ground, letting Chris's punches bounce off his rounded face and bald head with no second thought, or signaling of any pain to his brain.

Standing his ground, his left foot in front of his right, staring menacingly into Chris's eyes with a fiendish grin, all his size used as intimidation.

Chris was losing the so-called spar as time went past. With a couple of rounds done and dusted and into the third, he was getting pushed further and further back onto the ropes. Slouching onto them, cowering into a shell, hands tucked up by his head and elbows over his ribs as Roy's true nature poured out. Bullying Chris into a corner, he was pounding away at him like he was a toy, eventually resulting in Chris taking a knee on the ground. The big burly character told him to get back up, without pity.

Chris couldn't cope with Roy's strength and aggressiveness. He weakened as every second passed. He wasn't as fit as Roy either, which did him no favours. "Get on your feet, boy!" This was a savage way to spar. My Dad's preferred way to spar, brutal, so it would build up your resistance to pain.

It turned out Chris had to take a few more knees in that last round. Looking battered, exhausted and lost, with no real desire to continue. At the same time, knowing he couldn't stop, he just got on with it without searching for a way out.

"Right you. Out you come, boy." The burly character shouted at Chris from the opposite corner, flicking his head.

Out he came between the ropes, bruised and dripping in sweat, strolling slowly over to the water-fountain at the entrance of the gym. The burly guy signaled over to Tim. Glancing over at me, they talked quietly and in secret.

Tim then came over. "Mike wants you in for a couple rounds."

Chapter 8

The Spar:

"Really? On ma first night back?"

"Aye, you'll be fine. You're made o' that Tilly grit. Come on lad, just a couple rounds."

What the fuck, let's give it a shot. What was the worst that could happen? Not as if a punch would kill me, although I was extremely skeptical about my ability between the ropes after so many years.

Tim gave me a couple minutes to get kitted up with my gum-shield and headgear from the changing-room. Slotting the gum shield in after festering in my bag for so many years, it was fucking minging. Tasted like chewing a bit of grotty car tyre.

Strolling back through to the ring, the nerves were churning around in my guts at the thought of getting hurt again. As I say, 'It's like going swimming, can't go in the water without getting wet.'

I feared I was about to get drenched.

"No need for that thing in here." Tim nodded at my old head-guard. Having witnessed that two men go at it like a pair of bears scrapping over a river salmon, no way was I going in there without it.

"Think I'll keep it on, if it's all the same wi' you, mate."

"Aye, nae bother. Here, slide your paws inside these." My hands forced themselves into a pair of worn out 14oz gloves. The inside padding round the curve mostly disappeared with Velcro hanging off the wrist and not offering to stick.

"These are a bit past their sell-by date, are they no'?"

"Yeah, yeah, we're in need of some new ones, but you'll have to make do. Listen, I know you're knackered, but keep your chin down and your hands up. He's a bully, and likes to dish it out."

I took his words on board, but really it wouldn't help, I wasn't in any shape to stop him, being a good bit heftier than me and undoubtedly much fitter. I would just have to suck it up and get on with it.

As my first foot touched down on the inside of the ropes, that nervous churn in my gut came, which I hadn't experienced in years. "OK lads, you two ready, on you go." Tim instructed.

Fuck sake, what am I doing here? Time to roll back the years and get rid of the cobwebs.

Roy and I veered forward to have customary touch of gloves and a glance in each other's eyes before we started.

His look, confident and assured. A stark contrast to the look of anxiety in mine. Everyone in the gym stared in our direction. Waiting to see what this piece of fresh meat was capable of.

I stuck my head into my chest, hands up, hopping back and forth on my toes, left leg in front of the right, attempting to refresh my memory.

Roy shadowed me, impatient with my movement around him. With every little step he edged his 110kg towards me and there it was, the pain. Hitting me with the standard jab, usually the first punch you would throw. It landed bang on my kisser, coiling my head back like a rag-doll, sending a shock-wave all the way from my head to my toe. Falling onto his hairy chest, I tucked my chin in. He didn't like that, shoving me back with both gloves.

A straight right bounced off my chin, as he followed down to my body, clattering my kidneys with a wide swinging right, making me wince. I hung on the ropes looking for that moment to gather my breath and register the pain.

I tried to keep loose on my feet, snapping out a few jabs, but they were hopeless. Roy repeatedly backed me up onto the ropes and into the corners, draining my energy.

There was one thing helping me, the old boxing brain, helping me duck and dive my way off the ropes and into a bit of space, where I could get some air to breathe and a couple seconds of brief relief.

Roy didn't have much of a brain, just stalked me like a heavy-handed dumb dog. The creaky stiff wooden floor made his movements awkward and loud as he thumped his way round the makeshift ring.

What he did have was a stubborn streak and a lot of power. The pressure from his massive weight following me around the ring was sapping my supply tank. The longer the round went, the more success I was achieving but at the same time, my energy levels depleting with my legs becoming sluggish and my brain slowing down.

After throwing a punch, my hands would drop to my waist instead of protecting my head like they should, standard boxing dictionary stuff.

Two minutes down, Roy really let the onslaught begin. He had me sunk onto the ropes for the last minute, while he rained down blows. Head-hooks, body-hooks, and every other punch in the book connected. Thrown with ferocious power, a grunt, solid impact and the intent on seeing me lying flat out on the creaky floor. The pain was shocking, and I couldn't help but pray for this fucking round to end.

Finally, Tim announced the round was over. Roy looked at me from the corner of his eye, a cocky glint as the bully inside had loved every second of this. I got back to my corner, where Tim waited for me with a much needed drink of water.

"Shit, am fucked, give me a drink." I huffed and spat out the words as quick as possible. I was weak-legged from the heat trapped inside my head because of the headgear. Tim lifted the bottle of water to my mouth, and I gulped down as much as possible before taking a fresh breath.

"Right, you've a minute to sort out that breathing."

"Fuck that. I'm no' doing another round, am done."

"Don't be a fanny. Don't you want to get your own back after that?"

"Course I do, just no' the day." My head hung below my neck looking at the floor. The night's sweat had soaked through my t-shirt, sticking it to my skin. I'm in a state of shock, looking for pity and a way out.

"Stop being a coward, that's not the man I remember. One more and that's you for the night."

I lifted my head up with a blank stare, accepting I'd do another round.

"When he traps you on the ropes, open up on him with a couple of counters on the inside, a left-hook or a right uppercut should do the business. His hands hang low between punches, so use your counters. Let him know you can hit. He's stupid, he won't figure you out. Right come on, that's time."

He gave me a couple more sips of water before I returned to face the dumb dog again. The big geezer giving Roy a pep talk, slapped him on the back of his shoulder as he turned to face me, as if he was instructing him to finish me off.

I marched forward, determined not to let the bully intimidate me.

Rapidly hitting him with a one-two left-hook combo, connecting well with the sweat jumping off his face, his neck juddered as the left-hook landed. It had effect, surely it hurt. Shaking it off, he continued to pressure me again.

Getting more success this round, but unfortunately he was still wearing me out. Pretty much done, half way through the round finding a temporary home leaning on the ropes, I absorbed the assault. It had turned to a fight in my mind at that point, he wasn't holding back.

This was now a test of character. Pissing me off, all I cared for was to stand on the cunt's head once I'd knocked him out. Hearing him grunt with every punch he threw, pushing me to take a knee as he did with Chris. He wasn't far from succeeding, I'll give him that. As I felt my legs getting hollow, an added problem was the body punches sucking the air out of my lungs.

"Joe, remember what I said. Come on, get on wi' it." I tried to let my guard down to sneak in a couple punches through the rain of fire.

The first couple of times I missed, the third time, connecting, again with a heavy left-hook, following with a right uppercut, stopping him on the spot as his brain took notice. Allowing me a ten second, well needed touch of confidence.

For the first time, Roy had a look of respect, but catching me unaware as I gloated to myself, he began his assault again. I couldn't take much more of this punishment. Thinking - taking a knee would be easier to let this end - but the stubborn part of my brain said different. Fuck this cunt, stay on your feet, one more chance to fight back before the round, or I, was over.

Studying his upper body movement for that gap I needed. I dropped my hand.

Suddenly, silence, the sound died, like amps on a speaker being switched off. I lost my vision, seeing only dots of colours flickering in my eye-line. Losing the power to hold my body-weight, my legs began to buckle to the ground, left knee brushing the wooden surface, leaving little coordination in my brain and body.

Springing back up, I threw a right hand, feeling it clatter across his left cheek. Regaining part of my sight I saw his head ping across his neck and his bulky body coil to the ground with a big thud. Out cold, no movement whatsoever from the dead weight. I looked down on him, repaying his arrogance.

"Fuckin' hell, Joe! Where the fuck did that come from!" Tim gasped. He jumped into the ring, placing Roy in the recovery position, resuscitating him back to consciousness. The big guy in the corner glanced over to his smaller mate with a questioning look that said 'Who the fuck is this guy?'

I never held any remorse for Roy. A new feeling that was to become ever more common. I didn't care about his health, after all, he tried to bully, take advantage.

Analysing what had just happened, I reckon the big man who'd been giving him the pep talks, issued him with a free pass to inflict as much pain as he desired. Well it didn't work out quite as well as he thought.

Fuck them. I climbed out of the ring refusing to look back on the collapsed body on the ground, made my way over to the water fountain to regain my breath. Exhausted and weak, almost as if I wasn't all there.

I never figured out where that punch came from. I must have been storing it up for a while. Acting on pure instinct without thinking.

Chapter 9

The Aftermath:

I wandered back around the ring to see Tim helping Roy to his feet and over to a stool in the corner. Tim had the usual supply of smelling-salts to revive the weary, and Roy was definitely weary, confused and embarrassed from getting knocked flat by the fresh blood just in the door. Tim massaged the back of his neck and give him regular sips of water.

The bigger of the two guys Tim had been talking to slid out between the ropes, walked over to me and held out his hand for me to shake.

"Alright, Joe? The name's Mike and that's my partner Bull over there." He pointed to the back of the ring where Bull stood. "That was some punch you came out with there". His eyes weighed heavy, looking like a half-filled tea bag.

"Cheers, just instinct." I could see Roy limping up to his feet out the corner of my eye.

"Aye, he's a tough lad, he'll be alright in a few minutes." By the tone of his voice he didn't care much for Roy either. "Tim tells me you used to be quite the boxer, back in the day?"

"Aye, I stopped about eight years ago."

"I could tell by the way you moved around in there. You looking to fight again?" I suspected by the inviting way he talked, keen to compliment me, he was obviously fishing for something.

"Na, not really, just wanted to do a bit of training."

"Because you're a mate of Tim's, your welcome any time to come train."

The mood in the gym changed, everyone making their way out. Roy now on his feet and getting his bearings. Once out of the ring, he idled over and shook my hand.

"That was some blow, never saw it coming." His voice had a deep crackle and his mood was OK, given what had just happened, he didn't seem pissed off at all, just embarrassed. If anything, he was showing respect.

"Nor me Roy. You alright?" I asked, trying to be polite, but I couldn't give a fuck.

"Aye, am grand. Nothing a good night's sleep won't cure." He came across as a heavy-hitting stubborn tough-guy in the ring but now, he knew his place. I watched him coast his way toward the changing-room.

Tim was having a bit of a tidy up around the ring, trying to pair the gloves that sat loose on the sweat layered floor.

"Hey Tim, how am I getting home?"

"Well, it's not going to be Roy, as planned. I'll give you both a lift."

This was going to be a little awkward, sharing a lift with the guy who had just seriously collided with my fist.

Keen to get going, I waited in the car for them and reflected on the nights' events. As we left, I felt completely exhausted and didn't have the energy to speak. I slumped back in the passenger's seat and wondered if Roy should be taken to A&E, although I suspected hospital wasn't a top priority for boxers around this gym.

Knocking that bully out was something I was proud of and would repeat in an instant, given the chance. It felt as if I had just achieved something for the first time in years. It was safe to say I'd definitely be returning to Kilgours, super-keen on getting fit and losing some unwanted pounds from being a couch potato. That was the goal I set myself at the time, but there was a bigger goal on the horizon, one I couldn't predict.

Mike and Bull were last to leave, locking the shutters and the doors. Heavily paranoid at the thought of young rogues panning the windows and door in. Who wouldn't? Being situated in Tilly.

Before I knew it, Tim was nudging me awake. I was woozy and a tad confused. Roy had already gone.

"Cheers for the lift, mate. You fancy picking me up on Thursday?"

"Aye sure, lad. I'll pick you up, same time. You take care now."

"Sound. See you then." Tim gave the thumbs-up.

Getting in the door, I headed straight to the kitchen, needing some sustenance. Finding May sitting at the kitchen table, hand on her forehead with her hair ruffled up, trying to balance the books, figuring out which bill needed paid first.

She immediately noticed the small black-eye Roy left me with, hardly noticeable to me. Looking me straight in the eye, eyebrows raised with disappointment.

"Well, well, it's just like the old days, eh? Joe Rhodes. Walking about with black eyes?" Referring to my previous name, when I did stroll around with coloured eyes

"Ach, I would hardly call it a black-eye, May. Anyway, you should be glad it's not my nose that's broken." I tried to make light of the conversation.

"Don't be coming home with them all the time. The kids don't need to see that on a regular basis. Joseph." Her voice firm.

"I know what you're saying. Not the kind of thing I want 'em to see, either."

A big sigh "I'm off upstairs for an early night. My head's mince, looking at all these bills."

"OK babe. Night."

She slipped out the door, not willing to take me on. I didn't know if it was the bills lying on the table, or my black-eye that pissed her off. Sinking into the sofa, eating some leftover dinner, I felt content that I'd achieved something with my fists tonight. I was back!

Chapter 10

Good Feeling:

I got a warm, fuzzy feeling about myself over the next couple weeks, something I'd been missing for the past seven months. The extra spring in my step gave me some welcome relief from the stress. Tuesday and Thursday, I kept attending boxing.

My mind healthier, but body older now, weaker and stiff. Not able to afford the protein shakes and training supplements all the serious gym-goers were taking, I had to take the pain for a few more weeks before the muscle ache would fade.

What I wasn't enjoying was the constant search for a job. Truth being, I was beginning to settle into a life that I couldn't see a way out of. To be honest, I wasn't job-hunting as hard as I could have, the boxing distracted me.

The welfare payments transferred in my account every week. Sitting in the Jobcentre, explaining to the grey-faced, grey clothed dominatrix sitting opposite me, that I'm doing everything by the rules to find work, was like talking to a brick wall.

Just like a fight, I had to duck and dive my way towards getting the pittance of a hand-out they deemed 'enough'. I had to keep looking forward in the hope something would turn up.

Boxing had been going well and I could still fight, probably as good as in my teenage years. I was even surer of that when I took apart another boxer from the club, Toby. A real live-wire. Muscular, a good size for his weight and game as hell. A broad-shouldered 84kg, not a slice of fat to be seen. Five foot eight and a real stylish boxer as well.

Wasn't local though, had a southern Scottish lingo. Having a really friendly kind of face and a good manner about him, he didn't seem a bully like Roy, who hadn't been seen since I put him on his arse. He must have been too embarrassed to show face after getting sparked out.

It was easy to tell Toby was an experienced fighter. The way he glided, the speed of his punches and the different variations of combos he had at his disposal. No ego, just a workmanlike attitude.

We had our first spar a couple weeks after I exchanged blows with Roy. It started off quite relaxed but there he was, Mike in his corner egging him on. A few rounds passed when he thought he could take advantage. Being twenty odd kilos heavier than him, I was taking it easy. In the fourth round he started hissing like a snake as his punches started ploughing in. Following Mike's instruction from outside the ropes, he stepped up a gear. Really trying to trouble me.

Once his athletic body stood inside my space, he would hit and move round my slow frame, pull my guard down, land a combo then disappear out my sight. His brain full of boxing tricks.

Half way through the round, losing patience with the drip-drip effect his boxing was having on me, I dropped him with a hammering left-hook to the body. He sunk a deep breath as his legs couldn't hold his weight. That was a warning to him, but he didn't take it. Lifting himself back up to his feet, he returned to the same tactic, hissing aggressively as he threw random leather in my face. He was too game for his own good.

He got on my inside, opening up on my body, lightning quickly, he was hard to stop. My patience wearing thin, the kettle began to boil, I took it upon myself to drop him again, this time with a right uppercut in-between the narrow space showing in his guard.

Taking another knee, I hoped for his sake he stayed there.

No, the game son of a bitch got up again, gave Mike a glance in the corner, who nodded while he blinked and casually said "Carry on, boy." I let him finish the round, allowing myself some easy time to regain full lungs. Hoping for his sake there wouldn't be another one.

There was, one more. He went easy at the start of the round, must have learned his lesson. Keeping him at bay with my stiff jab for the time being, while Mike barked at him to close the gap and get back into my chest.

Toby went into overdrive. The cunt had some tank on him. Flat out almost every round, he was still fresh as a daisy.

It was at this point that I realised everybody in this gym must be on some kind of juice: steroids.

I was sick of the sight of this pocket dynamo. Stalking him until I could pick my moment, being patient, when the time came at last. It all shifted into slow motion.

His feet bore forward, trying to sink his face into my chest and force me back, but I glimpsed his legs move and threw a straight. It mauled into his face, terminating his advance, almost as if somebody turned the switch off, he crumpled to the floor. I had warned him. He needed to learn not to fuck with me.

The same rescue-squad came to his aid. Tim the first in there to help. Mike by his side, probably just to check he wasn't dead for his own benefit. Once Mike was able to feel a pulse, he left the ring.

"Boy, you've got a habit of doing this?"

"Tell your boys to stop taking the piss, 'en I might take it easy." A couple minutes of trivial chit-chat went by before Mike asked me about my past fights, then he turned to my job dilemma.

"Tim tells me you're out of work?"

"Aye, haven't worked for a while."

"You fancy making some money?"

"Doing what?"

"Looking for somebody to take a fight in a few weeks. Easy night's work. Interested?"

"Na, I can't." May would never allow it.

"£400 for a night's work. An easy night's work for a man of your talents." His compliments were meant to rope me in.

"I don't know, Mike." If May knew I accepted a fight, she would have a fit.

"Well, you have a wee think about it, Joe. Get back to me. I can tell you're a fighter."

Mike walked away at that point leaving me something to mull over. Four hundred quid for a professional fight would really help us out over the next month with all the bills piling up. Mortgage, gas, electricity and food all needed to be paid for, and I couldn't see any answer to my problems or any other way of bringing in money. I couldn't let May go through all the constant worry. I instantly knew I needed a cover to fight.

Chapter 11

Preparation:

The following day, the stacking bill problem really hit home. Through the post came the red letters: final reminders for the gas and electricity, the mortgage three months late and the phone cut-off, which meant no internet access.

No internet meant I couldn't apply for jobs at home. Hiding the gas and electricity bill from May for the time being, seeing her showing signs of breaking down, I didn't want the bill finding its way into her hands, just yet. She seemed stressed and snappy. That was so out of her character, normally so laid back, just taking things in her stride.

It was there and then that Mike's offer started to make a lot of sense. £400 for one night's work? That would cover some of the overdue money on the mortgage.

We could use May's wage and my welfare cheque to pay the gas and electricity bill. It would put us above sinking level for the time being. Give us a chance to breathe for a couple weeks. The last thing I wanted to do was lie to my family, but it seemed the only option.

Stuck between the family's need for money and my weakening morals, my decision was made. I was going to take the fight. I used the weekend to ponder how keeping it quiet from May would work. Coming to the conclusion I'd have to make up some kind of story about picking up some weekend work or a night job, sneak away, having Tim cover the story if need be.

The weekend was spent as usual, entertaining the kids and visiting May's parents in Stonehaven. It was pretty boring and I didn't really get involved either. I didn't gel with her parents anyway. My mind was too occupied on what was going to take place in the upcoming weeks.

Little did I know at the time how much this was going to change my life and me.

Tuesday arrived and I was very eager to talk to Mike regarding this fight. Tim picked me up as normal, 6.30 on the dot and I wasted no time in telling him my plans as I entered the car.

"Tim, I'm going to take that fight Mike offered me."

"Aye, why not, eh? You'll be fine. Fighting's in your blood." Tim replied.

"Need to keep it hush from May, though. Don't want her to know, so if you speak to her, I'll need you to cover any story I make up."

"Aye, nae bother. When we get there the night, talk to Mike. Find out if the fight's still on. If you're lucky, you'll be in."

Spotting Mike as I arrived at the gym, I wasted no time in approaching him. He was chatting to Bull. Those two were practically joined at the hip.

"Hey, Mike, can I have a word?" I asked.

"Fire away, Joe."

"Is the offer of that fight still on? If it is, I'll take it."

"Great, we can make that happen, as long as you don't go cancelling on us at the last minute. We don't take kindly to that kind of shit. Once your name's in the ring, there's no going back. You understand?" It seemed clear that cancelling would land them in the shit and me in a hole.

"This will be a good fight for you. Let's check your weight on the scales." Mike ordered and I made my way over.

"100.5 kg. OK, fine, but you'll need to keep working your ass off, get rid of those extra kilos. Tim will keep you posted about the fight details."

"Alright, cheers. When and where is it?"

"It's down in Dundee next weekend, Saturday night. Tim will keep you right. I'll give you a good spar the night, get you a little sharper." Mike said.

Turning away, I started skipping with the rest of my training partners. Never thought to ask how many rounds or what size of gloves it was. Presumed it was a pro-boxing show. It just didn't seem important, acquiring the money took precedence.

I put in extra effort that night, pushing it a little harder than usual, but it left me fatigued and thinking more about this fight tensed me up. It seemed to mentally and physically drain me that evening. Maybe it was the lie.

Nearing the end of the night knowing the sparring was approaching, didn't fill me with joy. All the other boxers were much fitter and topped up on juice. The 'roids charging blood through their pumped-up muscles, just helped them keep going.

"Right guys, sparring. Everyone can have a few rounds the night." Tim yelled, standing with his customary stopwatch around his neck. There were five of us that night, and I had a bad feeling I was going to get pushed to the limit here.

Tim came over while I refreshed my dry throat at the fountain. "Joe, you're in for a treat the night.

Three minutes wi' each guy here, a one-minute break between rounds. Just get through it best you can, and don't give up or coast through it. Mike and Bull don't want to see that."

"Seems like I'm the one you want knocked out the night." I tried to joke.

"Nonsense mate, you'll be fine," Tim replied.

Climbing through the ropes into the ring with my head-guard on and gum-shield in, taking a deep breath, Tim gave me a nod, asking if I was ready, although that was the last thing my mind was telling me.

The five guys outside the ring squatted against the wall, or stood with their gum-shields in and gloves on, ready to rumble. Toby was the last one lined up on the row and Chris the first. Good, the two hardest guys first and last.

All the boxers weighing over the 80kg mark. Chris and Danny were big, bulky bastards. Staring me down with a glint of fear in their eyes, showing I gained some respect around here.

"First two, ready." Tim mumbled as he side-stepped around the ring, taking the role of ref again. Bull standing in the other corner, Mike taking a casual stance at the back of the ring.

First spar, Chris. Looking pretty wary of me, he didn't come charging in, as usual. We exchanged combos in a more friendly fashion. I mean friendlier as in he wasn't trying to charge me down, or rip my head off.

The old boxing brain started to return, dipping and slipping punches, keeping the head movement working.

Half way through the round he stepped it up, started landing grinding hits, pounding my ribs was his specialty, which hurt like hell. Towards the end of the round, Mike yelled.

"Now Chris, NOW!"

He went to town on me for the last 30 seconds, hitting me with everything. Upstairs to the head and down to the body, I countered throughout his barrage with little effect. The round was soon over thankfully, we touched gloves and he left the ring.

Next up, Peter. One of the smaller lads. Quite young, nimble, in his early twenties. Short, fluffy ginger hair. Not built big, but owned fast fists.

"Right come on, let's go. Round two!"

The minute break wasn't long enough to settle my breathing back to normal. Peter was a raw brawler like the rest of the boxers here, but lacked size and difficult to hit because of light feet.

He might have lacked size, but didn't lack heart. As I battled my way to land a combo of heavy punches to bounce his body from side to side, he absorbed it all and carried on. I liked guys like this, loads of heart. If you didn't have heart you have nothing. Something Tommy Stevenson used to tell me. 'You can hit hard, you can be fast, you can be big, but if you've no heart, you're fucked.'

Three occasions during this round Mike shouted at Peter. I sensed a pattern.

"Now boy now, get on him!" Mike took pleasure in controlling what punishment I received.

I could see what was happening, Mike was testing me, pushing me, trying to find my limit.

Totally fucked by the end of the round, I needed more than a minute before taking on the next guy, but I kept repeating Tim's words in my head, not to 'upset' Mike or Bull, get through it best I could. The same one-minute break would have to do.

The third round, with Danny, a well-rounded plump fighter, kept relentless pressure on me. Danny had a hanging beer-belly, but boy could he fight. Blessed with a gift and he knew how to use it.

Targeting the body, leaning over me and keeping on the inside. As I had less and less energy to move, he punished my stomach and kidneys. I didn't like it. My energy drained, taking pounding thuds to my kidneys and rib-cage, not able to dodge the hits. My feet felt like they were dragging a ball and chain, heavy and weary.

The minute breather came in time, before I took a brush against the canvas.

Round four, they had seen the effect Danny had on me, keeping him in for this round, trying to take me down to another level, Mike pushing him to punish me, fast dancing legs combined with a huge belly, a combination not put together often, giving me the run-around.

Wasn't sure if I would make it through the fourth. My heart and skull ready to explode with lack of time to draw breath and heat trapped in my head, ducking, backing onto the ropes, taking a hurl of punches to the head, immobilising my movement.

In the fifth, I had to really push myself and try to get my credibility back with Danny. I surprised myself, considering how knackered I was, putting him down, and fighting on pure instinct. I could hardly breathe, fatigued and struggled to keep my hands up.

Every punch thrown was telegraphed before it left my side, and when they landed, they brought no weight behind them. In the last minute and a half, I was getting thrashed, but couldn't give up, not if I wanted to bring the readies home to May. That wasn't an option for me.

The last guy into the ring, was the pocket dynamo, Toby. Knowing his skills, he could break me, the fastest and fittest here. By this time, the pain ran throughout my whole body, my lungs hardly able to function, legs weak, eyes and forehead ached, standing tall sent a stabbing pain into the ribs. I just had to suck it up, get on with it. Mike must have taken pity on me, giving me just over the minute's break this time, but that wasn't going to help.

I slouched into the corner after the fifth round.

"Here Joe, get this down you. One round left!" said Tim as he tried to build the confidence in me, while pouring water down my throat and over my head "And for fuck sake, keep your hands up, your eyes are a fuckin' mess."

I tried not to think about what I'd look like after this. Just had to get this last round done and dusted.

"Come on mate, last round, let's see if that Tilly grit's still in there." Tim said.

Immediately at the start of the round, Toby flustered forward with a sharp combo, hissing like a snake each time his punches hit, but I kept my hands up so it didn't have the desired effect.

Remembering our first spar, I knew he'd be itching to make the most of the weakness showing in me. You could tell he was a well-seasoned boxer, judging by his speed, combos and elusiveness. Bouncing into my face again, slithering his chin against my soaked chest, connecting with a bouldering body blow then coiling his body back, he smacked me in the jaw with a wicked left uppercut. I clambered back, swinging a lacklustre left hook, missing as he weaved under my arm and floated back up, landing what felt like a bowling ball, shaking me to my boots. His eighty four kilo frame far too fast for me to cope with in my condition. My brain couldn't function, I went to sea, legs wobbling as if balancing on a wave, eyes seeing double and unable to focus, the sound numbed like the echo of a muted speaker, but, I was still on my feet, still looking Toby in the eye, or at least I thought I was.

Under two minutes of the round left. I wasn't going to make it. Suddenly he halted, refusing to take advantage of my wounded state, choosing to stand idle and wait for my recovery. Mike egged him on to finish me while I was handicapped. He either didn't have it in him, or was wary of my power when wounded.

Regaining my senses after fifteen seconds, I realised I had been let off the hook.

It was in his hands to drop me at any time, but he chose not to. I pretty much collapsed on the floor exhausted, as Tim signaled the end. Taking one last look at Toby, I turned and slumped out of the ring, not looking back.

"Well done, son. You've sure got the heart and guts for this game!" Bull bawled in a local accent and slapped his palm on my shoulder in a friendly gesture.

I didn't reply, too exhausted to talk.

"Joe, you're pretty bruised around the eyes, lad. Might want to get some ice on 'em." fussed Tim.

Once I made it to the changing room, I stole a glance in the small mirror hanging. May was going to go nuts!

Chapter 12

The Eyes:

Sheepishly entering the front door later that night, immediately tensing at having to face May and the kids...Oh god, the kids. I realised I had to deal with this head on, and strode into the sitting room where May was on the landline, chatting about nursing work. Hearing her mention the ARI, the cancer wards, the Anchor Unit, I was now annoyed with myself.

This wasn't on, allowing her go back to work in the hospital, knowing the emotional trauma she would have to suffer.

I would have to think quick, make up a white lie about picking up some work next weekend, and use the four hundred to stop May returning to a job that would destroy her. Had to think on my toes here.

Coming off the phone, she flinched.

"Holy shit, Joe! What the fuck happened tonight?!" Jumping back in her seat, placing her hands over her mouth.

"Well, sparring was a bit rough the night." I replied.

"Rough?! It must have been world war three, JOE! What are the kids going to say when they see you like this?" She was in shock at the state I was in.

"I know, I know," I replied, with hands up, palms towards her, trying to calm her distress. "I'll just tell them the truth. I was at boxing and took a few hits."

"A few? Jesus, we decided years ago this wasn't going to happen."

"I know May, I know. Look it's happened now, so give me a break would you. My body's in agony."

"Oh Joe, what an idiot! You need to get some ice on those eyes, right now."

Storming to the kitchen for some ice, as I glanced into the big, rectangular mirror over the mantelpiece. Her comment about world war three was bang-on and I was now dreading seeing the kids.

"Here, lie down on the sofa and stick this over your eyes, let the ice do the work."

I lay down and covered my eyes, realising this was the perfect opportunity to lie about the fake job, as I wouldn't have to actually look her in the eye.

"Got some good news for you. I managed to find a wee bit of weekend work next Saturday, down in Dundee."

"Weekend work? What is it?" She asked.

"It's a security job for a couple of days. Paying four hundred, cash. Met a guy at the gym who needs some help. It's a small weekend music festival, or some shit like that."

"Least you've got good news to go with those eyes. This a one-off, or you getting more work?"

"Oh aye, if things go well down there, I should do."

"Has Tim got anything to do with this?"

"Aye, he works for 'em as well."

"Is that his full-time job?" May asked.

"No, it's just something he does now and again to help out. They like hiring guys like us, in case there's any trouble around the beer-tents and that." The lies seemed to flow like an everyday event.

"Let's hope you don't come home with any more black eyes, then." She said sarcastically.

"Well, I hope no'." Thinking I'll probably come home with at least one damaged body part.

"That's really good news for us. You fancy a bath?" She asked.

"Aye great, thanks." This is going better than I imagined.

In my mind, there was no other choice but to take this professional fight. My father lied to my mam about anything and everything for years, ending badly for everyone concerned.

May never mentioned anything about the job she was chatting about on the phone, so I reckoned she was happy for the time being.

I really worried about what the kids would think of my eyes. Knowing from my own past, seeing my father come home bloodied and bruised all the time, it didn't paint a pretty picture.

I had to weigh up my options though, it was the desperate need for money, or risk getting thrown out of our home, or bankrupt. Just had to get through this at the moment, not able to see any other way. I wasn't going to lie to the kids. I'll just tell them the truth about my black eyes.

Chapter 13

Old Man:

Rising the next morning, my body felt the age of eighty. Limping around the house like John Wayne. My ribs aching and face in agony. During the night, my eyes picked up some unwanted colours.

The usual routine of waking fifteen minutes before the kids, starting on the porridge, the breakfast of champions, served every day. Usually with added extras like blueberries, strawberries, jam or honey, but we couldn't afford that kind of luxury, now replacing that with sugar.

Once the oatmeal was cooking, I would turn the lights on in the kid's rooms, this usually woke them, but I would leave May to sleep through the early morning.

First to come down stairs was Junior. Having my back to him as he entered the kitchen, stirring the porridge trying to keep the lumps out. Still in his PJs, he sat at the table, rubbing the sleep out his eye.

Laying his plate in front of him, I waited for him to point out the obvious. Peering out his sleepy eyes, just away to say thanks when he noticed. "Uuuhh, Dad, what happened to your eyes?" His voice whined, thinking it was cool to have black eyes. You know kids, we all liked to think our Dads were the toughest guys around and in my case as a child, it was very true. Leaning down to his eye-level, he continued to check out every colour in them.

"Junior, Daddy went to boxing last night and walked into a few punches. That's all."

"Does it hurt? It looks sore."

"Aye, it hurts a lot, son. Don't go walking into fists, it's not smart."

"Dad! Dad! Can I go with you next time?" bouncing up and down in his seat.

Just what I didn't want, my son getting interested in boxing. I wanted the family's fighting blood-line to end with me, but thought I'd better humour him a little.

"No, no, Junior you're way too young for that carry on. Maybe in a few years, I'll take you out to the shed and teach you a few things on the bag."

"But Dad, I want to do it now!" He huffed and sulked.

"Tell you what. If you do really well at school by the end of the year, I'll think about it. OK? School is way more important than boxing."

"Och, Dad that's not fair. I don't want to wait until the end of the year!"

"Sometimes life isn't fair, Junior. Now eat that porridge." I said firmly.

Junior definitely took after his Dad. Keen as mustard at any sport at school, and hated losing at anything. While playing Xbox, most of the time I had to let him win because he was such a bad loser. I definitely knew he was going to succeed in any sport he did later in life. I just didn't want it to be boxing.

Next up to see the bruised rainbow eyes, was Jess. She came down stairs and had a seat at the table. She wasn't really at an age to understand, but I did my best.

"Dad, what happened?" She asked rubbing the tiredness out of her eyes and sitting down beside her brother.

"A man at boxing hit me a few times."

"A man. Why did he hit you?"

"We were just training together. He didn't mean it." I answered, struggling to conjure up a way to explain it to her. It felt more awkward with Jess.

Half asleep, she started to munch into her breakfast and didn't say anything else about it. She was a little too young to understand and more interested in spooning the sugar into her bowl.

Walking the kids to school that morning, I was met with the evil eye from other parents. There weren't a lot of people who knew my family past in Inverurie, but most knew I used to be a boxer. God knows what they were thinking, looking at my face. Probably thought I'd been in some kind of drunken street brawl.

Once back to the house, I woke May and made her breakfast, well, I heated up what was left. "Morning. Get the kids to school OK?" She asked.

"Yup, nae bother. Got a lot of dodgy looks as well."

"No wonder, your eyes have more colour in them than a packet of Skittles. They look sore."

"I can't really feel 'em. Think the ice helped a bit. I'll be happy when they're normal again."

"You and me both. So when's this job?"

"I'll find out when I go back to the club. Am sure it's not this weekend, but next."

"You're going back for more of what you got last night?" She hoped I'd say no.

"Of course I am. I loved it last night."

70

"I know it's not costing us anything and it gets rid of your stress, but you can't be coming home looking like you've had a hiding all the time. The kids don't need to see that shit every week, and people will start talking."

"It's OK. I'll just tell people it's domestic abuse." I cackled.

"Well, you might just be telling the truth if there's any more of your cheek!"

"Ooh, good come-back." I complimented.

Before I could put her breakfast on the table, she flung her arms round my shoulders. "You know, I've still got more than an hour before work. Do you fancy heading upstairs?"

"Damn straight I do, baby." A big smile lit my face as I leaned in and met her inviting mouth with a deep kiss, then stripped her pink shorts and t-shirt off, revealing her flawlessly darkened skin. My body was in agony, but I forgot all about the pain soon as she was in my arms. The simple touch of her skin was enough to make me quiver. I flung her onto the kitchen table, we made love like teenagers, and left drenched in sweat.

She never did eat her porridge that morning.

Chapter 14

The Training:

When I woke up later on the sofa, May had already left for work. Making the most of an empty house four hours a day, I used the time to train in my garage in the lead up to my pro-boxing debut.

Our garage housed my own gym, which was converted a few years back. A big, heavy bag hung in the centre, a rack of dumbbells in the corner and a speedball.

I had the other equipment, a weight-bench, a big rectangle mat, skipping-ropes and a few medicine-balls. The walls were covered in boxing posters of Ricky Hatton, Tyson, Ali, and a bunch of others. Trophies, medals and pictures of my past hung on the walls. None of my Father but there was a few of Mom. It was good to know she watched over me

It was my church, my place to fuck off to from the stress of life, and take my frustration out on the weights and bag.

AC/DC often blasted out the speakers, or anything that would give me motivation to train and get me in the mood.

Starting my workout with a customary ten minutes of skipping, moving to the heavy bag for around six to ten three minute rounds depending on how much energy I had, with a thirty second break between rounds. Spent a good ten minutes on the speedball, before doing some weight work. That was the routine for three days and the other two weekdays would be sit- ups and stomach work along with cardiovascular circuits. Road work was done at the weekend.

This was my plan for the next couple of weeks until the big debut. It didn't matter how much pain I suffered, just had to train and it was a lot harder at the age of thirty-two, compared to when I was a young pup.

The one problem though with all the training, was food. Not being flush with cash, I just had to eat whatever I could. I would love to be eating steak and chicken, just couldn't afford it.

Attending boxing on the Tuesday and Thursday, I never sparred again over the next ten days. They probably took pity on me and besides, my ribs were killing me and my eyes needed to heal. Wincing in pain a lot over the next week. It wasn't nice. I hoped it would clear up by the time the fight came round.

I also spent a lot of time worrying about getting injured in this fight, or something terrible happening. What would May think about it? She wouldn't be happy once she found out I'd been lying to her. I say once, because lies always filter out in the end. Losing the fight wasn't an option. I needed the money, we needed the money.

Chapter 15

The Hard Truth:

The days ticked away until finally Saturday, the day of the fight, arrived. I agreed with Tim the fabricated story that would get me out of the house and into the ring without suspicion. Both of us working security at a music festival in the Dundee area for the Saturday night and most of Sunday. We would leave early on the Saturday, returning late home the next day. May thinks it's a two-day event, justifying the £400. She didn't have an inkling what amount of pay security guards got, but it damn sure wasn't 400 quid for a weekend's graft.

All that had to be done was fight, win and take home the money.

That morning I got up earlier than the household. I didn't feel the need to speak to them before leaving. The alarm sounded at 6.30am, I switched it off as quickly as possible so it wouldn't disturb May. Raising slyly and putting my clothes on, I sneaked out the room. Before closing the bedroom door, I glanced round at May. Stunning even when sleeping, looking at her bulb-shaped nose and the beauty spots on her cheek. I couldn't imagine a life without her, which made the stab of guilt even worse.

I tip-toed down stairs into the kitchen for some breakfast, having that feeling you get when you're a child doing something wrong, but in your head, you reassure yourself it's right.

I left the house heading straight for the bus stop, catching the 7.45 to Kingswells. The cover story required me to leave early.

I was really psyched-up for the fight and it reflected in my eagerness to get to the bus stop, itching to get between the ropes and have it over and done with.

The usual thoughts circulated my head leading up to a fight. Who was he? Will he be tough? Will he hit hard? Where's he from? None of that mattered, really, I only told myself not to be second best, don't be the mug that loses, be the one who takes home the candy.

The journey to Tim's took about forty minutes. He stayed in a really clean, established area, but his house wasn't up to much. Junk and pieces of scrap scattered around the garden. The gate hanging off, the aerial cables flying around the air in the wind.

Tim's house stuck out from the others and not in a good way. I knocked on the door, expecting the inside to be as rough round the edges as him.

"Joe, come in, make yourself at home."

"Alright, Tim. What's the crack?"

"Am fine, lad. Have a seat, I'm just cooking some grub. Hungry?"

"Eh aye, I could eat again. I'll need the energy for the night, I suppose."

Strolling into his living room, I had to slow my steps. The expression 'Don't judge a book by its cover' came to mind. Outside might have looked like a mess, but inside was something out of an edition of Tatler.

Absolutely spotless, expensive-looking black leather reclining sofa, big fifty inch-flat screen TV, an exquisite looking marble-topped bar built in the corner, with a stock of expensive malts.

The guy definitely had style. His house looked the exact opposite of him. Strolling around with torn-up clothes, bad hair, never clean shaven, yet drives an expensive Mercedes Benz and lives in an immaculate house.

Something didn't quite add up here. After a couple minutes I got bored and wandered through to the kitchen. Just as nice as the living room, heavily tiled floor, spotless white cupboards with shiny black work surfaces. All the mod cons, from a mains-powered tin-opener, to the huge free-standing Aga.

"Nice pad. No offence, but I wasn't expecting it, judging by the outside."

"Aye, she's not bad, lot o' cash in here. Just had a good security system installed. Never know what cunt's scoping out your house." His spindly arms lay on his hips, proud of his smart thinking. "Making the outside look like a dump, the less chance anybody thinks the inside will be any better." He was quite a contradiction, and thought outside the box.

"Where's the wife and twins? I was looking forward to meeting 'em."

"Dawn took them out for the day, a kid's party or something at the other side o' town, then she'll probably head for the shops to spend my wages. You just missed her."

"Spill the beans 'en? How can you afford all this stuff?"

"Hard work, mate."

"Come on, I won't tell."

"A deal here, a deal there." I knew exactly what he meant. The local Del Boy, he hadn't worked an honest day in his life. Having a scrap business in his name was just a front, even though he dabbled in it to cover his arse.

His house was packed full of dodgy goods. I didn't need him to tell me otherwise. Anything that was stolen from somewhere, ended up in his pad.

"So, what time's kick-off the night? When's the weigh-in?"

"It starts around sevenish. There's no weigh-in at these types of shows." I frowned, an alarm-bell going off in my head.

"What do you mean, no weigh-in? It's a boxin' show, is it no'?"

"Well, it is a boxing show, but…it's unlicensed." As he said that, he waited for my reaction.

"Fuckin' unlicensed show? You're havin' a laugh?"

"No, I'm not, Joe." Answering bluntly, I knew by the sober look on his face he wasn't joking.

"Fuckin' hell, Tim! You fuckin' serious!? It's bad enough am lying to May. Never mind it being a fuckin' illegal show." I turned away, massaging my temples, absorbing the unbelievable truth: he'd played me.

"It's not exactly illegal, but some o' the things that happen there can be." He was too casual about this, there was no reaction, it seemed second nature to him.

Stomping around the kitchen, holding my breath, furious. "Fuck me! Fuckin' Hell!" Had visions of throwing him through his patio-doors. What the fuck has he done?

Tim stopped cooking for a moment and looked at me, square-eyed. He could tell I was ragging as he stuttered, trying explain his deceit.

"It may not be illegal, mate!" I butted in "But, it's brutal. I've heard the story of Dad killing someone."

"Aye, I know the story. Carl Jenkins deserved what he got, beat to a pulp. Trust me Joe, you're made for this."

"Trust you? Piss off! What if I get killed, have you thought about that? Look, this isn't happening, am no' fuckin' doing it." Adamant I wasn't getting involved. It was wrong on so many levels.

"You have to do it, Joe. There's a gangster called Steve Dean running the show. If you don't turn up, I can't guarantee he won't come after you. Trust me, you don't want to fuck him over."

"This is just too fucked up."

"Look, just have the fight, take the £400 home. If you don't want to fight again then don't, but you can't back out on this one. It's too late." I was disgusted about getting suckered into this.

All the time, Tim had been cooking, avoiding my eyes. He laid a plate of eggs, overcooked bacon, sausage and beans in front of me. I wanted to plant it back in his face.

For some reason, I just stuck my head down and ate, pondering the situation I'd been landed in. Sitting silent at the kitchen island counter and munching my food with my hand round the plate, resisting raising my head, I could only come to one conclusion – I had to take the fight. It would cause huge repercussions if I didn't. There was a chance this Steve Dean could turn up at my door, putting my family in danger. This was the one and only reason I had to go through with this fight now.

"Fuck me! I'll have to do it. I can't risk putting the family in danger."

"You'll be fine. It's not as bad as you're thinking."

Tim was a lot of things, but I never saw this coming at all. It felt like he'd stabbed me in the heart. I'd been conned. Could have walked away, but the risk to my family would be a weight on my shoulders.

This was a shit situation to be landed in, stuck between a rock and a dangerous place.

I really didn't know what to expect from this fight now. Didn't even know if it was taking place in a ring, or what?

Absolutely livid, I couldn't talk to Tim. Wracked with worry about the whole situation. What was I walking into? It's possible I could end up badly hurt, or land in the morgue.

This was a bad road to travel down.

Chapter 16

Montrose:

Finishing my food, I headed out to Tim's Merc, totally ignoring him. He kept a keen eye on me as I walked out the door, making sure I wasn't doing a runner.

My cheeks bright red and fists clenched in my jeans pocket, I was annoyed but slightly calmer than ten minutes ago. All those years ago, I'd made the decision to hang up my gloves so my family weren't raised in a fighter's world, and now, I was about to walk into an unlicensed boxing show.

Agitated and out-of-sorts now, I just had to get this done and dusted. Tim wandered casually out of the house with a ring bag I expected was full of fight gear. Passing me as he walked round the car to the driver's door, I blanked him.

"Come on 'en. Let's get going."

Jumping into the car, I immediately laid it out. "Look, don't speak to me on the way down the road. I can't be fucked wi' you right now."

"Don't be like that, lad."

"I said don't fuckin' talk, just drive." I snapped at him, talking from the side of my mouth, burning a glance at his face, and he got the point.

"Alright Joe, whatever you say."

Staring out the window at the path I was taking, left me deep in thought about what I was walking into. What kind of world would this be? Who's this Steve Dean that Tim fears so much? I couldn't stop fidgeting in the car, using my phone to keep my hands busy, spitting out and replacing chewing gum every ten minutes. I was anxious about the whole affair, but at the end of the day, it was still a fight, a fight I had to win more than ever now.

The conversation was non-existent, apart from Tim taking a couple of phone calls. Things started to make more sense now. Kilgours was full of raw boxers loaded on steroids, dodgy characters and bad attitudes. It fitted the scene of the unlicensed scrappers. Kilgours was named after an old street in Tillydrone. Kilgour Avenue. The name changed to Alexander Terrace in the late 60's because of its notorious reputation for crime.

I always wondered why the sparring was so brutal and now I knew, now it made sense. The kind of bout I'd be in tonight, wouldn't be the kind you see on TV between two professionals. The rules might be there, but wouldn't be followed.

Guessed it would be more like street-fighting than anything. You could be up against any cunt, an ex con, ex-army, a psycho or an ex-fighter like me, I just didn't know what to expect.

About a half hour into the journey, Tim broke silence. "Joe, I've got to make a pick-up. It's a little detour through Montrose. Won't take long."

"Whatever." I couldn't go the rest of the day without speaking to him.

He reversed into an industrial-estate, stopping at the rear of a small, shabby-looking building with faded cream paint and no windows, just a roller-door big enough for a car and an entrance by the side. It looked like the back of a vacant shop.

Tim disappeared inside, leaving me alone in the car. The roller-door opened after ten minutes, letting me see inside the building, which was brightly-lit with a white light and untidy. I could make out a couple printing-machines and piles of scrunched-up, ink-stained paper scattered around.

Tim popped the boot of the car while I eyed him in the side-mirror, watching curiously to see what he was up to. A short, slimy bald guy sidled out carrying a couple of briefcases, his fingers and arms covered in ink.

Tim placed the briefcases in the boot and chatted for a couple of minutes. Out from the side door came another man. A malicious, dodgy-looking character, wearing one of those black puffed-up jackets, sleeves rolled up to his elbows and drawing on a smoke.

He stood, reading from a slip of paper in front of Tim. I couldn't make out the conversation, but it sounded like figures. Tim handed over an envelope, which I assumed was cash. Sticking it into his back pocket, the dodgy man glanced into the side-mirror, catching my stare, arms by his side, the fag hanging out his mouth. His evil, intimidating glare sent a shiver through me, an aura of pure hatred in his eyes. Turning his back, I stared at a massive swastika tattoo on the back of his head. One of these Nazi white supremacist types. Tim finished his business, shook hands, and returned to the car.

"What the fuck was going on there?"

"I can't tell you, lad. You don't need to know."

"You're into some dodgy shit, aren't you?"

"Just doing a pick-up, that's all."

"Need to know basis, I get it."

"The less you know the better, the way I see it."

"This part o' your income?"

"Nae exactly. I don't make any profit from this. I'm just doing Bull a favour."

This day was getting stranger with every passing hour. Bull seemed like a big-time criminal. I felt myself getting sucked in. I wanted to find out what was in the briefcases.

"So, how do you make your money 'en? Surely can't all be from thieving?" I asked.

"Thieving? Less o' the swearing. I suppose I can tell you, but it stays between us."

"Well, I don't think I'll be talking about this day for a long, time so I think you're safe."

"See this unlicensed show we're going to? Mike and Bull pay me to train the guys and find the fighters. I make a lot of money on the night, placing bets on who I think will win an' most of the time, I know. Plus, the thieving adds up, then there's the wee bit of scrap dealing I do."

The part about Mike and Bull paying him to find and train the guys, I figured out for myself on the way to Montrose. The betting I couldn't have known about.

"Bets? What bets? There's betting at these things?"

"There's always a bookie at these shows and whoever runs the show, provides the bookies. It's one o' the main reasons they happen. It's a major slice o' the profits."

"You betting on me?"

"Don't worry about that. Just do the business the night. I never bet on my own guys if I think they're going to lose. There's usually about three or four fights a night, so there's a good chance of making a few quid."

Things starting to fall into place, here. Tim thought he'd get me in the door, use me as a puppet to make some cash, not thinking twice about playing with my emotions, or my safety. Not sure he would be betting on me tonight, but my instinct told me he would.

We spent the rest of the journey to Dundee discussing how much money he made in the past. Tens of thousands, he said. Saying he had a gift, able to pick the winner just by the return of a look. Involved in the game for years, it became second nature.

I quizzed him on the rules for the evening, looking to ease my worry. The fight would take place in a ring, I would wear gloves. That was all I needed to know.

Chapter 17

The Venue:

Edging closer to Dundee, taking a slip-road off the dual-carriageway onto some country roads, Tim found himself lost, and me confused. All I could see was green Scottish countryside, fences, sheep and cattle. Pretty much in the middle of nowhere.

"I can't fuckin' remember where this place is."

"What kind of place we looking for?"

"A massive shed covered wi' blue cladding."

"Got a postcode?"

"No, I've not got fuck all like that. Been ages since I've been here. Got lost last time, as well."

We drove around a little more. Taking his time to get his bearings, although still seeming disoriented, Tim stopped dead in the middle of the road and pointed out the window.

"That's the bastard over there, the blue roof, you see it?"

It was pretty well concealed from the road, the height of the birch wood virtually hiding the shed. Driving a little further along the country road, taking a turning onto a farmer's rigid dirt track, where a row of ancient trees overhung the road on each side. The woodland surrounded the shed on the left hand side as the road opened up to a big patch of an uneven, hard, muddy surface. A large shed to the left and a farmer's cottage over to the right.

A collection of guys hovered outside the large roller-door, including Mike and Bull, the only two I recognised. Most of them dressed casually, except two guys who stood out, one in an immaculate Italian-cut, three-buttoned duke blue suit, smoking a skinny cigar, gold rings on his fingers, looking misplaced in this company.

Beside him was another well-dressed man. About the same height, but stockily-built, at five foot six. Dressed in sleek pressed trousers, t-shirt and suit jacket, all in black, standing watchful.

Passing them on the way to parking the Merc round the blind side of the shed, everyone fixed stares on us. We parked next to a vintage E-type Jag, which I immediately paired with the suit. The venue seemed perfect for an unlicensed show, middle of nowhere, hidden from the public and the main road.

"I need a word with Bull. Take a look around, wait by the front door and we'll take a look in at the place."

"Aye, nae bother."

We walked to the front door. Tim stopped by Bull, as I carried on past the hovering suspicious characters, head down, refusing to take anyone on.

Tim handed the briefcases to Bull and was thanked by a handshake. I slumped against the brick wall, waiting patiently. Stood like a loner, I could see Mike exchanging words with the suit, while having the odd glance around.

The suit and Mike strode towards me. I was immediately drawn to the deep scar on the suit's face, stretching from his right ear, down to the corner of his lip in a curved shape. You could tell a blade had been stuck in, deeply. He wore a pair of tinted glasses.

"Joe, I just want to introduce you to Mr Dean. This is his operation." An unusually polite introduction from Mike. His thick Aberdonian accent dulled into a well-spoken Scots.

"Heard a lot about you, kid. Hope you don't disappoint." Now I had a face to the notorious fifty year-old Steve Dean. My first impressions of this guy, he wasn't somebody to disappoint. He removed his glasses and rubbed his eye, seemingly sensitive to light.

The dark look in his eye and impeccable manners gave off a certain feeling of earned respect. The biggest clue was the way he was introduced by Mike. Normally not known for his manners, he was usually obnoxious and arrogant.

"Hope I don't either, Mr Dean." Answering confidently, I wasn't intimidated. He stood, glaring at me, sucking a long draw from his cigar, holding it with his thumb and index finger, swirling the draw around in his mouth, before puffing the smoke out above his silvery, gelled-back hair. He made an absorbing first impression.

"Well, you certainly are very relaxed, Joe. You must be looking forward to tonight?"

"Very much so." Looking forward to it as much as getting stabbed in the arm, but I wouldn't let on any other way.

"I'll be sure and tell Warsaw that you're looking forward to the proceedings."

"Please do, Mr Dean." I figured Warsaw was to be my opponent.

He cocked his head to Mike, then back to me, seeming irritated at my laid-back attitude, or thinking I was taking the piss. Either way, I wasn't sure. Sounded as if he held this Warsaw in high regard.

"OK kid, I'll see you tonight." At that point, Bull waddled his wide frame over, handing one of the briefcases to Mr Dean, who in turn gave him an envelope. Pacing away, he yelled to one of the men in the huddle. "Lukas!" Without hesitation, the man dressed all in black collected the Jag, then opened the door for Mr Dean. Lukas obviously was his right-hand man.

What was in these briefcases?

"Hey son, watch what you're saying to Steve. Don't piss him off." Mike jabbed his finger forcefully into my chest. I got the feeling he didn't care for me, or my attitude.

"What's going on here, Mike?" Tim finally appearing.

"Tell this stupid prick not to piss off Mr Dean. I don't want to be counting his body-parts tomorrow morning." Mike emphasised every word, rolled his eyes, then marched off.

"What the fuck have you been saying?"

"Nothing, he's just being a bit touchy."

"Well he's right, don't piss him off. That's a man that will cut you up without a second thought." I took it all in my stride, having bigger problems to think about. One of them, getting some food. I was starving.

"Let's get some grub, Tim. I'm fuckin' starving."

"Want a look inside first? 'En we can head into Dundee, grab something."

"Aye, suppose so."

We entered the shed through the small entrance door I stood beside. On the left, were a couple of shabby brick-built rooms. The shed was poorly-lit, cold from the levelled stone floor, wide and high. I immediately caught sight of the ring situated in the middle like a showpiece. It looked ancient. The canvas, once blue, looked more of a tea-stained brown. The same had to be said for the corner pads.

I leapt into the ring to get a feel for the occasion. The ropes slack as fuck and floor uneven, the chance of breaking an ankle, high. The fact there was a ring was a plus-point, so I needn't complain about that.

"Jesus, classy ring, this."

"It's seen better days, like. Anyway, I know who you're fighting now."

"Aye, I heard. His name's Warsaw and that can only mean he's Polish and if he is, that means he's probably hard as fuck." I jumped up and down on the loose planks.

"You're right about him being hard. In the Polish armed forces for ten years. Moved over here for work, just like the rest of 'em."

"That's great, Tim. Ten years, great fuckin' news, this. Not only do I have to have an unlicensed boxing fight, it's against a hard-ass Pole. Fuckin' great! Give yourself a pat on the back, mate. You deserve it." The pressure of the bizarre day had sunk in, so I tried to make Tim feel guilty.

"Look lad, I'm sorry. That's all I can say. But, you have to get your shit together if you're going to win."

"Don't fuckin' worry about me, mate. You got me into this, but I'll get myself out." I said, heckling in his face as I jumped back down from the ring.

"Right, come on 'en, I'll take you into town for some grub, on me, of course."

"Should fuckin' think so."

"I'll have to find out what time to be back. Jump in the car, I'll be there in a minute." Walking past the gathering of bodies, flapping my hoodie up, I ignored everyone again. Tim behind, stopped to speak to Mike.

"Got to be back around six. Three fights the night, you're on first."

"Thank fuck, first. Gets it done quickly."

As soon as he said I'd be first, an uneasiness started to build inside me over the event. I stuck it to the back of my mind for the time being while we got fed. I just kept repeating in my mind there was only going to be one winner.

Chapter 18

The Fight:

Arriving back just before six, the scene had changed dramatically. Seventy or eighty people hanging around the outside of the shed, guzzling cans of lager, making a holy racket of a noise. The car had to scuttle its way through the boisterous Dundonian crowd. A big fifty-seater bus sat in front of the farm-house

As we idled through, bodies parted, ogling through the windows to see the night's blood. The atmosphere was rowdy and tense, the crowd well on their way to starting their own brawl.

Into the shed, I followed Tim over to the ring, where a few men settled around a table positioned at ringside. Around twenty bodies in the place, most of them setting up two stalls at the rear.

One resembling a marquee bar, well supplied with crates of beer and spirit optics. The other must have been the bookie's, a blackboard pinned up at the back, with a raised stage. Mr Dean was at the bookie stall, roaring at some poor cunt, giving him a telling-off like a school-teacher.

Getting right up to the table, I could see an open suit-case full of cash with Bull standing over it, speaking to another heavy. As he spotted Tim and me approach, he slammed the case shut, and took a few strides away.

"Alright, Joe. Not long now?" He slapped me on the tricep in a friendly gesture." Feeling good?"

"Aye fine, Bull. Just wanting it over an' done with."

"Won't be long, bud. Am looking forward to it, should be a good scrap. There's a lot of people itching to see this fight." His round head bobbed up and down.

"Aye, me too." Appearing calm as always on the outside, I wasn't on the inside. My stomach doing knots, unsure of where that night would take me.

One thing I did figure out, the cash in the briefcases was counterfeit. The printers in the shed and paper scattered about all over the place, it made sense now. A handy little business venture to be running, while hosting an unlicensed show. I got the feeling the cash would be sold and distributed to occupants of the shed that night

Bull turned to Tim. "Right Tim, get your man out of sight. We need to open the doors."

"Will do. Better get in the warm-up room before anyone else."

Tim led me over to the brick-built rooms beside the small entrance door. Inside, it was bleak and dry, a table and two chairs in the centre of a poorly-lit room. Happy to get out of the way of the mob coming in, I could be alone with my thoughts. We listened to the invasion of yobs entering, chanting songs and roaring at the top of their voices.

"I've got to go back out to the car, get my ring bag. Have a seat, relax. I'll be back in five."

Relax? That'll be right. How the fuck could I possibly relax awaiting to fight in front of the most hostile crowd of people I'd heard? Dundonians were a raw breed of people, loud and in your face, loved a rumble and riot, most sporting the customary look of a shaved head.

Taking a pew on the manky floor near the door, I pulled out my headphones, plugged them into my phone, and stuck my hoodie up, starting to get my head in the right place. It needed to be focused and all thoughts of love taken out, meaning there was no room for May, Jess or Junior, for tonight. My foot shook uncontrollably, making my arm tremble as it sat on top of it, the anxiety kicking off.

The crowd were getting even noisier, the chants getting louder through my headphones. I turned the volume up, constantly reminding myself of the job at hand, trying to think of the situation as a normal boxing encounter.

Tim arrived in the room about twenty minutes later, with his ring bag and a multipack of bottled water. No idea what he was doing for so long, but it gave me plenty time to 'relax.'

"Here Joe, drink some water." He threw a bottle at my feet.

Full of nervous tension, my right leg still trembled, my mouth crisp and throat dry, I needed the water.

"We've got about thirty minutes to get ready. What you fightin' in? Those jeans?" pointing his finger down.

"Jesus, I never thought about it. I'll have to, haven't got anything else".

"Lucky I've got something in my bag, 'en."

"What?" I asked.

"Just a pair of joggers. They were for me, but you can use 'em."

"Sound." I never thought about taking anything to wear. Just slipped my mind. "You had one of these fights before?" I asked him.

"I did, aye."

93

"What happened?"

"Well, let's just say." He scratched the top of his head. "I wasn't cut out for this type o' fighting." What he meant was, he wasn't cut out for this game. Fighters can't normally admit when they know they've got a weak spot. Saying it out loud was quite a revelation, especially for a retired boxer like Tim, a well-known name on the streets.

Everyone has their role in life. It hurt him on the inside saying that. After all, he was a proud man, despite that weakness. One thing you had to give him credit for, was the fact he admitted it.

Instead of getting into the ring time after time, getting his head smashed in, he admitted that it wasn't for him, taking on a different role. That was smart, not weak, in my eyes. Besides, he had no need to do this. The man was rich in life. Had a lovely house - on the inside - twin, three year-old boys, a wife he loved and a stash of cash somewhere.

"Here, sit down. I'll wrap your hands." Tim slid two stacking chairs over and set them back to front. I sat floating my hand over the edge of the seat, while he got to work with bandages and tape. He looked as if he had done this a thousand times by way his hands moved effortlessly around my wrists and knuckles. I continued blanking out everything with my headphones in. I focused on the need to bring home the candy and tear Warsaw apart.

Tim focused on his task, eyes not willing to meet mine. He nudged me to remove my headphones. "When you get out there, just keep focused an' walk directly to the ring."

Well that was obvious, I wasn't taking the scenic route. "I'll be right behind you. I got you into this, the least I can do is see you out." His voice had certainty in it, he had been here so many times. Seen grown men shake in fear, seen men doubt themselves in their moment of glory. He spotted the doubt in my eyes, but in my case, it was what brought out that hidden beast. Despite Tim putting me in this position, I knew the right man was in my corner.

That was to be the case with every fight I would find myself in.

I didn't respond. I was entering that zone, that place where nothing matters but victory, and where pain is not felt. Willing to lay your life down to succeed. My stomach churned. The fear at its peak at this point. I felt the need to move, nervous and impatient sitting on this seat.

"Right, get your top off, stick these gloves on and I'll warm you up on the pads." Taking my top off moved my brain one step closer to entering the ring.

Tim handed me a shiny pair of plain black leather gloves. The finest you could get. Hadn't even seen a punch, as far as I could see. Wearing the 8 ounces felt like a tight fit, the knuckle could be felt through the padding.

"Smooth gloves."

"Aye, they're mine, but now they're yours. Call 'em a gift."

Just then Mike ventured in, hands in his pockets and fag loose in his mouth. "Don't mind me boy, just carry on." He pushed the table over to the side wall and sat perched on the edge.

"One-two's, just take it easy for a start, get the juices flowing." Tim said encouragingly.

I banged at the pads for a couple of minutes, nice and easy, but getting more pumped the longer I struck them. Then, the pre-fight sweats started. My breathing got heavier with the tension and my body tightened. The only thought going through my head was 'Bury the Pole.'

The feeling was different going into this fight compared to ones in my youth. Never did I want to hurt or win so bad. The thought of winning drove me on, losing wasn't an option. Losing meant no cash. No cash meant no food, mounting bills and an even unhappier life.

All those terrible years of childhood, plus the hard time I'd been having lately, was making its way to the surface, ready to cascade. But I had to push that out, no love in this game.

"Come on, harder boy." Tim banged the pads together, a loud echo rebounding from the walls. "Harder lad, come on!" Five minutes into our warm-up, it was time to step it up. "Hit these fuckin' pads as if it was your old man's coupon." Tim was getting into the rhythm as much as I was. That forgotten, petrified feeling before you enter battle returned from my past, like a euphoric high you couldn't stop.

As soon as he mentioned my Father, my eyes flared with vengeance and I snarled. I moved into a hyper state, full of hate, ready to shatter Tim's head against the wall. Momentarily, I stopped, and glared into his eyes with a burning urge to tear his tongue out. He dropped his pads to his hips, taking a half-step back. I had put the fear of God into him with a single look.

I knew then I was ready.

Instructing him to put the pads back up and get on with it, I could have broken his hands by the end of the warm up. Growling, screaming like an animal with every blow, I felt possessed. My chin buried into my chest, pupils fixated on each punch. I was boiled to the surface and ready to spill.

"It's time." Bull called from the doorway.

I had one last gulp of water, then Tim coated me in Vaseline. I could hear shouting in a foreign tongue. It was the Pole heading to the ring from next door. He must have been in the other room warming up. I couldn't understand the words nor understand the tone, but I knew he was as psyched-up as I was.

"Remember, ignore the crowd, head straight to the ring, I'll be right behind." He placed his hand on my left shoulder, looking solidly into my wild eyes.

"You know why you're doing this."

Totally enraged, I flared my nostrils and held his look. On opening the door, the atmosphere hit me like a Tyson right-hook. The population of the shed more than doubled.

I was so in tune with my anger, my heart beating into overdrive, a tingling of adrenaline rallied my nerves. A better feeling than any drug.

The light dimmed around the shed, apart from the ring, gleaming, inviting me in. The room filled with smoke, the crowd like a pack of wild animals, plastic beer cups and tins being thrown through the air. Despite the racket, all I could hear was my beating heart.

I barged past the drunk, blood-hungry crowd, some trying to block my entrance.

It only fueled me, snuffling like a gorilla. The adrenaline at this point overruling my head, the sweat poured from my body, the airless venue suffocating.

Warsaw awaited me in the ring.

He looked big, naturally big. Not defined with muscle but big-boned, all six foot of him.

Entering the ring, full of rage, adrenaline and excitement, my eyes fixed on Warsaw. Charging back and forth in my corner, I waited for that moment I could let go.

"Joe, look at me. Calm down a touch. Don't go steamrolling into this cunt. Use your boxin' brain. He won't have one." Wise words from Tim. He spent the next couple of minutes attempting to calm me down. I took in his words, I listened.

The referee, dressed sharply with a shirt and bow tie, had his last word with the judges.

They wouldn't be needed on this occasion.

The Pole, like me, wore joggers. Had ears like they'd been chewed by a Rottweiler and his nostrils spread like a buffalo's snout. A Polish Army tattoo on his right arm, looking around his mid-thirties, with the standard army hair-cut.

The Pole headed to the middle. I nudged Tim out the way and marched forward to meet him in the centre stage. Our heads were millimetres apart, catching each other's breath. His pupils flared and I could tell he had no fear. I knew he would be a handful, I could see a hardness in him. Not fazed, all I wanted was to put him away, get this done and dusted. The referee gave his instructions.

"No head-butting, biting, or low blows. Four, three minute rounds. Back to the corners and listen for the bell. You know the crack."

•

I walked backward to my corner, turning your back was a sign of weakness in my eyes.

The bell went. We both stormed forward, into a collision of heavy exchanges, neither giving an inch.

So much for using the boxing brain. It wasn't in his blood to take steps back, or admit weakness. Bobbing and weaving under his hooks, I rolled under, countering with my own thundering hooks, rocking him as he rocked me. Massive blows landed on my forehead, hurting.

Warsaw had a lack of boxing intelligence, which soon became obvious. He brawled and swung like a bear. Each time he connected with a big blow, the sweat rocked off me, but I stood my ground, as did he. Standing wide-legged, he left himself open to counters. My chance would come. His naturally big frame suited me, as he threw wide hooks, standing square on, I could get underneath them.

Easy to judge, I caught on to that quick. Unlike him, who ruled with aggression, I had the ability to think. He wasn't looking to land a jab or pick his moment, his eyes focused on the big knockout.

Knowing I was more intelligent than this cunt, I had to find a way to use that intelligence, pick the right time. After two minutes of carnage, he let an overhand right fly through the air, like a sledgehammer. It smacked into my forehead, careering me backwards. Seething, I cursed to myself and bit down on my gum-shield. Things didn't go too well for Warsaw after that. I slipped onto the back foot, took a few seconds to get rid of my agitation and think clearly, as he cruised forward with the same look of over-eager rage in his eye.

Waiting for the right haymaker to come again, like your alarm-clock after hitting the snooze button or a song on repeat, you knew what was coming. I went on the back foot and analysed his footwork.

There it was, the haymaker, rolling under with it, splattering a left-hook across the jaw and right hand into the flat of his face.

His legs weakened, I knew I had him. Walking forward to meet him again, using my boxing brain to finish the job. Feinting a left-hook with a small step forward, made him flinch and lean back.

Taking another half step forward, propelling my right hand into the hub of his nose, I felt it shatter and crumble.

The blood splattered.

Gushing everywhere, Warsaw fell to the canvas on both knees. The referee jumped in, started to count.

"1! 2! 3! 4!" The Pole stood, pushed the referee out the way, growled in annoyance, blood flooding out, and came for more.

Unfortunately for him, I was dead right. As predictable as he was stubborn.

"Finish him, Joe! Fuckin' finish him!" Tim yelled out from under the bottom rope.

Warsaw ran towards me in utter disgust at himself, because touching the canvas was a blow to his pride, his nose shattered, red gore flowing down his thick neck.

Pissed off to say the least, I used his anger against him. Standing still as you like, waiting for him to enter my range and throw the same right hand haymaker.

Rolling under his wild right hand with my eyes closed, slipping out to my left, countering with my right hand, planting it on the square of his face. The momentum of his charging frame landing into my fist, was catastrophic.

His legs buckled, he collapsed onto the blood-stained canvas like a toppling building. The ref pushed me to the side, placing Warsaw into the recovery position, avoiding his once intact, caved in nose.

There and then, I honestly couldn't tell you if he was alive or dead.

Chapter 19

The Buzz:

He lay unconscious in the middle of the ring. I felt no sympathy towards him, or what used to be his nose, or any interest in seeing him stand.

Standing, a lone soul in my corner, my hands by my side, taking in the crowd's roar as they cheered my victory. Now I could hear them in their full voice.

The tension and nerves sank from me as the Pole hit the floor. Proud as never before, body bursting with endorphins, blood soaring through my veins like a victorious gladiator standing in the middle of the Coliseum. Bruised, but still on his feet.

The audience roaring with satisfaction, pleased at the one-round battle they just witnessed. Racing through me was pure ecstasy, and if the feeling could be sold, I'd be a millionaire before the end of the week.

"I told you, Joe! I told you! You're made for this! Good job, lad." Tim came into the ring, digging his fingernails into my shoulders, looking proudly into my face. I was quite speechless for the moment, relieved the job was done.

"Let's get out o' here, back to the changing-room before this mob turns into a riot."

To be honest, I didn't want to leave. Standing in the ring victorious, my foe dormant on the floor, made me feel alive. The crowd still leaping over each other, throwing beer everywhere, added to my excitement.

Tim led me out between the ropes into the jubilant crowd, instantly mobbed by people tugging my arms and tapping me on the head. Feeding me praise and trying to shake my hand, I did my best to barge my way through to the changing room. It all felt a bit claustrophobic.

In the commotion, I lost Tim but continued on until I reached the room at the back, finding Tim already there.

Mike and Bull awaited, sitting on the two chairs, looking keen to praise and stood as I entered the room.

"That was quick, mate." Bull said raising his brows with welcomed praise.

"Cheers, Bull. Quicker the better, don't get paid for overtime."

"You gave the crowd their money's worth there." Mike said. Both the guys offered their hand, and I said I hoped that would be the last time I'd have to.

Their new-found respect for me, giving me an extra kick. People knew who I was now and I'd given them a fight to talk about, a fight to remember.

Mike, Bull and Tim talked about the fight as I took a seat, started to relax and let my head catch up with my body. Taking my gloves and wraps off, downing a bottle of water. I felt satisfied and happy I would be taking the £400 home to May.

May! As soon as she crept back into my head, I had to check if my face was marked. I rustled for my phone from my jeans pocket that lay on the floor and brought up the camera screen. My forehead and face ached from the hard blows and to my amazement, I was unmarked. A huge sigh of relief.

Another three bodies entered the room. One of them Mr Dean and the other two were the next trainer and fighter. Mr Dean shook my hand while the rest of the guys discussed that night's events. "That was impressive boy, very impressive." He removed his glasses.

"Cheers, it was easier than expected."

"You made it look easy Joe, that's why. I can see you're a smart kid, by way you dealt with my boy, Warsaw." His Fife accent was thick.

"It takes more than muscle to win a fight, Mr Dean."

"That's very true, kid. I hear you used to box?"

"Aye, in Aberdeen years ago, my Dad used to train me."

"Your Dad, eh! He done a good job, then."

"I suppose he did, aye."

"Well, hope I see you again. I'll keep in touch with Mike. Look forward to following your path."

"Sure, Mr Dean." I had no interest in becoming anything back then.

"Please....call me Steve, Joe." He put his glasses back on.

"Alright, Steve." We shook hands and he coasted out the door. He seemed like a rational well-mannered man, but everyone knew around here, he was anything but nice. A gentleman, but a very treacherous one.

"We need this room so we can get our man ready?" One of the two men said in a thick Dundee accent.

"Aye, sure. We'll get out your hair in a sec." Tim answered.

Tim started gathering the stuff we had lying around, while I began changing out of the joggers and wiping Warsaw's blood off my chest, still not knowing if he was dead, but I think if he was toast, somebody would have said.

"Let's put this shit in the car."

Took a quick exit out to the car in the cold October night. There were a few people floating around outside. Probably grabbing some fresh air from the smoke-filled shed.

Tim popped the boot of his car, threw his gear in, handed me a jacket, revealing a couple cases of beer.

"Have a beer, you've earned it." Tim said.

"Cheers mate, fuckin' need this!"

"You deserve it, after that pay day."

"Aye, so where's my cash, dickhead?"

"See Bull. He's the banker. Don't worry, it's yours."

"Sound. By the way, if you're drinking, how we getting up the road?"

"We're no'. We're crashing in the car." On such a high, I really didn't give a shit. Figured out how the rest of the night was going to pan out. Lots of beer, a few bloody noses and a bad hangover the next day.

"Joe, I'll have to get the bookie before the next scrap starts. Coming?"

"Nah, I'll stay out here, drink my beer and cool down."

I couldn't be arsed going back in, the drunken rabble was kicking off again. Stayed outside, drank my beer taking a moment to myself, thinking about May, Jess and Junior.

Done what I needed to do, won the fight, won the cash. Happy I'd be returning home without a mark on me. The noise escalated from inside the shed, curiosity got the better of me, so I headed inside with my pockets full of beer.

Chapter 20

The Hangover And Ride Home:

The next morning, waking in the back of Tim's car, with the morning glare of light beaming into my eyes. I rubbed my hands through my hair. Tim sleeping in the passenger's seat, still snoring. I realised I was rough as fuck. Head pounding my brain, living two seconds behind my sight, I could tell that day was going to be Hell. My mouth as dry as the Sahara.

I rummaged around amongst the empty beer bottles in the car looking for water, only to remember it was in the boot.

I gulped a bottle down and reached for another. It tasted good. Kept a hold of the other one, because I knew I'd need it pretty soon.

Taking a look around, there was nobody to be seen. No indication of what went on here last night except for the ground, strewn with alcohol cans and bottles. It was just past eight. The open space in front of the shed had turned to mud with overnight rain.

I decided to take one last look inside the shed. The place was a tip, rubbish everywhere, a few bodies lying flat out on the concrete floor and one guy using a six-pack of beer as a pillow.

The place reeked of stale beer and cigarettes, I turned and left. I didn't need any more memories of what I had taken part in. Just beside the door, I heard footsteps approaching me, it looked like Warsaw. As he galloped towards me I thought, "Christ sake, he's coming for a repeat of last night." Stopping a few steps in front of me, he looked menacing.

His right eye bulged like a golf ball. I doubt he could see out of it, his nose caved in like a smashed juice tin. He looked in a bad way. He stood for five seconds without speaking, just glowering at me with his good eye, eventually muttering something in Polish, shook my hand and walked away.

I headed in the direction of the car, spotting Tim vomiting uncontrollably outside the passenger's door. Watching him throwing up, set me off. I started spewing next to him. Tim finished before me.

"What a pussy!"

"Piss off, you went first!" I spat out between a couple more chucks.

We both started laughing, chuckling away with sick hanging down our chins and over our tops. We both took our jumpers off and wiped our chins. We looked at each other and started laughing again, hysterically, like a couple of stoned kids hanging out at Seaton Park.

"I can't go home stinking like this. I'll need a shower." I said. The smell of vomit mixed with stale booze from our breaths.

"What time you need to be home?"

"Any time after seven."

"We could go to mine. Dawn can wash your clothes and you can grab a shower, you'll probably get fed as well."

"That's a plan. Good of you to help me out."

"It's the least I can do, after getting you into this." Tim said.

"Talking of that, where's ma cash?"

"Bull gave it to you last night, you no' remember?"

"No, do I fuck." I rummaged through my pockets. Sure enough there it was, a pile of notes. I counted it. Five hundred. "There's five here, instead o' four."

"Bull and Mike decided to give you an extra ton." Fucking hope it's not that counterfeit paper.

"Let's get the fuck out of here before Mr Dean shows up. He usually does a bit of snooping the next day."

"Definitely, let's get to fuck."

Speeding off down the dirt track road, we reeked of sick. The only thing I wanted to do was sleep and it wasn't long before I nestled my head up against the window conking out, not waking up until fifteen minutes from Aberdeen. The snooze did me good. Feeling half-human again. All I needed was a good wash and clean clothes. Getting too old for this drinking carry on.

"Alright, lad. Woken up at last."

"Jesus, I needed that."

"We'll be at mine in a half hour, so you'll get a shower."

"Sound, cheers for this."

"No problem. Say, just wondering, you ever hear from your Dad?"

"No, I disowned the prick once Mom died. I looked for him for a couple of months, but couldn't find the cunt."

"He used to carry quite a name for himself around here. Never lost a bout, as far as I know."

"I know fuck all about his past. Just know he was a vicious cunt. I'll never forgive the fud for what he did. I'd love to catch up with him some day."

"Is that why you changed your last name?"

"Aye, I didn't want to be associated wi' it." Davie Rhodes.

"You and your Mom had a hard life with him, eh?"

"It wasn't nice, mate. When he took me to boxing, I thought things would change, but it just went further downhill."

"He was always giving you a hard time in the gym, too. Made you tough, though?"

"Aye, that's true. One thing he taught me, was not to end up like him."

We got back to Tim's around one o'clock and I was finally able to get a shower which was refreshing and well needed, staying in it for twenty minutes. His bathroom was as luxurious as the rest of his pad.

The room was marble-tiled all around in black, white and grey with the usual woman's touch of bright yellows in candles and flowers. Finished up in the bathroom, stuck on spare clothes Tim handed me, and headed downstairs.

"Joe, this is Dawn."

"Hi, nice to finally meet you." I leaned into her plump body and gave her the customary kiss on the cheek.

She had a kind face, a friendly attitude and sounded distinctly Irish.

"Nice to meet you too, Joe. I've heard a lot about you."

"All good, I hope?"

"Yes, almost." She smiled. "Have a seat, relax, it will be a little time before your clothes are ready. There's a Sunday roast cooking, you'll get a good feed soon."

"Cheers, think I should come here more often."

Sitting down, I could start to relax while watching TV with Tim for the rest of the afternoon. The smell of the roast wafted through the house. Tim started to count his winnings from the night before, stacking it in piles of hundreds on the floor.

"Holy fuck, mate. Is that what you made at the bookies?"

"Aye, sure is. Five grand."

"Five grand?! A nice little earner. Is any o' that courtesy of me?"

"Na, Joe. I never bet on you."

"So, does that mean you thought I was gonna lose?"

"Na, it just didn't seem right betting on you. Maybe will in the future though, after seeing what I saw last night."

"Look, it's a one-off. I have a family with a wife I love. It can't happen again."

"That's a shame, you could make a pile of cash in this game."

"I might as well tell you now, I'm not coming back to boxing either. Need to stay away from the scene. You'll have to let Mike and Bull know."

"Fair enough, I understand. It ain't for everyone."

He finished stacking his notes, disappearing out the room.

Dinner was ready, we tucked into it around the kitchen table. The roast was amazing and just what a hungover body needed. Dawn was a great cook and I complimented her on it. She seemed like a loyal women and knew exactly what Tim did on the side. He was very open and chatted about it over dinner. Something I'd never be able to do in my house.

111

By the time we finished eating, my clothes were dry. I said my goodbyes to Dawn and thanked her for the lovely meal.

Chapter 21

Back to the Same Old Same:

"Cheers for the lift, mate."

"No problem. You sure you're not coming back to Kilgours?"

"Definitely not. I'll keep in touch, though. We can grab a beer some night?"

"Aye, sounds a plan."

At that, I left the car, Kilgours and Tim behind.

Approaching the door, I realised I'd have to make up more stories about this security job, and quickly at that.

"Hi, am home!" I shouted, as soon as the door shut behind me.

Little Junior ran through to me clinging onto his Ironman and Spiderman toys. Jess must have been in bed.

"Hi, Daddy! You're home!"

"Sure am, kid." I ruffled his sparse hair, then put my arm around his shoulder, fortunate and proud to be a father. "Where's your mum?" I asked him.

"Mummy's watching TV."

May stood up and greeted me with a kiss and a big hug. Happy to be back in her arms. "How did the job go?"

"Really easy money, babe." I replied, trying to put on the most confident face I could muster.

"And look at the wages, an extra hundred."

The cash pulled out my pocket in fifties. Her eyes sparkled and her face lit up, which I hadn't seen in the past few months.

"What's the extra hundred for?"

"There was a few no-shows, so they paid us extra. No trouble either, a hand-out really. I'll use most of the 500 quid for the fuel bill, you can have the rest for a little shop."

"I'll put it aside for the mortgage, Joe. We're three months behind. What we going to do about that?"

"Look, something will come up, I'm bound to get a job soon." Tried to reassure her, but I had no idea where the cash would appear from. The stress was getting to her. Most of the £500 cash was to keep the power on. "Just have to do the best with what we have at the moment."

"This is no good, Joe. We need money. What if we ask my parents?"

"What, take money from your Father? No fuckin' way. I'll never hear the end of it. I've had a rough weekend May, I want to relax."

"What if I run a little bath for the both of us?"

"Mmm, someone's missed me this weekend, 'en."

We lay in the bath together almost an hour. Relaxing in each other's company was brilliant, after spending the previous night with a bunch of maniacs.

Getting up at 7.30 the next morning, a hell of a lot fresher than the previous day, I slipped back into the usual routine. Getting the kids up, making breakfast, the school run and home to wake May.

I realised how much I'd missed my family over the weekend. I promised myself to do everything I could to find work and keep our heads above water. I wanted my kids to have everything, unlike my past. They didn't deserve the pain I had to endure, and I would do everything in my power to protect them.

That morning, I paid the £315 fuel bill, then headed down to the estate agents with £185, the rest of the blood-money to pay into the mortgage.

"Sir, are you aware of the outstanding balance on our account?" Like I could forget.

"Yes, course I am, do you think I like you reminding me every time I come in here?"

"I'm sorry, sir. But, it is my duty to see that your account is kept up to date." What the fuck did she want me to do or say? £1500 in the red, what the fuck were we going to do?

Quickly as I could, I left, not able to face the thought of our mounting debt, week by week, month by month. I couldn't give her what I didn't have.

Back to the same old problem, no cash. May would use her whole pay-cheque for the mortgage this week. Twenty-seven quid left in my bank account. Least the kids would get fed.

On the way home, I picked up the local paper. Nothing in there for me. All jobs you needed qualifications for. I had none, except fighting, but that wouldn't get me anywhere.

Frustrated, I got up and headed to the Jobcentre and searched on their computer system. A few jobs in Aberdeen, thought I'd try them. I would find something where the bus would commute to. There were four jobs taking my eye.

A slaughter-house trainee butcher, a yard-labourer, but you needed a fork-lift licence, a green-keeper at a golf course in Aberdeen, and a dispatch storeman in Inverurie. I applied for all jobs using the email service at the Jobcentre.

Spending so much time down there, I was on a first-name basis with the staff, my CV saved onto the desktop of their computer.

Once back at home, I went through the usual afternoon routine, cleaning, picking kids up and laundry.

Fucking sick of it, this was no way to live as the man of the house. I didn't mind doing it, but repeating the process day after day with nothing to show financially, was mentally draining me.

Another week passed before hearing back from the yard-labourer job, telling me they'd employed somebody with a fork-lift licence and my application had been unsuccessful. Just the usual disappointment.

I still hadn't heard back from the other three, but wasn't expecting anything positive coming from them. The reminder for the council-tax bill had arrived, but couldn't be paid, yet again. The phone had been cut off, that meant the kids had no internet for their games.

Benefit day was approaching, so at least I'd get some cash. Yet again another trip down the dole office to convince them I was actively looking for employment.

This was seriously damaging my pride.

Every time I walked in the door, it made me feel ashamed. The entire staff could see it in my face. "Don't worry, Joe. Something will come up."

Yeah, right. Nothing ever comes up.

There was only one way I could make cash.

Chapter 22

No Choices:

Fighting was the only thing I knew, and I kept remembering the euphoria of knocking out Warsaw, standing over his paralyzed shell. The buzz, the adrenaline, the roar of the crowd. It was a big difference from doing laundry, pushing a Hoover around, babysitting and knowing I could make more money from fighting, and money's what we needed.

A month after the fight, in the Jobcentre claiming my stake again, sitting patiently for my turn, with the usual shame and embarrassment. My time came and I unwillingly looked the lady in the eye while she probed me on my job-hunting. Each question examining my life, this was my Groundhog Day. Walking out onto the street that day, I'd had enough and reached my breaking point, making a decision that would define who I would become.

I made my choice.

The first thing was to get to a payphone and call Tim, nowhere near the right decision, but virtually having no choice. The house close to getting repossessed, bills everywhere, no funds to pay them, hiding the eviction threats from the May.

She became so worried, turning into an angry person, losing her temper with the kids and me, on the verge of having a breakdown. She made a decision to return to nursing. She started proceedings to get her old job back in A&E.

Returning to any kind of nursing job would mean massive emotional trauma for her.

"Hello?"

"Aye, Tim. It's Joe."

"Alright, what's the crack, lad?"

"The crack is, am broke. I need money. Can you get me another fight?" He felt my desperation down the line.

"You sure, Joe? I can lend you some cash if you're struggling." I paused, seriously considering his offer, but that wasn't my style. Bad enough probing the government for cash every two weeks, never mind my mates.

I knew he wouldn't mind, but the point was, I would. If I took his money, that meant I'd be deeper in debt and didn't want the extra pressure of paying it back.

"No mate, don't want that. I'll never be able to pay you back." Thinking about what that money could do for me and my family.

"Well, the offer's there. You're welcome to it anytime. Joe, you still there?"

"Aye, still here. Can you get me a fight, 'en?"

"I'll speak to Mike, see what he says."

"There's boxing the night, is there?"

"Aye, you want a run?"

"Please mate, if you could."

"No bother. I'll pick you up, usual time."

"Alright, see you then."

May didn't question why I never attended boxing the past month. Guess she was just happy that I wasn't going, keeping quiet about it in case talking about it would lure me back. But, I'd have to tell her I'd be going tonight. Getting another scrap would mean I'd have to invent a similar story to the last one.

After the phone call, I did the usual, picked the kids up from the school and walked them home. Jess seemed tired, Junior hyper as normal. He stayed in his room with his Xbox and Jess sat in the living room as I stuck on a movie to keep her quiet and send her to sleep on the sofa.

May arrived home just after four, catching me going through a couple loads of washing. She looked happier today. "How was your day?"

"Boring as usual, May. Same shit, different day."

"Yeah, I know how that goes. Got some reduced stuff from the shop. Beef-olives for supper."

"Nice one, haven't had that in a while. I'm going boxing the night by the way, get rid of this boredom." Scratching the back of my head, it was awkward mentioning the word boxing.

"Really? I thought you stopped? You've not been in a few weeks."

"Aye, I know. But am going tonight. Tim's picking me up."

"It's your choice, I suppose." She spoke under her breath with disappointment.

"Well, I better get started on supper. You won't want to be dancing around with a full stomach."

I gathered my boxing gear from the upstairs cupboard. The gloves Tim gave me still in the bag covered in dry patches of Warsaw's blood. Throwing the bag at the bottom of the stairs, ready for a quick getaway.

I helped May with the rest of the supper and set the table. We chatted, sitting across from each other. Strangely, the subject was the first time we met in 2002 at the Beach Ballroom, in Aberdeen.

Fighting on the show, my Dad my corner-man. I was nineteen at the time, training like a man possessed.

A spell in my childhood when Dad actually stuck around a lot.

He warmed me up in the conference room being used for the home stable. Burning me out, before getting into the ring.

The nerves terrifying that night and getting the better of me. The fear my Father sunk into my core as a child, had that effect. Waiting for the MC to call me into the ring, trembling, standing in my Dad's shadow.

I only wanted to get in the ring and hear the bell, because that meant three minutes not in his company, gaining my own sense of freedom for four, three minute rounds. Walking into the ring that night, I felt the shiver of a glare. Three hundred people in the ballroom, but I only felt one set of eyes.

Entering the ring, Dad had his usual final word with me. "Right boy, don't let me down, straight into him."

He had a word with the ref while I turned to bury my face in the corner pad, taking a moment before the bell sounded. That's when I saw her.

This petite girl, neck long, black hair curved into her cheek. Naturally dark, olive skin, looking absolutely stunning, wearing a tight, thigh-length black dress. The moment I saw her, I knew she was the one. Making my legs go weak at the knees, forgetting that I had to hurt someone, turning me to mush with only a look.

Needless to say, the fight didn't go to plan. The entire bout, I couldn't get the better of my opponent. Overly nervous and trying too hard, getting a bit of a battering. Sitting on the stool after every round, Dad yelled at me, steam pouring from his ears. He didn't understand the more he yelled, the less effect it had on me, but that was Dad.

"What the fuck are you doing in there, boy?! Waken up, for fuck sake! Where's yer fuckin' head at?!"

The truth was, I couldn't concentrate. The only thing interesting me was the girl that caught my eye.

The fight ended. I lost, which wasn't a surprise, that tended to happen a lot the older I got. Dad did the usual, ignored me for the rest of the evening and stood at the bar.

I got cleaned up then plucked up the courage to introduce myself to the girl. Standing in the middle with a bunch of her mates surrounding her, I was more nervous approaching her than walking into the ring.

"Hi, there. How's it going?"

"Good. How's you, after that fight?"

"Aye, just fine, thanks."

I asked her about herself. Telling me she was nineteen, from Stonehaven, a town fifteen minutes south, moving to Aberdeen to finish her last year at university to become a nurse. She had a job lined up in Aberdeen Royal Infirmary.

We hit it off as soon as we started chatting, and there's hardly been a day since that we haven't talked. I couldn't believe my luck. She should have been way out of my league. So beautiful, laid-back and naturally kind. She was so easy to get on with. She reminded me a lot of my Mom.

We chatted about it all while supper was cooking. I felt privileged to be surrounded by such a wonderful family, making the stab of guilt going through me deeper.

Chapter 23

Back To The Slog:

A cold, miserable, dreech November night, Tim picked me up at the usual time of 18.30. Never minded picking me up, he got to visit his Gran, who he cared for dearly.

"You just couldn't stay away, eh?"

"Don't have a choice, mate. I need money, am sick of having none."

"You don't want a loan?"

"No, fuck that. I'll just have to pay it back. I'd rather earn ma cash."

"It's your choice. Gave Mike a call, told him you're coming back and looking for another fight, think he's maybe got one."

"Really? Who?"

"Fuck knows. Ask him the night."

"Good, hopefully it's no' far away, I need the cash."

Straight into the changing room, I changed from my winter clothes into shorts and t-shirt. Walking into the gym, only four guys there that night. Danny, Toby, Chris and Peter. Everyone took time to say hello. I wasn't a stranger any more.

Mike pulled me aside before I had a chance to grab a rope "Hey, Joe. Come over here." I strolled over to the front of the gym. Mike stood by the front mirrors with his usual slouch, hands in his front pockets and those baggy eyes.

"Hear you're looking for another fight?"

"Aye. Need more cash this time."

"Making demands now, boy? I'll decide how much you get paid."

"Well if I don't get more, I won't be fighting."

Considering I needed the cash more than he needed me, that was a bold demand, but fuck him, he wasn't the guy risking his life. Looking me up and down, his left eye and cheek twitched, wondering what to say. "OK son, I hear you. I've got a fight for you, in a fortnight in Montrose, if you want it."

"How much?"

"Two grand to the winner. Loser walks away with nothing. Usual fix."

"Two grand! That's more like it."

"Just a one-on-one. Last-man-standing. Your man will keep you right."

Mike was a horrible man to share a conversation with. Obnoxious, thought he could speak to you as he pleased, or maybe he held a grudge against me. Last-man-standing was old-school boxing rules. Once you're knocked down, you have a minute to stand, or you lose.

"Alright, cheers." I gave him a nod of thanks, then started skipping.

Two grand would end our money worries, pay the mortgage. Allow us to breathe without feeling trapped.

Tim took his usual place at the front of the four men, five including me. Barking out instructions as usual. He took a casual approach, taking one on the pads, leaving the others to their own devices.

He gave me a pair of punch-mitts the MMA fighter's use. He wanted to speed up my hands and take the raw power out. Not arguing, he knew his trade. Pushing me hard, giving little breaks, making me earn this two grand.

Finishing up on the pads, I felt keen for a spar with an overwhelming itch to hit somebody.

"Sparring the night?"

"No mate, no' the night. Next week, wi' Toby."

"Why Toby?"

"He's got a scrap in Watford in a few weeks, and for fuck sake, don't knock him out, you'll mess up his confidence."

"Watford? Why you taking him all the way down there?"

"It's serious business, this game. Travel up and down the country. There's a lot of cash floating around. Especially around London and Liverpool."

"Who the fuck's he fighting?"

"Some hooligan making a bit o' a name for himself down south."

"How the fuck do you know people down there?"

"I don't, Mike does. Knows all the gangsters and lowlifes up and down the UK. There isn't anybody worth talking about he doesn't know."

"Who's this geezer I'm fighting?"

"You've seen him."

I knew it. The guy from the counterfeit deal.

"It's that guy from Montrose, is it?"

"Aye, that's the guy. They call him Skinner 'cos o' his skinhead, and the fact he's one of those white-power fanatics. And Joe, he's an evil fucker."

"Aye, I figured that by the look of him."

"It'll just be a one-on-one, no gloves, but punch-mitts."

"Well, there's nothing like getting thrown in the deep end."

"You'll handle him. Think of the good the money will do."

"Easy for you to say, pal."

He leaned in closer and spoke under his breath. "One more thing. Skinner specifically asked for you. Think he's taken a shine."

Well, this would be interesting. A scrap with Skinner wouldn't go as well as the one I had with Warsaw. Call it fighter's intuition, but I could tell a lot about a man just by the look in his eye. I'd had my fair share of bare-knuckle scraps as a teenager around Aberdeen, in the Union Street graveyard, where private scraps were set up to end personal biffs, or down at Broad Hill, where I joined in with the Aberdeen soccer casuals meets with rivalling firms, just for the fun of it. When the fair came into town, that's where the real fun happened. Boxing-booths where you earned a tenner if you could knock your opponent out with a single blow. But this was the real man's world, not a teenagers' gang fight that would end in a couple minutes, and followed by a team brawl.

Why did Skinner fight without gloves on?

Maybe he couldn't fight with them on, maybe it would be too much of a disadvantage for him. I needn't worry about the circumstances of the fight, only the two grand I desperately needed.

Chapter 24

More Lies:

We locked up for the night and I headed home to tell more lies to May. I would use the same 'fairy-tale' security story. Couldn't say I was going to Montrose though, a bit close to home. Couldn't say I was going to get two grand either. Who gets paid two grand for working security? If that was the case, I'd have been working as a security-guard full-time.

Tim must have been sick of couriering me every Tuesday and Thursday, but it was in his interests. It was like his job and in a way, I was his employee.

Saying adios, I walked up the drive towards the door. Just before I turned the handle, I paused, taking a deep breath, wrecked with guilt that I'd be lying again, but it had to be done, or maybe I told myself that to justify it.

"Hi, am home!" I shouted.

"Hi, I'm in the living room."

She was working her way through a massive stack of ironing, standing in her Chinese-style black and red robe, her luscious legs inviting.

"I've got good news for you. I've got another weekend's work with that security firm."

"Really?! That's great. Where? When?"

"Up in Inverness this time."

"Nice, least you're getting around, then. What is it this time?"

"What you mean?"

"What kind of event is it?"

"Ooh...it's eh...a music thing." I stuttered a little, and eventually got the lie out.

"Same pay as last time?"

"Aye, same pay, £400. Well, presume so."

"That's great, that's the mortgage paid this month, then."

"Aye, that's what I was thinking. I'll leave you to that pile of ironing. I need a wash."

Upstairs, in a refreshing hot shower, letting the water pour over my head, I felt reassured that the story was sorted.

What was I going to do with the spare sixteen hundred? Presuming all went well against Skinner, I'd have a chunk of cash that I couldn't tell May about.

I'd forgotten about Skinner for a while. Recalling the evil in his eye, this wasn't going to be like fighting your everyday Johnny Boxer. Some men are born with a certain amount of good and bad, and he didn't hold much good.

And another thing, why was he desperate to fight me? What was his interest? I got the feeling that the money wasn't what he was after.

Time to get rid of the thoughts and keep the head fixed on the cash. The harsh reality that I wouldn't be arriving home without some scars, would have to be accepted.

I didn't bother going back downstairs after my shower. Didn't want to speak to May, I'd told enough lies for the night. Coming out the shower, I jumped onto my bed, towel still wrapped around me, and drifted off to sleep.

Chapter 25

Bad Memories, 2003:

I woke during the night, tossing and turning, drenched in sweat and full of terror, springing up, disoriented in the darkness, unsure of my surroundings for a few seconds.

Turning on the bedside lamp, and saw it was too early. Looked round, saw May sound asleep and felt instant relief I was here and not stuck in the past, where my dream was set.

I dreamt of Mom, who committed suicide and the reason she did it...my Dad.

A savage man who was never happy with himself, or me, and didn't have a single moral, or a bit of goodness in his heart.

From as far back as I could remember, he was always drunk and raging, and terribly cruel to both of us. His heart as dormant as his brain, it only worked when he needed to fathom out a way to earn cash.

His sense of humour also non-existent, but that's how he was, that's how he was raised, I suppose. Mean, callous and dry.

Davie Rhodes was hardened by his upbringing in the brutal streets of the Gorbals, in Glasgow. His father, a Navy man, had his arm blown off in World War Two and had moved to Glasgow to help design and build ships. He married a local girl ten years younger, and raised a family of six. Four boys and two girls.

Davie, the outcast of his family, uncontrollable as a young teen, upset too many men in Glasgow including The Godfather, forcing him to go on the run.

Davie was a Titan of a man, all six foot four of him. His face, hard-skinned from a life of self-abuse, hard living and scraping. He kept his thick, light-grey hair slicked back, always carrying a comb in his back-pocket to keep it in check. Dressing loose and ragged during the week and visited his local pub at any hour he chose.

On a Saturday night, his appearance transformed, dressing smart with pinstripe trousers and plain shirt, top buttons open to show his St. Christopher gold medallion. Hair heavily gelled and clean shaven. Wads of cash at his disposal and not shy in showing his stack.

He had that 'old gentleman' look about him when he scrubbed up like this, but there was nothing gentle about him. He was forever coming home steaming, regularly beating the fuck out of Mom, and me too.

At a young age, I would hide in my room, sitting in a crouched position, putting my arms round my knees, rocking back and forth like a coward, scared shitless, crying, or in bed with a pillow over my ears to block out the screams, every now and then removing it, to listen. Had it stopped?

Fearing for my own life, would he come looking for me? Would I be able to get out of my room after it had stopped, and would I be able to face Mom, knowing I did nothing to help, knowing I could do nothing to help, except for putting my arms around her? But only when the coast was clear.

That's how life was, growing up, listening to Mom getting helplessly banged around, hoping she would make it through the beating.

Mom was a wonderful, very simple woman. Jessica, adorable and soft-hearted, with beautiful, cherry-coloured hair and misty eyes. Her manner equally as lovely, patient, calm, kind, gentle and so loving and helpful to me. She had that old-fashioned Aberdonian gift of making you feel you'd known her all your life after a single conversation, and was much loved by the community.

She treated me as a Mom should treat a son, always looking after my needs before hers. As a young kid, I would sit beside her, trying in some way to console her after Dad finished his handiwork. She wouldn't leave the flat for days after a beating. Hiding the shame that she carried around on her face.

A year or so before she killed herself, the wear and tear of Dad's work became all so clear on her face, wrinkles appearing prematurely. This went on for years growing up in our top-floor, two bedroomed flat in Alexandra Terrace, in the heart of Tillydrone. A street that used to bear the name of Kilgour Avenue, was a hot-bed for violent crime. The authorities thought changing the name to Alexander Terrace would end its reputation, but it had no effect.

An area in Aberdeen that was notorious for trouble, if you weren't local, you'd find out soon enough. Dating right back to post-war times, crime became a way of life. It wasn't any different in the late eighties and throughout the nineties. It contained the majority of the city's drug dealers, vandals, thieves and the odd murderer. Seaton

Park, in the neighbouring region of Tilly, was a magnet for sexual assaults and junkies. If you weren't thick-skinned growing up here, you'd get torn apart.

The most dangerous clientele lived there, and my old man fitted in like butter on toast. When he disappeared from time to time, sometimes months at a time, it became a scarier place to be. Dad is a lot of things, but he was hard as nails and feared throughout the Granite City. Nobody bothered us when he was around.

People often arrived at the door asking him to sort out their personal biffs and worries. Remembering one time, I was around twelve years old, a couple of eighteen year-olds from the block of flats across the road came round asking Dad to find some geezer, give him a doing, and they'd pay him 500 quid.

I was hiding outside in the lobby listening in. If caught, that was the kind of thing that would earn me the back of his hand, or a thrashing from his belt. I could count on both hands the amount of times he beat me, but I recall every time as if it happened yesterday. Imprinted in my memory, it would stay there until I had my revenge.

Dad disappeared after Mom committed suicide, when I was twenty. Having enough of the beatings, pain and her reflection in the mirror, she just couldn't take it anymore.

I'll never forget that day. I got home from boxing on a summer's night, finding her sat in his seat, an empty bottle of vodka in one hand, and a near empty packet of 7mg Zopiclone sleeping pills on the side-table.

I can't explain the feeling of hopelessness that flooded me after opening the living-room door. My whole body paralysed, my heart cold, stopping momentarily, waiting for my head to register. I stood dormant on the spot, staring at her motionless body, petrified at what I was seeing was true. I didn't bother checking if she was alive. It was obvious, she was gone, so far gone.

Coming round to what I saw, I tip-toed toward her, trying to tell myself it wasn't true, this can't be happening. Lifting her stone-cold head up from the base of her chin, slumped onto her chest like a dead weight, I saw Dad's handiwork. Her left eyelid glued shut with the swelling the battering caused. Her right eye misty, open wide, her cheekbones caved in. Dad had done a proper job this time. Then, I noticed an envelope down the side of the seat, with my name on it.

Dearest Joe

> *My lovely son. I want you to know I love you with everything I have. You are the one reason that has kept me breathing over the years of abuse inside this flat, and I'm eternally grateful for that.*
> *I will forever miss your blessed face, humble way and love you showed me through the pain I've suffered. You are the most beautiful, caring son I could have ever hoped for. I'm proud of the man you've become and know in my heart that you will be an amazing father one day. Don't be long in making May an honest woman. Girls like her are rare, never let her go, Joe.*

Sometimes life makes no sense and reading this will make no sense to, you but I can't stay in this life any longer. The pain has to end for me, I'm empty inside, I have nothing left. I want to move on, I don't want to see his face any more. I don't want to wake up any more.

I feel awful for abandoning you like this, but you are your own man now and a special one at that. I don't want you to blame yourself because I know you will. Don't, it's my decision and I hope you can understand my reasons for this.

I know we will see each other again, that I'm sure of, but just now, I have to go. This is my time and I will forever love you with all my heart.

Love

Mom xxx

I burst into tears, and didn't stop for hours.

Mortified and ravaged with guilt ever since that day, I constantly punished myself, asking why I hadn't done something about the abuse before this happened. I should have found the balls, there was no doubt about that. And why wasn't I at home? Ironic really, because my Dad was the reason I was out of the house at boxing in the first place.

It felt like someone had smashed into my ribcage, ripped out my heart, then sliced it in half. The sight of Mom's mangled face, slumped down in Dad's seat, will forever haunt me. That really confused the fuck out of me. Why was she in his seat? The only person allowed to sit there was him. I didn't dare sit there. Almost as if she was saying 'You did this to me, Davie. Now, you will live with it.'

This was one of the times Dad had turned up, back from his never-ending disappearances. Hadn't been seen for three weeks, word on the street he was down in Liverpool again.

Not knowing where he was, I didn't care.

My Dad taught me a lot about boxing. Trained me regularly when he was around, that was the only bond shared. Never speaking about anything else, never asked how my day at school or work was, and I didn't repay the favour. Forcing me to start boxing when I was fourteen, I just kept going throughout the years. It was something to focus on and don't get me wrong, it's something I loved doing, being blessed with great skills, so people kept telling me.

That day, he came home full of even more hate than usual, beat the fuck out of Mom for whatever selfish reason, then buggered off down to his local, The Fountain Bar.

Chapter 26

The Fountain:

My heart pounded like a beating drum, full of guilt and hatred. A violent rage flowed through me. Picking up plates from the sink, smashing them to the floor, punching holes in the walls, howling like a wounded animal. Launching the side-table, crashing it through the living-room window over the top of Mom's corpse, plummeting it to the ground from the top floor flat.

I had to find him. Knowing he would be hovering around his second home, The Fountain, guilt-free, supping from his nip glass full of whisky, tin of export beer by his side. I legged it out the door, sprinting the distance to the local.

Usually a fifteen-minute walk, it only took me two minutes to get there. Boiling with fury, picturing decapitating my Father, drove me there in a hurry. I wanted to grip my hands around his throat and squeeze until he begged, squeeze until life left him.

I burst through the double doors. A half dozen men sitting and standing around the bar with a couple playing pool. The jukebox blasting out Bob Segar, 'Old Time Rock and Roll.'

Each breathe one of rage, saliva spluttering out, eyes spread wide, staring at my soon to be dead Father. Standing at the bar with his back to me, in between two men seated on stools either side of him.

Barging past the pool player in mid-shot. He swore at me, shouted at me, he was ignored. By the time I got arm's length with Dad, he turned, his huge frame fight-ready, drunk and oblivious to what he'd done.

"Aye, can I help you, boy?"

Unwilling to answer with words. I clenched my fingers together as tight as possible. Visualising him dead on the ground in a sea of red gore. My jaw compressed, body tightening. I threw the most violent right-hook with enough force to flatten a rhino. Landing perfectly across his left jaw, his head flinching to the side, followed by his body weight. It didn't have the desired effect.

As his head turned slowly round, he locked eyes on mine with a murderous look. "You've fucking done it now, boy."

Lifting his right hand, spreading his fingers wide, grasping my throat, his trademark, but my hatred for him consumed me. Swiping his hand away, snarling, unleashing another right-hook, knocking over his two pals, while Dad staggered to his left. Left, right, left-hook, kicking him behind his knee, him falling to the beer-stained floor. Leaping on top of him, losing all control. He begged for mercy.

"Stop, boy." The first time I'd had ever seen a hint of weakness in his eye.

"Fuckin' stop?!" I said.

Without one ounce of remorse, I drove my fist downward into his face, intending to finish him while he was weakened, while he was there for the taking.

Face cut open and badly beaten, I could have killed him. Psychotically blanking out, I couldn't see his two pals come to his aid, dragged me off, gripping a hold of me under my arms and pinning me to the ground. Using their weight keep me there. I wriggled and struggled, screaming at them to let me go before Dad stood, knowing he surely would.

Rolling onto his side he started to rise, first to his knee, taking a moment, gazing at the floor. Gradually lifting his head, discovering me pinned on the ground by his two pals. I stopped struggling. Paused, Dad looked at me. Cheek burst open and eyes badly bruised. He was contemplating my punishment, thinking about the pain he'd inflict.

"Let me go." I softly told the two men to let me go. I had no other choice but to face my fate.

Dad cocked his head at both men, signaling to let go. They released their grip and I stood, petrified, holding his eye contact. The most intimidating sight I'd ever seen.

The man had hands the size of slabs of steaks, built like a lumberjack, dripping in blood, desperate to kill me. The Devil himself. This could be the end of me.

No words, no sounds, he stepped forward.

Frozen with fear, I could see it all happen in front of me, but helpless to stop it. The fear freezing me to the spot. Dad threw a couple punches, left-jab then right hand, standard. Both making contact, square in the face.

Losing consciousness, I hit the deck. His massive foot booting me in the ribs, taking my breath away. Laying there on The Fountain floor struggling for air, coughing and spluttering, spitting out blood, in terrible agony.

I had that feeling of helplessness Dad had embedded in me over the years with his violence. In that position, there's nothing you can do but ride it out, senses gone, replaced with overcoming your pain, survival.

Dad mumbled something, standing tall over my body. Unable to hear what he was saying. His bear-hug, gripping my waist, lifting me from the floor. Screaming like a complete psycho, crashing me onto the slot-machine, shattering my back, glass falling to the floor. Releasing his grip, I hit the floor, landing on shards of glass. He continued his assault, belting my face.

• "See? You're still not man enough yet. Boy." A cocky wink and a cheeky smile, proud of his achievement in thrashing his own son.

I tried over the years to stand up to him, but every time, I failed and failed again. "You don't know what you've done, do you?" I spat out, lying on the ground.

"What the fuck you on about?"

"Mom, you fuck! She's dead." I'm dizzy, head spinning.

"Don't talk shit, you lying, weak bastard."

"Go home, you'll see. She's dead, she killed herself."

Looking down, a long pause, then realisation. Fixated, looking straight into his reflection in a mirror. He knew that something like this might happen one day. You couldn't treat somebody with such disrespect for so many years, and not have it affect them on an emotional level. He was far from a stupid man.

Turning his head round to meet the whole bar gawking at him, not in fear this time, but in disgust. His Goliath frame stood over me, then gazed down, this time with shame, and just like that, he turned and left.

I struggled to stand and go after him, but I could hardly move. The only place I was headed was into the back of an ambulance. I'd been badly battered. Little did I know, it would be the last time I would be in my Dad's company.

Chapter 27

Coffee:

Getting up that morning at 06.05, I needed a shower to wash off the sweat that poured during my nightmare. I suffered from delayed grief for my mother. Never coming to terms with it, the night-terrors were my coping mechanism. My way of dealing with all the regret trapped in my subconscious that forever haunted me, like a soldier with PTSD.

Dad still occupied my darkest thoughts, sometimes for weeks at a time, unable to escape them, like an unwanted plague.

The funeral was eight days later, leaving the mortician to conduct a post-mortem. He discovered her jaw and two ribs broken, and confirmed the cause of death was an overdose of sleeping pills, prescribed a week before by the local GP.

To me, she had planned it. Years of a dire life, she wanted to leave, needed to be at peace. I couldn't hold that against her. I understood her reasons, understood her need to end the agony in her heart and the demons in her head, and bed.

The next two and a half months were the lowest of my life. Hitting the bottom of the barrel almost every day. Living on self-destruct mode, suicide came to mind more often than not. Alcohol made it worse, easily disposing of a bottle a day, of whatever came into my hand. Lager for breakfast followed by whisky for brunch.

Running out of drink in the house, meant a journey to the local shop. 11.30 in the morning one day, in the gutter already. Stuttering my way to the shop, demanding two bottles of blended whisky from a sweet old lady behind the counter. Only to be refused.

Eyes widening with fury, blood-shot and not a care for anyone, I jumped over, ignoring the shopkeeper, filling my hands with 70cl bottles of spirits, then legging it.

Other days I went to The Fountain, arriving at 12am, stumbling out at closing time. Some nights not making it home, taking refuge in people's gardens, up against walls, even in the middle of the road.

There were periods I couldn't handle the pain, grief, regret and bouts of complete rage. How I managed to come out the other side, a miracle. May was the one and only reason my heart kept beating. Didn't matter how badly I treated her, didn't matter the state I'd get in. She just cared for me through it. Having achieved her nursing degree, at that time, delaying starting her new position in A&E to help me.

Erupting in bursts of anger, throwing the plates of food she would make me onto the floor, ignoring her, vomiting on her. She was my rock, all she tried to do was turn me back onto the right track. Eventually it happened, and I'm eternally grateful for that. I owe her my life. Strange as it sounds, this brought us together, sealing a bond that should have lasted forever.

Grampian Police did their best to track Dad down and eventually gave up, no information on his whereabouts. The whole of Tillydrone attended the funeral, a flattering turnout, showing the community's love for my dear Mother and support for me. St George's church pews filled, mobbed out the door, huddles of people gathering on the grass outside. The service planned entirely by May and Mom's sister, Betty, living in Aberdeen.

Betty was a rare sight. She hissed at the mention of Dad's name. Hated him to the core. She knew what went on behind our doors. Spending years trying to release Mam from Dad's grip. She gave up and through stubbornness, they stopped communicating. Betty too living with regret that she wasn't there for her sister.

Gradually as time passed, I calmed down, learning to live with the agony in my heart. Taking two months off work to recover.

Brian Stevenson, brother of Tommy, my coach of the once glorious Drones Gym, now Kilgours, was the reason I had a job in the Mill in the first place. Sharing the same shift, he drove me there every day.

A bit of a chore when he went on holiday, having to take two buses to the end of the long road that entered the Mill. Telling HR of my stressful time, they took pity, holding my job open. There were nice people in this world.

Chapter 28

Blood:

After the monotonous chores were over, I spent the rest of the morning in my shed. Blasting some Guns 'N' Roses from my iPhone speaker. I did the usual warm-up of ten minutes on the rope. Wrapped my hands good and tight with faded-out yellow wraps. Placing the gloves on, then turning the stereo up, 'Welcome to the Jungle' echoing out my shed.

Beginning my bag-work, memories of Mom still fresh in my head. The longer I shuffled round the bag, the more the past started pouring out.

Working with the timer today, three minute rounds with a minute break. My bag work aggressive, engrossed in imagining Skinner lying on the ground, cock-eyed and fucked up.

After four or five rounds I ditched the gloves, hitting the bag with only wraps on, feeling the need to toughen the fists. I banged away for the next few rounds, tearing my knuckles apart with the rawness of the soft leather. My brain didn't register.

Three rounds later, my knuckles torn and bloodied. Pounding the bag like a man possessed. The bag soaked in red. My head went to that place where pain doesn't exist, where passion and aggression take over.

My t-shirt removed, chin sunk into my chest, eyes fixated on the bag, my Father's face glaring back at me.

Forty minutes gone since entering the shed, I switched the music off, sat down on my weight-bench, looking at the state of my hands. The skin on my knuckles worn, my faded yellow wraps now blood-stained and my skin left splattered on the bag.

The past taking over, and the money worries, my head was fucked-up. Mind you, it had been fucked-up for years. You couldn't have had a childhood like mine and come out normal.

I tried over the years to hide my demons from my children, but now and again, struggled. It was important to me that the kids have a good upbringing, not be brought up witnessing a life of violence and crime.

That was the sweating over for the day. Entering my kitchen, I rinsed my hands under the kitchen taps, washing the red gore into the drain. While the skin was tearing in the shed, I didn't feel the pain, I felt rinsing it under the tap. Stinging like a bitch, I knew I'd made a mistake.

Collecting a basin of soapy water, I scrubbed the blood from the bag and traces from the floor. Putting my clothes and wraps in the machine, I had to get them cleaned before May got home.

Coming back into the kitchen, I worried now what May would say about the mess of my hands as I poured vinegar over my knuckles "Holy fuck!" I belted out, making my neighbour look in from his kitchen window.

I waved and said I was OK. Treating my knuckles with some antiseptic cream and allowing it to soak into the bare skin, then relaxing in front of the TV.

Later on, picking the kids up, I left the house with a pair of woolly gloves on to hide my knuckles. Being November it was cold, good excuse to cover the hands.

Holding Jess's hand while walking home was really painful, as she kept rolling her little icicle fingers over my knuckles. The wool from my gloves sticking to the open flesh. Getting them home, the kids settled into their after-school routine of homework first, then TV and Xbox.

"Hi!" May shouted, as she came in, closing the door behind her.

"I'm upstairs. I'll be down in a sec."

May was talking to Jess in the front room, asking about her day. Having my jumper on and stretching my sleeves out, holding it with my thumb against the inside of my hand. Acting shifty, she instantly caught on to me hiding something.

"Joe, why are you standing like that?"

"Like what?"

"Let me see your hands."

"What you on about, woman?" Taking rushing steps forward, grabbing my forearm, pulling back my sleeve.

"Fucking hell! What the fuck…Joseph?" Swearing in front of the kids was frowned upon in this house, and there's Joseph, again.

"I don't know, May. It just…happened, OK."

"Just happened?"

"AYE, just happened."

"How can you do that to yourself? Is there something wrong with you?"

"Well, there fuckin' must be."

"Where you going?"

"Going for a fuckin' walk, woman."

I couldn't handle the aggravation. The guilt I had, scratching away on my insides. Yelling at May before storming out the house, taking a walk to cool down for a couple hours. It felt as if I was falling apart from the inside, on the edge of losing it. May sometimes forgot what I went through in my past. Having a normal upbringing, she didn't understand the heavy weight of childhood misery, the unfixable damage burning inside.

I was hanging on by my last thread, like there was only one piece of me gripping onto reality, it almost felt like I needed to be checked into a mental-home, before losing control.

Chapter 29

Wounded Knuckles:

The weekend went by, didn't do any training because of the knuckle situation, plus I spent all weekend with the kids. May dumping them with me. She was upset, needed space and went to visit her parents by herself. Did she see the beginning of my own destruction?

During the weekend, I also didn't get the chance to think about Skinner. Jess and Junior kept me busy, as kids do. Junior having his debut football game Saturday morning. Absolutely Baltic cold, we stood pitch-side watching his every move. Jess enjoyed watching her brother running around the park having the time of his life, slipping, sliding and leaping into puddles of muddy grass. He played in central defence and owned it. Above average height for his age, I think that's why he was positioned there. The team won, beating Formartine boys club 4-2, and Junior was buzzing with pride. Happy to see the boy so chuffed, it made me proud to be his Father.

On Sunday, we visited the park, leaving Junior to play with some of the neighbouring kids in the area. The park busy with other young kids, Jess in her element running about, joining in, burning herself out, and jumping on any play activity.

That weekend was great, spending all that time with Jess and Junior. More knackered after two days than a week's training.

May came home Sunday night and organized them for bed. The conversation virtually non-existent, so I flaked out on the sofa, staying there all night.

It was the usual routine during the week at home, training in the shed during the day. Due to the state of my hands, there wasn't any striking of any kind.

It began to feel a relief being home in the quiet with nobody in the house. I just had too much shit running through my mind.

I walked into the gym on Tuesday, Tim by my side, holding my kit-bag around my shoulder. Mike standing just inside the entrance, outside the changing-room. My fists were the first thing he saw.

"What the fuck you done to your fucking hands?"

"I got a bit carried away on the bag."

"Jesus, boy. I better not see you hit fucking anything. I'm putting the money down for this fight." His arms flapped about like an unhappy child.

"Don't worry, Mike."

"Don't, fucking worry?" He leaned off the wall. "WHO THE FUCK do you think you are? This isn't a fucking playground!" His index finger jabbed into my pec, inching me back as I stayed cool.

"Your money's safe." I sneered back at him, actually happy I was pissing him off, it amused me.

"Get out of my sight boy, before I hurt you!"

Majorly pissed off but happy I'd wound him up, I strolled into the changing-room. Finding out that Mike was putting up the grand for me, I wondered why? What was he making from the fight? If I won, Skinner's grand and Mike's grand would be mine, and if I lost, he'd be a grand down.

It all sounded a bit wrong to me but then, nothing in this game should have surprised me anymore.

I worked away on the skipping-rope, pull-up bar, stomach work, and shadow-boxing. It was so boring not being able to hit anything. I watched Toby spar with a few of the lighter guys at the gym. He was in good shape, picking his sparring-partners apart with his fast pace and quick combinations. Getting pushed hard from Bull, who was seeing to his corner, Tim helping Toby's sparring partners.

Toby got the same treatment I got before the Warsaw fight. Doing three minute rounds with only a minute's break in between. His sparring-partners had been brought in from local gyms, weight-coordinated. He pretty much beat them all to a pulp. Toby seemed a seasoned fighter, but I just couldn't see him in illegal fights. He was way too much of a technician rather than a scrapper, yet he looked pumped and fired up that night and ready for Watford.

I discovered that Toby's past was just as troubled as mine. Training as a boxer from a young age, professional at the age of twenty-one. Training during the day and working the doors at nights, he lived the life of the early professional until one night, getting in a scrap with a punter, resulting in him knocking the man to the ground. The back of the guy's neck clattered onto the kerb, paralyzing him instantly from the neck down. Toby had to do time, but released on early parole due to good behaviour. He decided he had to move away from his home in Edinburgh, away from the gossip, bad name and trouble that followed him, making a fresh go of things up here in the Granite City.

His love for boxing never died, though. There would never be a hope in Hell of him being granted a boxing licence, so he turned to the cold underworld. Shame really, he had a lot of talent and was a really nice guy. Goes to show, everyone has a past they want to forget.

That evening, I only trained for forty minutes. There's only so much you can do without hitting something.

I relaxed and watched the sparring, for a change having a pretty easy night. The state of my hands made Mike even moodier than normal. He didn't take anyone on, especially me. He let Bull do all the talking, just leaning over the ropes, watching his man Toby spar.

It was hardly sparring at this gym, more like survival of the fittest. Sparring got harder the older you got, well except when Dad was around. He felt the need to knockout every cunt he was in the ring with, whatever his age.

The coach I had at the Tillydrone club as a teen, was Tommy Stevenson. An ex-pro featherweight fighter, a damn good one at that, knew everything about the game. Every angle, trick, or technique and most importantly how to get under your opponent's skin, beat them from the inside out. That was the most valuable lesson he passed on to me.

I couldn't figure out how much knowledge Dad had, he just wanted you to batter everyone, end of story. He said you learn the most about yourself when you're hurt, trapped in the corner, and have to find the beast within. He wanted whoever sparred with me to do the same, come full pelt, and test me.

Dad and Tommy never saw eye-to-eye, but Tommy took me under his wing, took it upon himself to teach me the art of boxing. Dad turned up at the gym, sometimes regularly, sometimes randomly, teaching his way of all-out war.

Just like everyone else around Aberdeen, Tommy knew not to cross him. Tommy rented the gym and ran the club, but powerless against a man like Davie Rhodes.

Dad would just stroll in appearing to own everything in the gym, belting out instructions, pushing me to the limit.

Tommy was a good guy, I missed his coaching, and Toby fought a lot like he used to coach, very technical and smart.

At the end of the night, while I was waiting for Tim, Bull and Mike locking up, Mike caught me on my own.

"Don't bother coming on Thursday. There's no point, with hands like that."

Standing casual "Aye, Mike. Whatever."

He wasn't impressed. To be honest, I was getting a kick out of winding him up. Couldn't put my finger on why, but there is something to be said for your gut instinct.

"Your about as annoying as your Father, boy. I'll see you Saturday. Bring your balls with you, you'll need them."

Chapter 30

Mike and Dad:

"Tim, you know that Mike knew Dad?" That was first thing I said, as Tim came over to the car.

Tim hit the button on his key unlocking the doors, stopped and looked over the roof of the car. "You figured that out, 'en?"

"Something Mike just said. How does he know him?"

"Better get in the car, it's a long story."

Tim fired up the car.

"Well, come on?" Slouching into a comfortable position, preparing for a long story.

"Back in 1990, Davie was pally wi' Mike's brother, Carl Jenkins. They used to do the odd job together."

"Jobs. What kind o' jobs?" Asking quickly, not giving him a chance to continue his story.

"Thieving, sorting boys out, that kind of thing. They were on the hunt for a pair o' lads in Aberdeen that ripped off a gangster in Glasgow, Jamie Dean, a relation in some way to Steve Dean. Their job was to find them and hold them until Jamie Dean made his way up to Aberdeen to finish them off."

"Aye, carry on."

"Right, Davie and Carl spent a couple weeks looking for these two, they'd all but given up. Unbelievably, both men walked straight into The Fountain when Davie and Carl sat at the bar." Tim paused for breath.

"What happened next?"

"They couldn't believe their luck. Two weeks of looking for these two bastards, and they walked right into the palms of their hands. Carl clicked onto who they were right away. He'd carried a photo in his wallet for two weeks. He signaled Davie to follow him into the toilet to hatch a plan. When they left, Davie headed outside, waiting for them to come out."

"Who were they?" I was totally engrossed in the story.

"Well, Carl knew who they were, he picked up the job and told Davie what he needed to know. A couple o' knife-thugs from Glasgow. The kind of boys who grew up in the slums, and carried a blade like a fashion accessory."

"So, what did they do to Jamie Dean?"

"The word was, they intercepted a huge haul of drugs on the way to Jamie Dean. Pills, if I remember right. When they found out they belonged to Mr Dean, they disappeared from the city. They'd been shifting it up our way."

"What happened to Dad when he went outside?"

"The plan was for Davie to head outside and wait. Carl was supposed to follow the two guys out once they left. The thing is, once they left the pub, he just sat on his seat sipping away at his pint."

"Dad got left to deal with both men outside?"

"Aye, he tried. He stopped them in their tracks as they came outside at closing time. He was waiting for Carl to come out and back him up. He didn't."

"You're going to tell me he got stabbed and ended up in hospital?"

"Aye, that's right. Davie tried to take them both on at once and in normal cases, he would've been successful, but he wasn't prepared for these two

155

cunts being armed with blades. I don't think they lifted their hands to him, but what they did do, was stab him five times. Once in the upper arm and four times in the chest and stomach."

"Jesus, I remember that. Me and mum visited him in hospital. Carl didn't come out?"

"Here's where the story grows another leg. Your Dad was shagging Carl's bird at the time. Carl knew and wanted to get his own back. He found out, but didn't let Davie know that he knew. Carl didn't bargain on Davie living. God knows what was going through his head. Like Mike, Carl was a grumpy, back-stabbing jealous bastard."

"Fuckin' prick, shaggin' other birds. Tim, you know more about my old man than I do. He must've been lucky to make it through that."

"That's what I've been saying. Your Dad is one hard son of a bitch. The nurses said to your mother that they'd never seen somebody so close to death and be able to walk out the door as if nothing happened."

"All this is why Mike's a bit funny wi' me?"

"The story isn't finished yet. You know the story of your Dad killing someone in a scrap, aye?"

"I've heard the stories, aye."

"Three months later, once your Dad was fully fit, he tracked Carl down and challenged him to a fight. Last-man-standing rules. Carl, the stupid cunt, agreed. A big fucker like Mike, but wasn't the fighter your Dad was. He just said yes 'cos he knew your Dad wouldn't stop until he got his own back. Carl just wanted it over and done with, but little did he know. Mike was only twenty at the time, and had no influence over his older brother."

"Last-man-standing?"

"Jesus man, I thought you'd know that. It's when somebody gets knocked down, the round ends they go back to the corner, or they have a minute to come to, then the round starts again. And no hitting when the man's down. It's frowned upon in this game, but happens a lot. Old-school rules, as they say."

"The fight? Dad killed Carl, right?"

"Aye, that's pretty much it, Joe. Bare-knuckle. In the top floor of the Bon Accord parking lot. Davie kept winding Carl up about his bird saying stuff like 'She was gagging for it, I taught her what a real man feels like.' Carl got sucked in and kept coming. Davie kept putting him down, round after round. Somebody counted Carl was down about sixteen times, but once he went down the seventeenth time, there was no getting up."

"Killed him?"

"This is what Mike told me. Carl was on the ground on one knee and Davie cupped his chin with his left hand and nailed him as sweet as you like across the jaw with his right fist. Game over. Carl was in a permanent sleep. Got told from an older guy I know that it was the most vicious punch he'd ever seen. Davie played with him the whole fight, knowing he was going to kill him."

"You're telling me that Mike witnessed all this?"

"Aye, he was there and seen it all. Like you, he's desperate to get hold o' your Dad."

"No wonder he's so fuckin' touchy wi' me. And, he can join the queue."

"Don't worry, he's touchy wi' everyone, not just you."

That was a lot to take in on the way home from Kilgours. I remember the time as a young boy. I didn't really understand what was going on with Dad in hospital. Five stab wounds and he survived! If he ever got his hands on those two Glaswegians, they'd live to regret their actions. It was sad that Tim knew more about my Dad than I did but hey, I didn't want to know him growing up.

I was getting more curious to know how much other dodgy shit he got up to. This road I was walking down was teaching me as much about my Father as it was teaching me about myself.

Chapter 31

Ticking Clock:

Later in the week on Thursday, I was checking my emails on the Jobcentre computer. I had a request for an interview for the dispatch job the following Tuesday. One of four jobs I'd recently applied for. Not a job I was at all interested in, but it meant steady cash coming in and an end to the rut we were in.

I emailed back straight away, explaining I would be very happy to attend their interview.

It was great news, though it didn't mean I would get the job.

The fight getting closer, the two grand in my grasp, I couldn't forget that.

Still mystified as to why Skinner burned to exchange fists with me. Surely a look wasn't enough to entice him into a fight?

The anticipation of the bout and the apprehension of fighting without gloves on was making me snappy with the kids. I spent most of Thursday and Friday, lazily moping around, ignoring the mundane housework. Choosing to watch the pish daytime TV.

I called Tim on Friday morning, arranging the cover story and plan for the weekend.

"Alright, Joe. What's the crack?"

"Alright, pal. What's happening the morn?"

"Leaving around six. Mike tells me the fight's around the back of eight."

"Right, I've told the missus I'm working in Inverness. I'll have to be out the house early, but not too early. Around ten?"

"Aye lad, that's fine. I might be out doing a couple o' errands, but I'll tell Dawn you're coming. She won't mind you hanging around until I get back. You taking the bus?"

"Aye, that's sound 'en. She can rustle up some o' that fine grub while I'm waiting. Aye, I'll get the bus again. Should be there around eleven some time."

"Dawn will probably make you feel more at home than me."

"She's a good one, your Dawn. Listen have to go, I'll see you the morn, 'en."

"Joe, take it easy, lad."

That was that sorted. I packed my rucksack with some essentials, and hid it in the bottom of my wardrobe ready to pick up in the morning. All I had to do now, was pick the kids up later on, fill in the night with them and May, and try not to worry about the scrap.

I knew Skinner was the complete opposite of me. I was a family man fighting to put food on the table, keep the roof over our heads. He was probably doing it to feed his fix of aggression, his ego or fill his pockets.

Couldn't picture him at the dinner table, or putting the washing in the machine. He would be more like the kind of man my Father was, no morals, no scruples, no heart and only looking out for number one. Probably avoiding the tax-man and loading his pockets with illegal pounds.

My Dad always had tons of cash, throwing lumps of it at Mum, trying to justify his behaviour. A clue he was getting ready to do a disappearing act, would be leaving hundreds on the bedside-table.

Now, I knew where it came from, fighting, thieving, betting, or debt-collecting. He may have had it figured out, though. Look at me, I'd had a punishing life for years, worked hard, looked after my family and I'm left with nothing. Being honest doesn't earn you money.

Chapter 32

In Anticipation:

I slept in a bit on Saturday, letting May handle the kids. The alarm belled and I dragged myself out of bed into the bathroom for a shower and shave.

Looking into the mirror, I saw an aging face, untidy hair getting greyer by the day, roughening skin, and eyes haunted by a life too hard.

Having had a restless sleep and hearing the kids making a racket downstairs, I wasn't in any kind of mood to deal with them along with my feelings of doubt, fear and worry, not knowing if I would come out of this weekend in one piece.

I pictured how the fight would go as the water cascaded over my back in the shower. 'Bloody' was the only way I could picture it. No gloves, just mitts.

I hadn't felt the punch from a knuckle in years, not since my teenage days of street-brawls. I imagine wearing the mitts would have the same unforgiving bone-to-bone impact.

I walked into the living room to see Jess and Junior play-fighting. Jess armed with a cushion trying to batter her older brother, while he crouched in a ball on the corner of the sofa, playfully taking a beating from her.

"Stop! Stop!" Junior shouting "I've had enough, you win!"

"Yes, I win. Junior is the loser! Junior is the loser!" Jess boasting, as she ran round in circles, delighted with herself.

I butted in. "Hey, what's going on here? Sugar overdose, or something?"

"Daddy, Daddy! I beat Junior!" with her smile as wide as a clown's.

"I see that Jess, calm down. It's far too loud for a Saturday morning. Junior, you big fairy."

Junior whispered in my ear. "I just let her win, she wasn't really beating me up."

"Mmm, I'll take your word for it. Listen do me a favour and keep the noise down while I have some breakfast. Stick the telly on."

"OK, but after that can we go have a kick about?" Asking with the excited twitch young kids get when they're itching to do something.

"I can't, I have to work this weekend. But, when I get back we can, maybe Monday night?"

"Noooo. But, Dad! I want to have a kick about today!" He was tugging my jeans as he asked.

"NO! boy, I already said I have to work. Now sit down and watch the telly with your sister." I raised my voice louder than I should have. I wanted some peace and quiet, it was first thing in the morning, for Christ's sake. Just before I left the room, I was drawn to our wedding picture, hung above the wall and struck with a horrid flood of remorse.

I headed to the kitchen where May had made breakfast. I thanked her with a kiss.

I really didn't want the breakfast as my belly was already full, with anxiety over what I was about to do. Playing with my food, I was in a daydream.

"Do you want toast? Joe! I said, do you want toast?"

"AYE, OK!" I shouted, making her flinch.

The noise of the kids from the sitting room and over-thinking the fight made me snap. Feeling trapped in my own house.

I threw the food down my neck, drank my tea and had to leave.

"So when will you be home? Sunday again?" May asked, peeved because I raised my voice. The friction could be felt in the air.

"Should be Sunday night."

"Well behave yourself over the weekend." She joked.

"Since when do I not behave, woman?" I angrily answered back.

"Fucking hell, Joe. Calm down!"

"Right, am out o' here. See you later." I picked up my bag from the wardrobe, grabbed my coat and slammed the door shut on my way out just as May shouted.

"You not even going to say 'bye to your kids?"

The obvious answer was no, but I couldn't believe I left my house and didn't say 'bye to my kids. Stepping out the door was such an almighty relief, I wasn't going back in.

I used the slow march to the bus stop to clear my stressed head. It was a cold, frosty November morning. I had left far too early, but was happy to be out the fucking zoo.

I arrived at Tim's at quarter past ten. Dawn welcomed me into the house. Her twin, three year-old boys were at it. Both of them sobbing, clinging to their mother as she hovered around the kitchen.

"Mummy, we want to go to the park. Mummy, please, Mummy!"

"Jesus, you two drive me crazy!" She belted out at the twins. "Just keep quiet, will you? We can go later."

Thought I had left this childish crap behind me an hour ago, I really wasn't in the mood for anyone else's kids.

"Really sorry about this, Joe. They've been driving me crazy all morning. I'll get them out your hair and you can chill out until Tim gets back."

"That's OK, I've got a boy and a girl at home. Am used to it." Pretending to sound supportive.

"Our house is your house, so help yourself to anything you want." Which is just what I did, helping myself to a chilled bottle of juice from the fridge, and settling on the sofa.

She left about an hour later, wrapping her kids up warm.

The house was finally silent, I could relax.

Tim arrived home a few hours later carrying a couple of heavy cardboard boxes. I got up to greet him.

"About time dickhead. I've been waiting three hours for you."

"Sorry lad, I couldn't get here sooner. Where's Dawn?"

"She fucked off hours ago, took the kids to the park."

"Aye, she'll be round at one o' her mate's now, drinking tea and gossiping. Irish women are good at that."

"What's in the boxes?"

"Eh, just some shit I need to shift."

"Like?"

"Some PlayStations, Xboxes, games. You want some?"

"Aye, give me a couple games for Junior."

"Take your pick."

I rummaged in the boxes and pulled out a couple, knowing they were hot, but least I could give something to my boy. He didn't get much these days.

"Cheers, these will do. How much?"

"Na, it's alright."

Well that was a first. Tim giving you some of his merchandise for free. It would be a different story if this was the old Tim. Back in the day, he kept a black book for his accounts. Letting people pay in instalments, interest added of course.

"Hey, make some grub, will you? I need to shower, it's been a long night. Just rustle something up from the fridge."

Disappearing upstairs, I opened the fridge, abundant with food, unlike ours. When he said "It's been a long night", I presumed he meant he was on a night-time raid, hence his boxes full of goodies.

While we sat eating, I asked about Skinner. "What's he all about?"

"He's what you would call...a bit of a wild card. He's English. I've spoken to him a few times, and can't quite figure him out."

"Mike says he's an evil cunt?"

"Remember that day we picked up those briefcases?"

"Aye."

"The briefcases were full of fake paper. He's a master at his trade. The banknotes are almost flawless. He's done time for everything, from shoplifting to fraud. Mike uses him for fights now

166

and again. He doesn't play by the rules. Very unpredictable."

"What you mean, unpredictable?"

"He doesn't care about anything, he's a bad egg, that's it."

"The cunt better turn up, so I can collect my cash. I need it."

"Aye, the sounds o' things, he's probably heard about your last fight and wants a piece of you, take you down a peg, so I don't think he'll be a no-show."

"Does he fight a lot?"

"Well, not really, just now and again. He's took a few fights from Mike and Bull. I've only seen one, he pretty much tore the boy apart in the first round, the second he played with him. The third he put the guy in hospital. Booted him in the ribs a few times, broke five and busted up his face pretty bad. He's an animal, he doesn't live by rules and won't put a pair of gloves on. His fights are always behind closed doors, with a small, selected crowd."

Once Tim had given me the low-down on Skinner, my first thought was, he's a bully. Someone that thrived on seeing you in pain. If he was so keen to bully me, he's in for an almighty shock because that's the last thing that will happen. His big advantage is that I can't wear gloves, the fight won't be in a ring, and he's from the street and that's how they fight.

So be it. I'll just learn quickly. This cunt doesn't know who I really am, he doesn't know that I carry the blood of Davie Rhodes.

Chapter 33

Pre-Fight:

The rest of the afternoon we lazed about, ate plenty and talked shit until it was time leave. Tim grabbed his usual ring bag and threw a six-pack of water in the boot, along with my bag.

The journey down didn't take long, maybe an hour. Enough time to put my head down as I liked to do before fights, but I couldn't sleep, fixated on what was about to happen. I was more wired than usual. My head over-thinking the worst scenarios. In a way, I think I was doing this to prove something to my Dad. Maybe I was looking for him to accept me, love me in a way that a Father should.

No gloves, just mitts and definitely not in the ring. This was taking me well out of my comfort-zone and deep into the lion's-den. So disturbed by this I could hardly speak, keeping my head up against the window, sliding into my jacket.

Traveling to the south side of Montrose, we drove through an open, green-painted steel gate into the massive parking lot of a motor garage. The building long and low, with eight roller-doors and lights turned on in the inside. The car park filled with vehicles.

"Before we go in, I just want you to know everyone's betting against you here. Only the big rollers are here, so there's a lot of personal bets going around."

"Aye, so every cunt thinks this prick will do me over?"

"Pretty much aye, but not me. I wouldn't let you do this if I thought otherwise."

"Well, I'll give you the best tip for the day."

"What?"

"Bet on Marks." I sounded confident, but was faking it.

Heading into the garage on this cold frosty night, the sky covered over in black, fifty spectators scampered around under the bright yellow lights in front of eight car ramps, each with a roller-door.

A heavy, oily smell matched the greasy surroundings. I only recognized Mike, Bull, Peter, Mr Dean and Lukas, the rest a selection of suited-up businessmen, paper gangsters and the odd piss-head. When the door shut behind us, a silence spread throughout the garage.

Our footsteps clunked as we walked in the direction of Mr Dean. He stood with tinted-glasses on and a gleaming long black overcoat, his aura marking him out from his acquaintances. I say acquaintances, because he didn't come across as a man with many friends.

"Mr Dean." I offered my hand.

"Joe…how you feeling tonight?"

"Not bad, Mr Dean. You?"

"Aye, I'll be fine if things go my way tonight."

I could only think he was relying on me to carry out the execution.

Mike Jenkins peered over, seemingly jealous of the respect Steve and I had for each other, then pulled Tim aside. They turned their backs, deep in conversation.

I chatted with Mr Dean. An interesting, elegant man, and a very dangerous one. He ran a sprawling criminal empire and had connections from the local council office, to Scotland Yard. There wasn't a problem he couldn't handle.

A group of four hovering close by us were having a heated discussion on a fighter they called 'The Reaper' from England. Apparently he hadn't been beaten, putting many in hospital, and called him a Barbarian.

"Who's The Reaper they're speaking about, Steve?"

"He's climbing up the ladder in England. I know the guy that looks after him. Says he's a killer."

"A killer, eh? Where's he from?"

"Liverpool. A Scouser. Jack Gallagher looks after him. A good friend of mine."

"Sounds like a hardy cunt, by the way they're talking about him."

"Hard! He's the business." A rare moment of excitement crossed his face.

Tim appeared back and pulled me aside. "What do you want to do before the fight?"

"Chill out somewhere quiet."

"The only place I can think o' is in the car. I'll come and get you thirty minutes before the kick-off."

"Where we warming up?"

"I'll get the boys to set up a quiet corner. I'll need to wrap up those knuckles first."

With my tension over the fight, I completely forgot about my half-healed torn-up knuckles. With just over an hour to go, I took myself out to the solitude of Tim's car. Preparing my head, I looked out a pair of headphones, starting my usual playlist on my phone, flopped back in the seat, and began to move into the zone.

As time ticked by, I let all thoughts of love and family drift out, replacing them with my pent- up hatred of my Father. I could only think about Skinner and decapitating him, ripping the bully apart, leaving him lying in a pool of blood. That same feeling I had prior to the Warsaw bout came over me once again. I had no interest in Skinner's well-being, I only wanted the money.

"Come on, lad. Get out the car. I'll tape up these hands." Tim startled me, tapping on the window.

"Not inside?"

"No, do it out here. Keep those hands hidden."

Tim was right, and good advice, too. He popped the boot where I sat with one leg on the inside and the other on the ground. Bitterly cold outside, the chill of the frost made me shiver. Tim went faster than normal to get it done. He looked more like a doctor performing surgery. Cutting short bits of zinc-oxide tape, sticking them to the top of the bumper ready to use. Opening up a couple bandage packs, placing them down. Using two types of scissors and a strict procedure to combine all the items.

"Think I'll call you the doctor from now on." Joking with him.

"I've had somebody tell me that before. I've done this so much, it's second nature to me. Here, drink some water, stay relaxed." The usual worried look layered on his face, as he concentrated on my hands, reluctant to look me in the eye.

"What's wrong, worried about me?"

"What the fuck you on about, Joe? There's nothing to worry about." Knowing he was lying, I could see the concern on his face.

172

"What were you and Mike talking about in the shed, earlier?"

"Forget that. You need to concentrate on what's happening now. This guy will tear you apart if you don't sort that head out."

The chit-chat turned my thoughts off the fight, so I stuck my earphones back in to keep my cool. My body started to swap nerves for that first tingle of adrenaline, my heart pounding like a drum. Tim carried on taping my hands, me winching with pain due to his over-exuberant bandaging, patting and pressing.

Taking a massive gulp of water to quench my parched mouth, I glanced at Tim's watch. Twenty minutes 'til show time. And, there was something odd about Tim's behaviour. Maybe the idea of his mate getting hurt might be the cause. I didn't give that a second thought. Having that mind-set would leave me on the edge of defeat. Instead, I switched all thoughts onto inflicting pain on Skinner.

"Joe…you know it's last-man-standing the night?"

"Aye, I'd worked that out for myself."

"You know what it entails? I know we spoke about it the other day."

"Round starts and ends when somebody hits the deck."

"Then, you've got a minute to get back to me, or stand. If you don't, you lose."

"A minute. No problem, Doc." I felt cracking a joke might lighten the tension.

"Seriously, Joe. A minute, that's all you've got. There's no ref as such, only a guy holding the stopwatch." Tim paused for a few seconds "Listen, a piece of advice. This prick is going to try and do

173

you when you're down, it's what he does. Like I said, he hasn't got any principles and don't forget it."

"Aye, I'll keep an eye on him. Don't you worry." The wrapping job on my hands done, I grabbed my gum-shield and black mitts, Tim picked up his pads and we headed inside out of the freezing cold night.

Back inside, we plodded past the growing throng towards a quiet corner. No sign of Skinner.

I decided to fight with my jeans on and removed the rest of my clothes to let the baying crowd see I was in good shape, shoulders and arms now starting to bulge, a well-defined chest, but still my gut overhung a little.

Sliding the focus-pads on, Tim was ready to warm me up. My hands wrapped so tight, I had to force them into the mitts. Tim held the pads up, instantly each strike echoing the building with loud slaps.

19.50, still no sign of Skinner.

The stable of spectators now glaring over to the corner while Tim took me through the motions on the pads. The bodies in the room had created a warm buzz in contrast to the earlier temperature, and the warm-up was a sweaty one. It was simple to open myself up now.

Three things that tuned my mind: Dad beating me, Dad beating Mom and the sight of her battered head hanging over his seat, dead. After five minutes, almost breaking Tim's hands with loud grunts of fury every time I made contact, all thoughts of normal life left my mind and body, filling my head with pure hatred, my fists clenched tight and my eyes in a trance.

Where was Skinner? I was ready.

"Joe, drink some water." I gulped down a few mouthfuls of water, letting the overspill roll down my chin.

I heard the door open, and everyone froze in mid conversation, gazing. In walked two short, bald skinny men, wearing tight black trousers and black bomber-jackets, the door momentarily closed, before Skinner stalked in.

My intensity skyrocketed.

Chapter 34

Skinner:

He stood with his muscled back to me, displaying his tattooed shrine to Germany, the back of his bald head portrayed the Swastika tattoo, coloured in a deep black, on the rear of his shoulders an outline of the Nazi eagle.

Covering his back, a portrait of Adolf Hitler in front of the Swastika flag, the writing 'The Third Reich' underneath.

Turning to eyeball me, he carried that same cold stare, shooting shivers up my spine. We exchanged deep scowls, waiting for the proceedings to begin. Neither dared to blink, or break the staring match.

Momentarily he glanced left, to Mike leaning up against one of the roller-doors, taking a long slow drag of his fag, blowing it out and returning an acceptable nod. A strange move, considering I was fighting for Mike!

"Right men. You both know what's about to happen here. Two rules. One, no hitting when the other man is on the ground. Two, when you're knocked down, you've got a minute to rise. Play by the rules, gentlemen. One minute to go."

This was it, time to go to work, time to fuck this cunt up. My heart rate thumped uncontrollably through my chest, but I held my cool on the outside, as did Skinner. Couldn't give away my fears.

My blood pumped at a rate of knots. Turning to Tim, my mouth dry with fear, he knew to feed me some cold water and soak my gum shield before slotting it into my mouth, still showing the same anxiety in his face.

Tim inhaled a sharp breath. "No guts, no glory."

Eyes focused, I didn't take him on. Knowing what I had to do. Mr Dean walked out into the middle of the floor between the car ramps and roller-doors, the slight chatter in the room dulled again. This was it.

A single word of "Begin." Shouted by Mr Dean.

Marching forward hanging my guard, swaying my left and right hands below my chin, getting the feeling-out process over.

He plodded, slowly, arrogantly towards me. His lean muscled frame, his veiny arms hanging by his side, sinister eyes burning through my forehead. Half a smile layered across his face, he analysed my every move.

I was in no mood to fuck about, the intensity ruling my mind. Leaping forward, a jab landed square on his jaw, shocking my wrist with the collision. I forgot punching a jaw was agonising without gloves.

His head rocked back, repaying me with a smile. Cheeky cunt, let him come closer and I'll make that smile bigger.

Repeating the move again, but this time a left-jab, then a right hand, right down the middle, flat on the kisser it landed. The right burst his lip, nearly breaking my hand in the process. Blood dripped, and I made the mistake of thinking this was going to be an early night.

How wrong was I to be? He put fingers over his mouth, realising it was leaking. He spoke "You'll drink my blood, you fuck." He groaned in a London twang.

I'd pissed him off already. At this point, I didn't know if that was good or bad.

He started hunting me down, looking to inflict pain, and it didn't take him long. Trying to avoid him, I shuffled round on my feet, waiting to get the feeling back in my right hand. He cornered me between a roller-door and a section of crowd, instantly grabbing my throat with his left, turning me motionless, four short rapid rights in a piston motion rebounded off my face, feeling like the stump end of a metal bat.

I slumped to the ground, Skinner towering over, globules of blood dripping from his chin down past my eye, collecting with the foul stew on the ground. Breathing heavily, Skinner itched to carry on his assault. I heard a welcome voice. Mr Dean.

"Round over, back to your corners."

This was the first time I'd heard the spectators. Cheering and grateful at the sight of my underdog frame slumped in pain. Picking myself up, I wasn't hurt, just stunned.

"What the fuck had just happened? Definitely wasn't Queensberry rules in this game."

"That's what you call bending the rules, Joe. Don't give him an inch. If you want to come out of this fight walking, you better wake up to what's happening. You're the smarter fighter. Don't stand still, he won't be able to hit you. Don't fight his fight. Make it your fight."

Standing beside Tim, keeping my back to Skinner, taking in his words of wisdom, realising I could be out of my depth, I had to adapt to survive.

"Time." Mr Dean shouts. His man Lukas was holding the stopwatch.

Skinner was already waiting in the centre when I turned. I had to remember what Tim had said, be smart.

Skinner, repeating his plan with the same half-smile, followed my dance around the floor. Over-anxious for him to lose patience, I cracked first with a left-hook, ducked to his left side, took a wide swing with my right hand, landing in the solar- plexus, winding him and hearing him wince, but he soaked up the pain like a sponge.

I had to quickly shuffle away to avoid his hand grasping for my throat, and now he was stalking me, waiting impatiently for his own moment to pounce, closing me down as I lurked closer to the same trap again. Forcing my right arm towards his face, he caught my fist cleanly in his right palm which impressed me, but I was the broader man here, and I could not let myself forget that.

He squeezed, bending my arm out to the side, ogling me with a smirk, mixed with determination and bloodlust, then pounced with the same rapidly fired punches, this time six of them.

Falling to the ground, blood spurting from my nose, shouts of cheers from the gathering mob filled the shed as they showed how the thrill of a man down was what they wanted. Taking ten seconds to get to my feet, lifting my head and eyes until my head cleared.

"Skinner. You'll have to do a lot better that that, big man."

His response, the same blank, angry evil look that hadn't changed.

Mr Dean again stepped out from the crowd. "Back to your corners."

Walking back, I knew Skinner's punches were stunning me, but never going to finish me. My advantage would be to box him. Tim got quite animated. "Fucking hell, mate! What the fuck you playing at?"

"Pissing him off."

"By getting your arse handed to you? Stop fuckin' about. I don't want to carry you to the fuckin' hospital!"

"Relax, Tim."

"Jesus, wake up! This guy will kill you!"

"No, it's me who'll be doing the killing."

Giving me some water and wiping the blood from my nose and chin with his towel, I understood what he was saying. I knew I was in trouble, big trouble, if I didn't get my head in gear. Pissing Skinner off would result in him making mistakes. Beat him from inside out. Turn him against himself.

The next round here.

With blood clogging up my nose, I snorted it up, and spat it over his golden rigger-boots. That was it! His boots! He couldn't move around on them quick enough.

What a dick.

Putting the 'Don't stand still' plan into action even more, knowing I could be quicker on my feet, shifting around him smoothly, slipping in and out of his range like a coiled spring, landing some blows, and avoiding his counter-tactic of gripping my neck.

That round, I cut open his left eyebrow.

Four more rounds went by, Skinner caught me time after time, sending me to the hard ground, which was fast becoming an unwelcome friend.

I was getting fatigued, trying to keep on my toes was hard work. He seemed to expel next to no energy.

It was the seventh round before there was a change to his style. Starting to box me, throwing jabs and some combos. Aware of his own frustration, he visibly tensed up. I carried on in and out, slipping his punches and countering with mine. Hurting and frustrating him more as time went on.

After five minutes of the seventh, the longest of all the rounds, my sweat and blood spattered my body. I thought he was there for the taking, but he was judging the timing of my movements perfectly now.

I slowed for a few seconds looking to land something that would take effect. I began to see him weaken with frustration as I refused to fall. There I made the mistake, standing idle in front of him as a thunderous right-hook stunned me. Standing immobile on the spot, he floored me with a left.

I was back lying on the dusty, oily, bloodied floor, disorientated, broken and searching for Tim through my double vision, in a state of panic only knowing I had to stand, get on my feet or it would be over, I would be the loser.

Getting onto to my hands and knees, three massive blows rammed into the side of my ribs sickeningly, shattering my ribs, the pain immense. Gasping, it felt almost impossible to breathe. I could hear Tim shouting. "Get up! Get up!"

It took everything I had in me to rise from the depths of defeat. But, the pain woke up another part of me. Unsteadily standing, determined, my stubbornness was now controlled by rage. I would be no loser.

"You'll have to do a lot better than that, big man." Repeating what I said earlier, telling him I was no mug, continuing to dig under his skin.

I had provoked a long-awaited response. His eyes softened for the first time, and his body language changed. He knew he had started something he couldn't finish. Hearing Tim in the background. "Joe, get back here!"

I waited until Skinner turned round and headed back to his two midgets.

My body in more pain than I ever wanted to feel again. "My fuckin' ribs are broken."

"Broken?"

"They're fucked!"

"You can't go on, Joe. You're in too much pain. I can see it in your face."

"Time!" Mr Dean shouted all too soon.

"I've come too far to give up."

"No! Think about your kids. Don't do this."

"That's why I have to carry on."

Getting back to the centre of the circle dividing the crowd, I stood ready for Skinner, holding my bust ribs with my right hand, my left fist clenched at my chin, blood running down over my mouth.

He looked at me with irritation, not expecting my return, standing there for several seconds trying to figure me out. I could read his face now. He glanced at Mike again, who stood tall and rigid, uncertainty in his eye. There was the customary nod of his head as if to say 'Finish him off.'

Everything became clear. This was a set-up, and Mike had stitched me up. Now I was pissed. Skinner must have thought 'Another couple of blows and he'll be finished.' Peering through the crowd to Mike rather than Skinner, another massive right-hook slammed into my jaw, jerking my neck. Almost blacking out, my memory suddenly burst into action.

I could once again see my Dad, fists pounding into my Mother, her slumped, dead body. Now, with no coordination, no sight, and only functioning on raw instinct, I launched a vicious punch at Skinner's smug face, a right-hook that landed with perfect accuracy, shattering his jaw.

He fell like a clattering tree, onto the ground, thumping onto his left shoulder. The force of the punch left me exhausted, on one knee. I loomed over the racist bastard as he squirmed on the blood-splattered floor, his jaw hanging from his face, his hand held up, begging me to stop his pain.

His call of mercy wouldn't be met. Rising to my feet, I lifted my leg high, showing the sole of my trainer, ready to smash it into his face.

His only saviour was Mr Dean, pulling me back from Skinner's crumpled, broken, empty shell.

"That's it, boy. That's enough, you've won."

Chapter 35

The Victor Claims The Spoils:

Mr Dean held my left hand aloft. "Winner, Joe Marks!"

A shockwave was still rocketing through the garage. No one expected this.

I stood beaten, in pain and mentally exhausted, the high of the blood-soaked scrap second to none. Money now took the place behind the victory. The atmosphere vastly different to the Warsaw result, where the crowd chanted my name.

Judging by the deafening sound, silence, the mob were awe-struck. Fighting and winning had totally consumed me. Combined with the black-market for fists, added to the adrenaline buzz I felt, looming over Skinner on the ground suffering, his shattered jaw was a dark, bloody and brutal mark of victory to me.

Skinner couldn't move, or talk. He just held his broken jaw in place with his hand, the massive blow to the head concussing him. Looking in his eyes, all the arrogance and evil had gone, replaced with sorrow and weakness.

His ego and body broken, was hurried out the door.

Some of the crowd were arguing frantically about the result. Many had lost a lot of money and pointed their frustration at Mr Dean and his chauffeur.

Didn't anyone have a few quid on me?

Tim helped me over to sit on a stack of car tyres. "How you feeling?"

"My ribs are fucked, my hands are fucked, my jaw is sore, but I'll live."

"Where the fuck did that punch come from?"

"The same place they all come from. Hey, this is a set up." By Tim's expression, it was obvious he knew something.

"Mike told me to make sure you lost. I didn't know how to say."

"Fuckin' knew it." I said, as Mike casually walked towards us.

"He's coming over. Don't let him know that I've got it figured." Mike must have put up Skinner's grand as well, so he was now two-grand down with nothing to show for it. Skinner must have been banking on a two-grand grand payday.

"Got it." Tim said.

He strolled over, his hands in his long, leather jacket pockets, eyes mostly focused on the ground, probably in disappointment or embarrassment, offering his hand. I welcomed his gesture. Knowledge is power, and he had made the wrong decision.

"Well done, boy. Bull's got your cash."

"The sooner the better. I need to get out o' here."

"You make sure and get healed up. I've got to go take care of some business." His tone blank, with no feeling. I could tell he was rankled as he turned and walked away.

A deadbeat loser of a drunk stopped him in his tracks.

"Mike, you cost me a lot of fucking money tonight!" He slurred through the haze of alcohol.

Mike spun and back-handed the drunk's face. The sound echoed throughout the shed, demanding everybody's attention. Tossed in the air with the force of the slap, the man retreated back into his shell. About a hundred and twenty kilos in that slap. Lucky it wasn't a punch.

"Somebody's pissed off."

"I couldn't tell you, Joe. I was stuck in the middle. I'm sorry."

"Tim, you weren't to know it was a set up until you got here the day. Just get me back to yours. I need a strong dram after that."

"It's the hospital I'll be taking you."

"No hospitals, I hate 'em. We can sort it out at yours."

"Sort it out?! Your ribs are broken."

"Ribs heal on their own."

Before leaving, Tim took off my mitts and wraps, as I sat on the stack of tyres. The skin of my knuckles hanging off in a threaded mess of red, had to be peeled away as the bandages were removed.

The adrenaline wearing off, the pain started to sink in. Using the mitts had left my hands shattered. My body started to shake along with my hands. I couldn't control it, as I retreated back into a normal state.

"You're shaking man, go with it, take it in." Tim frowned, worried.

Sitting there, hands in agony, face bruised and ribs broken, it was all his doing, in a way. He felt guilty for what he had done. Every time I took a breath, my ribs ached. I couldn't be sure they were broken, but by intense stabbing pain, it felt like they were.

The audience started to leave, while Bull ambled over, his slicked-back black hair shining under the yellow light. I wondered if he knew anything about the setup, but my instinct told me he didn't.

"Here's your money, mate. You earned that, well done." He sounded proud and even happy to hand the cash over. You get what you see with Bull, and I didn't think he had anything to do with the double-cross here.

The only people that knew, were Mike and Skinner. Mike, knowing Skinner was a sinister bastard, thought he would take me apart outside a ring. The feud with my Father tore him up inside. Little chance of ever catching up with him, and deciding to end the feud with me.

"Cheers, Bull."

"How's the ribs?"

"They're fucked mate, but I'll live."

"Make sure you get healed up and I'll see you back at the gym."

I had no desire to return to the gym. That was it for me, I couldn't put my family through this.

Tim helped me up and led me out the door.

I painfully entered the car, and Mr Dean appeared with his chauffeur, Lukas. He never spoke. Dressed in his usual black. He seemed to do everything for Mr Dean. A loyal servant, by the looks of it. An intriguing character.

"Hey, Mr Marks!" He shouts.

By this time, I was already in the car, the aching body made it too hard to exit to greet him. I wound down the window.

"Good fight in there, boy. How's the ribs?"

"Ah, they'll heal, eventually."

Steve slipped his hand into the inside of his pocket, took out his business card and handed it over.

"Give me a call if you ever need anything. I've got a good fight in mind for you, if you want it."

"I'll mull it over, Steve." I said with curiosity, already thinking about the next pay-day.

All I wanted to do for now, was get out of here, back to Tim's for a stiff drink and some pain-killers.

•

Chapter 36

Sunday Morning Blues:

"Holy fuck. Get me to a hospital. I'm in serious pain, here!"

"Aye! Told you! Should have taken you last night."

"Just help me off this couch!"

Waking up on the couch in agony, I knew straight away I had to see a doctor. My heavily-bruised ribs making it hard to manoeuvre, wrists and hands feeling like they'd been trying to punch through a wall and my knuckles scabby, torn-up with skin festering around. To be honest, I couldn't decide where the most pain was.

I had to get the thinking-cap on, conjure up a story for May.

And the kids. I didn't want this, but I'll be taking home two grand with me. That should count for something.

We drove to Aberdeen Royal Infirmary straight away in Tim's Merc. Mostly looking forward to getting some pain-relief. The paracetamols swallowed last night, washed down with Stella and whisky, had worn off, replaced with gut-wrenching pain, mixed with a nasty hangover.

Going to this particular hospital was a risk. I'm sure somebody would recognize me as May worked here eight years ago. I had little to no options.

Tim dragged me to a seat in the waiting area, while he checked me in at the reception desk. Filling out the necessary paperwork.

Approaching 09.30 on Sunday morning, the waiting area empty. All the weekend casualties more or less gone. We were quickly seen by an older nurse, Elaine, taking me through for an X-ray first.

Returning, I waited on a bed, in a small, closed-off area from the waiting room. I sat upright staring forward, my eyes glazed-over, bloodshot and tired, waiting patiently for the doc to appear. A nurse flashed past, who I recognized straight away from a past staff party.

Chloe, I'm sure her name was. Taking a second look as she strolled past, but I wasn't sure if she clocked me. I couldn't be certain either way, but something else to add to my worry.

Finally, after twenty minutes, the Indian doctor made an appearance, and I hoped he was here to fill my pockets with anaesthesia.

"Hello, Mr Marks. You look in a lot of pain here." Getting straight to the point, poking around my ribs, making me wince and shiver. Under the glaring white light of the room, colours sparked in my eyes. Grabbing a certain part in the right side of my rib-cage, I could have strangled him. My eyes turned cock-eyed. "Whoa, doc! That fucking hurts, you know!"

"Sorry sir, I need to be thorough. Well, I've a little good news, there's no breaks showing up on your x-ray." No breaks!

"So, what's the damage down there?"

"Looks like they're badly bruised and maybe cracked, so take it easy, Mr Marks. You won't be able to work for a few weeks. I'll give you some pain-killers for the ribs and I'll get the nurse to wrap them up. You need to keep the movement in them to a minimum. Now, what's wrong with your knuckles?"

"Ah…nothing, I had a tumble and scraped my hands down a wall…very drunk!"

"Tumble, did you?" He knew I was speaking absolute shit. "OK, I'll get the nurse to tidy up the skin hanging around there and wrap it up. I'll prescribe you some Dihydrocodeine, strong paracetamol and cream for your knuckles. Stay out of trouble for a few weeks Mr Marks, your body needs a rest."

"OK, doc. Thanks very much, I appreciate it."

"The nurse will be with you, soon."

Another twenty minutes, a male nurse called Gavin turned up. No Chloe, which was a relief.

I let him do his stuff, wrapping my ribs up quite tight, after picking the skin off my knuckles with a small, sharp, curved, stainless-steel knife, disinfecting them and rubbing some cream on before wrapping them up with a complicated-looking bandage technique round my fingers and knuckles.

"OK, Mr Marks. Keep the bandage on until tomorrow morning, apply the cream three-four times a day and make an appointment with your local GP for a check-up. Here's your pain-killers and instructions on how much to take."

"Thanks very much, Gavin." Glad all that was over. I ripped the boxes open with my teeth like a depraved junkie as I limped back into the waiting area. Not bothering to read the recommended dosage, I swallowed a couple tablets from each box.

"Tim, let's get the fuck out of here, I'm starving."

"Sure, good idea. Anywhere you want to go?"

"Head up the road to Murdo's." Famished, light headed and feeling a stone lighter than the day before, I needed a good meal before facing the wife and kids.

The thought of last night weighed heavy on my mind, giving me a guilty conscience, while all I wanted to think about was the cash tucked away in the glove-box.

"Can we have two full breakfasts, with a pot of coffee, please?" Sitting down at the first free table we seen as we entered the lounge at 11.15am.

"Sure, no problem. Should be around a ten-minute wait." Said the stunningly hot, blonde waitress. A great rack and toned butt, squeezed into her snug black leggings, Tim's eyes were glued to her as she sashayed away, wiggling her cheeks with perfect precision.

"Jesus Christ mate, check that." Tim said.

"Perv! But, I wouldn't say no, like."

"Better get in line pal, I'm first."

Tim's mobile rang. 'Withheld number.' Answering, his eyes opened wide, he then handed it over "It's for you."

"Hello?"

"What the fuck have you been doing?"

Chapter 37

Job Prospects:

"Hey, get up, you've got work to go to."

"Aye, calm down, woman. I'm getting up." Fucking half-five in the morning, what a chore this was. Half dead, slouching out of bed, pulling my jeans up at the end of another ordinary, boring week at the wholesalers.

Still shockingly cold in the middle of April. Never mind. I just had to get on with things. Get to work, finish the week, my probationary period, and earn a few pounds for the piggy-bank.

This was the usual way I dragged myself out of bed for work. May shaking and shoving me to turn the irritating alarm off. The days of making the breakfast when I got up were over. The new routine now involved putting the kettle on, filling the 4-slice toaster, trying to wake from my zombie-like state.

It was now May's job to get the kids up, while I went to work.

I wasn't able to attend that interview for the dispatch job, after being banged-up from Skinner's bent-rule tactics that shattered my ribs. Feeding them the same story I tried to tell May.

Five guys jumped me at the music concert, and I wouldn't be able to attend due to the state I was left in. Having a good chat with Angela, the head of HR on the phone, putting on a BAFTA-winning performance, I got the feeling she felt sorry for me, insisting I went to the top of her list for the next available position.

By a miracle, the guy they ended up hiring was a bit of a waster and sacked after four weeks, giving me the opportunity of the job at the turn of the New Year.

The interview went really well, to my big surprise, and by the second week in January, I had a job. By then, the ribs and hands healed, but my relationship with May hadn't. Getting dropped off that Sunday, I tried to feed her the same story, but she seen straight through me as she always did.

Quite openly, I revealed the truth about both fights. Explained the reasons why I felt I had to do it: for the kids, house and her. She understood how trapped I felt, but couldn't come to terms with the dark world I'd been involved in. But, worst of all, she couldn't believe I could lie to her that easily. What other lies are there, she asked, over and over.

Regularly after that, she became distant with me, gave me the cold shoulder every time I tried to get close. Time after time, it made me feel continually useless and guilty about the damage I'd done to our marriage. Midway between conversations, she would choose to ignore me and sometimes just walk away, leaving me talking to myself.

Getting sick of the situation, I would sneak out of the house on occasion, nipping round to the pub for a couple pints, some welcome company and conversation with the locals.

That morning was the end of my three-month probationary period at work, which would see me fully employed with all the usual working benefits, thirty day's holiday and a fifty-pence pay rise.

The job was shit, full stop.

I worked at an industrial wholesaler in Inverurie, stationed in the dispatch section. Monitoring the stock and compiling the data onto the computer-system and taking orders from a Neanderthal of a boss. Once started, they placed me on some courses, fork-lift, manual handling and a pish safety course. It was difficult adjusting from months of unemployment into a Monday to Friday lifestyle. 6.30am-3.30pm. The two grand of blood money I earned from the Skinner fight was put back into the house, but only after a few days of argument with the wife. More educated, and from a better family than me, she had a strict attitude when it came to breaking the law. She seen the money as dirty laundry and didn't want any ties to it. It took a bit of convincing, but she came round. The debt on the mortgage was paid off and we were now living comfortably again. One thing I couldn't stand about my job, was taking orders and being made to feel like a school-pupil, especially from the boss who was a complete fud. He treated his job as if he was the President of the United States. He didn't realise there was more to life than loading trucks and keeping stock. Many days I had to bite my lip and keep my fist in my pocket as he spoke to me like a dim-witted child. I longed for the weekend as soon as the alarm went off on Monday morning.

I hadn't seen my pal Tim since dropping me off that day. I missed the cunt. Didn't have any real friends in Inverurie. Sure, I had neighbours, work-colleagues and people I talked to in the pub, but I could never have conversations with them as I would with Tim. I could speak my mind with him, and we roamed in the same circles since young, tearaway teenagers.

Texted him from time to time to see what he was up to, or what illegal activity he'd been mixed up in. May couldn't know of that, banning me from speaking to him, or seeing him. It was hard to take. In May's eyes it was him, or her. It annoyed me, as I'd just gotten to know the guy again.

I kept some stories to myself regarding the underbelly of unlicensed boxing. To her, it was obvious Tim was the start and end of it, and in many ways, she was right, he was. But, I never held a grudge on the guy. There wasn't room for a new grudge in my troubled mind. Why waste your effort holding a grudge, unless the grudge had history, like the one I held?

May and me scraped as much cash as we could manage, for the kids at Christmas.

I tried my best with her over the festive period, finding out I wasn't the only person in this house carrying a stubborn streak. Her parents visited for Christmas, bringing lots of welcomed presents for the kids.

When Jack and Margaret visited, May's attitude to me changed for the better and it felt as if things were looking up for our relationship, but no, she put on the show for them.

Her parents were up their own arses. Her stuck-up mum Margaret never liked me, she couldn't accept her prized daughter married a man like me, or should I say, a man from a family like mine. Fucking cow, looked down her nose, not letting go of that 'Better than you' streak to have a decent, human conversation. The only time she would, after a few gin and tonics, the guard would drop and the 'Lonely at home housewife' would pour out of the bottle. Seeking the attention from younger men, flirting and becoming very touchy-feely, looking for them to make her feel a young woman again, and willingly, she would let them.

At the age of fifty-two, Margaret Wood still had her looks. It helped that she wore the best clobber, expensive jewellery and a face-full of lippy and slap, standard cougar get-up. Felt she was upper-class, coming from an above-average rich family and her husband Jack being an over-paid offshore driller. A stereotypical gold-digging housewife, but earned her crust putting up with an arrogant English arse-hole.

Tolerating Jack did have its benefits for Margaret. Plenty of peace and quiet to get the local handyman round a couple of days a week, and unlimited use of his credit card, plus the luxury of driving around Stonehaven in his brand new Range Rover Sport.

Jack Wood was a chunky, broad, average height man in his late fifties, already gearing up for retirement. Rich and gullible to his wife's carry-ons, while he was 'Freezing his ass off in the North Sea' as he put it. He was an easy-spending, happy chap that would happily write a big cheque to help us out, but would hold it against me forever, with sly remarks and 'witty' comments.

He was a simple guy at home. Bought a paper in the morning, walked the dog and jugged a few cans of lager a couple of nights a week. Loved a bit of illegal hunting on estate properties with his shotgun, giving the old guy a sense of feeling young again. A spot of fly-fishing on a Saturday morning wasn't out the question, either.

I didn't mind Jack in small doses, but patience would wear thin with him. I could sink a few beers in his company no problem, until he would boast about working offshore and the big coins he earns.

All the time I'd known Jack, he had never offered help in any way. Until that boozy Christmas night sitting at the kitchen table, sharing too many beers he offered his hand. "You ever thought about offshore?" Sure I'd thought of it, many times but I hadn't the money to sort it out, and he knew that.

"Aye, all the time Jack, but I don't have the cash or experience to go anywhere." It was never supposed to sound like a cry for help, but unfortunately it came across like that, making me sound pathetically helpless. Leaning in closer to me by sliding his forearms across the table, he offered his help.

"Well, I can help if you want it?" Cheeky cunt, basically making me ask for his help, he was. What was he going to do? Write me a cheque, get me a job or make me grovel? The idea of letting him help me and owing him, wasn't thrilling me. "I could call the office set up an interview for you as a roustabout or roughneck, put you through all the necessary courses to get you on the chopper."

OK, this sounds like not a bad situation at all, but I couldn't get under his grip. I would hear about this for the rest of my days. Sure, I'd be better off and financially sound, but was it worth it? Taking his constant remarks about how he helped out his down-and-out son-in-law get started in the North Sea.

In all fairness he was trying to help, but in a patronising way.

We were both well on the way, with a mountain of empty tins sitting on the table and getting on like a house on fire, but the longer I sat at the table that night, the more I wanted to give him a slap.

Well, it ended up I didn't need his help. I called him up and said I'd managed to get a start at the wholesalers. It was considerably satisfying for me, but it was a kick in the stones for him, and brushing off his help made my day.

Chapter 38

Working Life:

"So, Mr Marks, your probationary period has finished as from today. We are very pleased with you, perfect attendance, your clock-in times are excellent and I'm told by your manager you're good at your job and you're getting to grips with the computer-system. We would like to offer you the job on a permanent basis." Said by the double-chinned specky wholesaler manager Mr Mackenzie, as he leaned back on his leather office-chair, interlocking his fingers, all superior. Seeming to be the most vital man in the company, he was just a puffed-up nonce, oblivious to the only reason I had to work here: to feed my family, and keep a roof over their heads.

"Thanks, Mr Mackenzie." I paused, thinking of my long-term future: I could be stuck here forever. "I would be delighted to have the job, thank you."

I wasn't delighted, far from it. Having no interest in getting out my bed when the alarm went off, or walking in and out of here every mundane weekday.

Thinking of quitting entered my head on a regular basis, this wasn't the place for me. Being somebody's mug, somebody to be barked orders at by arse-holes. That was the treatment I got at the Mill, and look how that ended up.

"Good, Joe, that's good. As from now, your pay will creep up a little and you are allocated twenty-eight day's holiday for the year, plus the usual bank holidays: Christmas, Boxing Day and New Year. After all, none of us like to work those days, do we?" Glancing up from reading paperwork on his desk, looking over his oval glasses, his double-chin desperate to fold over his buttoned-up office shirt. With his daily sweat patches and skin the colour of over-used chip fat, he was an undesirable man, to say the least. After a little more chit-chat about the benefits of being employed here, I was bored with him.

"You can go back to work now, Joe. Thanks for your time."

Back to work, I tottered back into the dispatch position, longing for the day to end. It was Friday though, a couple of days-off coming up. A couple of days of noisy kids and a mood-swinging wife.

There wasn't much I could do right by her any more. There was a constant atmosphere, and it continued to piss me off, my patience and temper about to unravel at times. I did my own thing at home, cracked open a few tins, sat with my feet-up holding my new Sky remote, recently installed. That at least kept me entertained at home.

My head was pounding that day, I had no interest in being at work. There was a big order to complete and a truck to load before I could switch off for the weekend. Mr Mackenzie decided he was donning the work-gear for the afternoon and joined the rest of the staff, barking unnecessary orders out, making my headache worse. I ached for that feeling of freedom for the weekend.

Once home, I slipped my trainers off at the door, and sank into the comfort of the sofa.

I couldn't be arsed with the family coming home frying my head, and decided to go for a pint.

Taking my phone out my pocket, searching for the contact, Brian. I had told May that Brian was a fellow work-mate. It was Tim. I wondered what he was up to. Keeping in touch by sending Whatsapp messages to each other, May saw his name pop up on the screen from time to time, so best she thought it was somebody else. It would only cause more arguing, knowing I was still in touch with him.

"Alright, mate. How's it going?"

"Not bad, Joe. What's the crack?"

"Nae much. What you up to?" Hoping he had a thirst for pints and a good catch up, I missed the scruffy cunt.

"Fuck all, not long woke up, late night."

"How about telling me about it over a few pints."

"Aye, why not? Where you thinking?"

"Fountain?" I didn't quite know why that sprung out as we both stayed in different towns, but we had to meet somewhere. I hadn't been in there since I was on my ten week bender after Mom died, so many years ago.

"Sounds dangerous. I'm up for it, I'll grab a shower and meet you there. You bussing it?"

"Aye, afraid so. I better jump in the shower before May gets home. Meet you there, 'en?"

Chapter 39

Paranoia:

The Fountain was a proper man's establishment. Dull, with no natural light flooding in, full of good crack and boisterous punters. Owned by Margaret Williamson, the landlady. She ran the pub for the past eight years, and made you feel like part of the furniture.

Her hard-work and attitude made the place what it was. We all respected her. Losing her husband five years ago to throat cancer, the bar became her whole life.

In her fifties, her face showed her hard life. But, she always dressed her best, taking pride in her appearance and had that sarcastic Aberdonian humour which entertained the locals.

The main bar never changed over the years, with vintage, eighties décor. Paneled wooden walls, scattered with framed paintings of alcohol and newspaper cuttings of the great Granite City and AFC, Aberdeen Football Club.

The wall just inside the entrance displayed photos of locals from the surrounding areas of Woodside and Tilly. The same people packed the bar that night.

"Another pint, Tim?" We were situated around the near side of the u-shaped bar that dominated the room, close to the pool table. The jukebox blaring classic rock, pub filled with workers desperate not to go home, still in their scruffy working clothes. Tim was playing a cagey game of pool with Micky MacDonald.

"Make mine a dram." Tim was a whisky man, loved an expensive, peaty malt and loved it even more when he didn't have to pay for it.

Pennies were prisoners with Tim. I'm sure he had one of those safes hidden under the carpet, carved into the floorboards of his house, somewhere. Locked up with a number of safety features to stop anyone like him breaking in.

"Micky, you for one?" I shouted, him in mid-shot as he stared down his stick, his chin sliding back and forth, lining it up like a pro, causing him to miss the crucial black, playing for a dram.

Banging the tip of the cue over the table, he returned my shout with a lingering look of disgust. I struggled to contain my laughter.

"Fuck me. Joe, you prick!" Micky MacDonald, a leery character, oozed jail-time. In and out like a yo-yo over the years.

He had a nervous twitch and slabs of paranoia. Always skittish, and on edge. Ready to erupt in argument with anyone who offered a serious confrontation, which was a common trait in an Aberdonian. His shifty demeanour came from years of watching his back in the nick and care-homes, where you had to sleep with your eyes open

That afternoon was the first time I had met him, and we grew to know each other really well over the next few months, under circumstances I couldn't predict.

"Sorry, Micky. I'll get you a drammy for that." Holding my hand in the air in a gesture of apology.

"Fuckin' right you will, cheeky bastard." Tim finished off the game with an easy pot on the black, snickering away at Micky, who was taking an adult hissy-fit, turning himself around in mini-circles, poking his head in and out, cursing "Fuckin' wankers! You cunts!"

"Aye, well-played anyway, Micky. We'll have a rematch later." Tim stuck his hand out, but Micky brushed it aside comically and headed to the toilet.

Micky was a wee nimble guy at five foot five, but exuberant, full of life and high as a kite most days. His runty frame and sloppy clothes made him look quite harmless, but soon as I spent ten minutes in his company, I saw something chilling about him.

His 'Desperate Dan' chin and beady eyes told me he was the sort that could tear you apart just by dragging his fingernails across your cheeks, if he had to. The kind that would take a chunk out of your ear, if he felt it necessary.

You knew exactly where you stood with Micky. Most would give him a wide berth, but I took to him straight away. We had a mutual respect for one another. Cut from the same cloth, Tim as well, we all were.

Tim and Micky were like Burke and Hare, with their sticky-fingered midnight runs. Their activity was never talked about in public, keeping their criminal operation working at full capacity, without unwelcome heat from the filth, or busy-bodies.

Not sure how much the locals knew or rumoured about their antics, but they were respected, left alone by the youth of the pub, and were well-liked by the older clientele.

That night, the young team started to overrun the back of the pub, but kept their distance. They got rowdier as every hour passed, feeding the jukebox, more often than not heavy rock, or punk music. The pub had a hard-core image, sometimes you had to yell from your gut to get a conversation going.

Getting close to 10 o'clock, I realised there were seven missed calls from May. We were all pretty drunk. Tim getting irritated with the racket spewing from the youths, hovering at the rear of the pub.

Micky was a breath away from dishing out a hiding to a random guy who constantly thrashed everyone at pool. Billy, a suave asshole, dressed in light, cream-coloured chinos and a tight-fit shirt, showing off his athletic upper-body. Light-brown skin with a bald head, he thought he was the boy.

Moved around like butter wouldn't melt, swinging his cue round his fingers in a kind of karate style. A bright, gold chain gleaming on his chest, and swaggering around with his pointy brown shoes, well out of place in this joint.

He would be more suited to the west end of Aberdeen, with the stuck-up oil-tycoons. This was a working man's joint. Only here to win drinks, and the odd game for money.

Taking advantage of his natural gift with a stick, thinking he was The Fountain's version of Paul Newman. He'd been on the table for the past two hours, beating Micky five times. The handshake after each game came unwelcomed, like the smirk from the outsider. He had no class about winning, cocky as fuck, and to my knowledge, no one knew him in here.

"Fucking prick, this cunt." Micky uttered to me, sitting a couple of metres away from the table.

Minced on a cocktail of cocaine and vodka, every passing minute sent him closer to the edge. Paranoid after snorting a gram of coke, his beady

206

eyes blatantly burning a hole into the outsider, arms crossed and fists tight, the inevitable coming

The poor bastard didn't have a clue what the inevitable would be. Micky's fifty wing was on the table, he waited with patience.

Racking up the next game, one ball at a time, softly placed into the triangle, half-open bloodshot eyes lazily stared across the table. Engrossed on his phone, Billy blatantly ignored Micky.

He ambled over, sniffing the leftover mixture of coke and bogeys running from his reddened nose, perching a coin under his thumbnail. I think he knew exactly how much pain he was prepared to inflict on this poor bastard that night. Guess he'd had enough by this point, coke and the relentless supply of vodka controlled his actions. It was inevitable he was approaching the breach stage.

"Heads or tails, brother?" Asking quite politely. Billy, the stupid cunt, ignored Micky and kept texting on his phone. Me and Tim watched, both quite content to see this big-headed twat get a slap.

"He's going to do him here, just watch." Tim slurred.

"What the fuck is he away to do?" We knew there was a plan ticking over in Micky's head, he hadn't spoken for the last half-hour, downing nips, glued to his bar-stool, glaring in Billy's direction, itching to pull the cue from his hand and wrap it around his neck.

Comparing the two physiques, Billy being a well-toned athletic guy, automatically would be your choice victor. But, he was in a solid amount of trouble here.

"Excuse me? Heads or tails, brother?" Micky asking again, pulling his shoulders back, poking his chin at Billy, standing face-to-face this time, politely asking once again. Tossing the coin high into the air, Billy's face followed the fifty like a cat following a ball of string.

His head came back down to eye-level. Before he could reply, Micky, veins in his skull pulsing, head-butted Billy, and he hit the floor. Without a split second's thought, Micky launched himself on top of him.

Now the entire pub paid close attention to Micky MacDonald and the scuffle. A huddle of people arrived at the scene. Pinning him to the floor, Micky looked like he was trying to do the front-crawl, bombarding Billy's face with fists.

Still conscious, Billy tried to wriggle away, but the ferocity of the attack meant he was helpless.

Two punters tried to pull Micky off. He wrestled them at the same time, wriggled out to punch one and kicked the other to the ground, leaving him winded.

Turning his attention back to the outsider, he watched Billy trying to escape, dragging himself across the parquet floor, reaching the exit.

Micky was a complete maniac once the switch flipped. He grabbed Billy's feet, towing him back inside the pub, flipped him over, dropping his ten and a half stone weight over his biceps, and pinning him down. Stretching his right hand out, Micky scooped the white ball from the table and using an axe-wielding motion into Billy's face, with saliva spewing from his mouth, he continued to pound. His uncontrollable rage was frightening. We had to stop him before Billy got killed.

Micky MacDonald had previously done two stretches for GBH, grievous bodily harm.

Chapter 40

Weekend Blues:

Walking out of the District Court on Queen Street on a Monday with Tim by my side, our eyes were blinded by the sunlight, but a welcome relief.

Charged with assaulting a police officer, resisting arrest and breach of the peace, police liked that one. It went on top of most charges dished out at weekends.

Tim received the same. Saturday and Sunday stuck in a lone cell in Aberdeen police station was the longest time in my recent years. Lying on a flat, padded, blue rubbery-type mattress, staring at four plain white walls was enough to make me overthink every situation that went through my head. Work, life at home, Dad and Mom. It's torture, believe me. No wonder Micky Macdonald's brain was a deluded mess.

The smell of shit and piss lingered in the air, belching from the stainless-steel shitter in the corner, no escape from the foul stench.

Walking self-confidently out of the court in the morning, there's one thing I wasn't looking forward to. The wife's wrath.

I called her on Saturday morning. Hungover, body aching due to four policemen attacking me with their truncheons, forcing me into the back of the police van. The abuse of power they just loved to dish out, giving them their fix of control. I made them all struggle with me, right into my cell. Cowardly bastards, they were.

Dad hated them, and so did I. Filth was a precise term, bending any rules to suit them and not a hope in hell of a bit of rational thinking. Common sense was out of the window. Hit first with no concern for their victims. Scum in my eyes, complete scum. Criminals, every one of them.

"Hi, it's Joe." Muttering cowardly to May, calling from the cells.

"Joe, where the fuck have you been?! I've been worried out of my mind!" Her love for me not in doubt, it shone through her worried voice.

"The Fountain. I went for a couple after work." Just delaying the inevitable, dreading telling her I was in a cell.

"What?!" She barked down the phone, as I had to pull it away from my ear. "And where are you now, then?!" Her anger drowning out any compassion she had for me.

"I'm eh...in the jail, in town." It was hard to say, and it must have been tougher to hear.

A long pause as she realised the worst, this could be the start of some bad shit to come. She had seen me when I was down and out after Mom's death, ten weeks on a bender. I hardly washed, hardly ate, and treated May like a piece of shit.

Lost, full of regret, a different person, only longing for the sight of Davie Rhodes, so I could tear him apart.

I knew May better than she believed I did, I knew these thoughts would automatically enter her mind.

"Oh, my God, Joe! Don't tell me! Fighting?! You bastard!"

I stayed silent, I didn't know what to say. The only person that I could depend on in this unbalanced life, was livid with me. And I didn't blame her one bit, but the scary thing here was, I couldn't give a fuck.

Locked in a cell over Friday night, just because we covered for Micky so he could get away. I felt rough as fuck, aching, physically and mentally drained. I didn't need her shouting down the phone at me. How was that going to improve my situation here?

"I bet that Tim was involved, was he? What about your kids? Did you spare a thought for them before you went to the pub? Junior had a game this morning, he was asking for you. I had to lie to him, Joseph. I can't believe you've done this to me!" My head just about had enough of this conversation.

"I know May, I know OK! I've fucked up. I don't need this shit just now. I'm feeling bad enough." I felt bad in the sense I was hurt and hungover, not in the guilty way. "Look, I'll be home on Monday, after court." Looking for an end to her shouting, the policeman shadowing me on the phone, feeling like I had little time left.

"Court?! Fuck me. Make your own way home, arse-hole."

Well that was that, she hung up the phone and PC Plod took me back to my cell.

I was interviewed later in the afternoon by a temporary detective, Graham Munroe, and Detective Sergeant Barry Magill, a right cut-from-the-cloth career man in the CID. Heavy Glaswegian accent and thrived in thinking he was the real deal in the force. In his mid-forties, experienced, thinking he could wrap me round his finger, the prime example of why I hated them. Trying his snide strategy in reeling me in, by making idle chit-chat and broken promises. I would get off with a slap on the wrist, if I grassed up who beat Billy Duncan within an inch of his life.

"Well Mr Marks, if you're not going to talk, you'll just make this embarrassing situation harder on yourself. You're sitting here without a lawyer, looking at a little stretch inside for assaulting my colleague last night. It doesn't sound very smart keeping quiet, does it? We can help you out of this situation, you know." The fumes from his coffee breath enough to shame a skunk's scent. "Don't you want to go home, put your feet up and see your family?"

Sounding cocksure, leaning inward over the coffee steam evaporating from his polystyrene cup, he underestimated my willingness not to talk. I was screwed anyways, no doubt there. "You know Mr Duncan's in a pretty bad way in the hospital. Do you realise how serious this is?"

I don't know why he thought I was prepared to talk, fifteen minutes I sat there and not a peep out of me. His colleague Munroe equally silent, only observing his older mentor take the field of play.

The door opened, a plain-clothed women handed over a sheet of A4 to Mr Magill. He examined the paper for a minute, then wrinkled his head and arched his brows, a new purpose in mind. I wondered what truths were written on this bit of paper. "So, Mr Marks, how's your Father nowadays?"

Stunned, I sat forward, glaring into his slimy eyes. "What?" I grunted, breaking my code of silence for the first time.

"Your father, Davie Rhodes. Where's he hiding?" I leaned my back up against the wall sitting side on in my seat, taking Magill on for the first time. This was a development not foreseen. Was Dad still remembered by the police around these parts after being gone for years? Or, had he been hovering around somewhere ducking the feds for some reason?

"Fuck knows. You tell me, I'd love a Father son catch up." If this bent fuck knew anything about which rock he was hiding under, I needed to know.

Chapter 41

Junior:

Heading back into work on Tuesday, explaining to HR that I worked the doors in Aberdeen at the weekend, getting into a bit of a scruff and was wanted by the police for an important eye-witness interview. They believed me.

May was furious, I'd never seen her so upset. My head had a massive bruise up my right side where the coppers slammed me to the ground. My thighs and hamstring battered by their truncheons.

My monotonous tasks at work bored me to the core. The constant computer work, keeping the stock in check and dealing with my boss, started to frustrate me to the point I wanted to flip two or three times a day.

Some nights I spent time playing FIFA with Junior. One night gathered in the living room, I did something awful, something I never thought I'd be capable of.

We were all in there that evening. May sitting on the sofa at the end, Jess standing in front of her getting the knots brushed out her shiny blonde hair, now half-way down her back. Junior crouched about two metres back from the telly, the Xbox remote glued to his hand. Me sitting on the edge, bent over with the excitement of playing FIFA.

"Dad, stop beating me, it's not fair." He moaned like a girl, and now eight years old. The age when you start playing up. If only he knew what happened to me at that age. He just kept getting more and more frustrated each time I beat him.

"Come on then, one more game, then it's bed time."

"Oookaaayyy" lengthening his answer, as he sulked about not winning. We were past half-time and still no score.

Junior was getting very animated, shouting instructions to his players, sounding like a real coach on the side-lines at Pittodrie. Then after eighty-four minutes of game-time left, Robin Van Persie slotted the ball home 1-0.

"Not fucking fair!" he shouted, livid, chucking his remote over the TV, leaving a dent in the wall.

Jumping out my seat, a red mist descended, taking a vice-like grip round his nimble wrist, lifting him off his crouched position, his head pinged to the side with the full force of my slap.

The echo sickening the entire family as they gasped in disbelief, before I realised what I had done. Junior's head hung at the floor, afraid to look at me, body trembling with tears, I couldn't let go of his arm.

He tried to wriggle free by leaning his body weight away from me towards the door. I still couldn't let go, I wanted to say sorry, but I didn't know how to. Wanted to take it back, somehow.

"Let go, Joe. Let go." May spoke softly placing her hand on my shoulder, trying to calm me. I let Junior go. He sprinted out the room to the safety of his own. The poor guy was terrified, I never thought about it, it just happened, never registered in my head what I was doing.

Jess was left stunned as well, she started crying frantically. May picked her up, grasping her into her arms tightly, leading her up to her room. I stood alone in the sitting room.

What had I done. What's happening to me?

Chapter 42

Phone Call:

Sitting in The Fountain a few weeks later, waiting to meet Micky MacDonald for a cold one on Saturday afternoon, the place was quiet. The usual heavy-rock music from the jukebox wasn't blaring. A few regulars sat at the bar sipping their drams and a collection of Leeds United fans were glued to Soccer Saturday. A couple were throwing darts up the back and the plump Margaret tended the bar.

Three weeks passed since the trouble that night, the old-timers full of questions about the incident. I suppose the gossip lines were at full speed the past few weeks.

The regulars spoke to me with more respect, and a willingness to share a conversation. Everyone had heard who my old man was, and that went a long way to explain my actions outside the pub, knocking out a cop.

Billy Duncan was carted off in an ambulance, spending the next eight days nursing facial injuries in hospital.

Micky had been in hiding, today being his first day out, he would still be welcomed into the pub, but like Royalty this time. People in here stuck up for their own, and knew we would do the same for them, without question.

15.30, the main man came stuttering in looking relaxed and casual in his white trainers, tracksuit bottoms, and plain t-shirt.

"Well, well, if it isn't the man of the hour. How's it going, Micky?" Looking pleased with himself, proud as punch and delighted he had dodged the filth for three weeks.

The double team of Magill and Munroe were definite that Micky was to blame. They didn't have the proof though. No witness would speak and the camera system was conveniently broken that evening. Margaret, the lady of the bar, sorted all that out.

She had a soft spot for Micky, he was a good cunt really, especially to Margaret, who needed help from time to time with troublemakers she couldn't handle. Micky was the first port of call for her.

Spending his youth in and out of foster care due to his unstable parents, he saw Margaret as a bit of a mothering figure and was quite protective over her while she worked. And newcomers found that out pretty quick.

"How's it going?! I'll tell you how it's fuckin' going!" Said sarcastically, puffing his chest out. "Fuckin' beautiful. I gave that CID scum Magill the run-around for three weeks. It's me who's been watching him, fuckin' Muppets." Proud as muck he was, and straight out with his story of where he's been. "Been hiding in ma' Aunt's shed over in Torry. The thing's practically a miniature bungalow. Bar, TV, kettle, heating, bed and three weeks of throwing darts. I've been on holiday, chaps." Loving life at the minute, he was.

"Game of darts 'en, Micky?" A sixty something year-old man with a bushy Captain Phillips white beard asked, taking a sip out of his whisky with his pinkie up.

219

"Fuckin' game o' darts, you've no chance, geezer." Winding everyone up, he set the scene for the rest of the afternoon. He had a seat at the bar next to me.

"Get a round in for everyone, Margaret, please."

"No probs, Micky." She seemed as happy as everyone else to see the energetic local back in the pub.

"£18.50 please." Micky took out his tri-fold wallet, opened the cash section and handed over a wad of notes totalling 300 quid.

"Thanks a bunch, Margaret. Keep the change." Gave her a little wink of his beady eye and a salute of gratitude. She accepted it with a smile, showing her feelings for him.

"Fuck me, Micky. Robbed a bank?"

"Well, you've got to keep your friends happy. So, Magill give you a good grilling, did he? Cheers for keeping hush, by the way." Gave me a 'good lad' nudge in the elbow and picked up his pint.

"Aye, he tried to. I said nothing. Getting done for assaulting an officer and resisting arrest." I didn't bother to mention the breach of the peace charge. That was a given, Micky knew that.

"Lawyer, who's your Lawyer?"

"Some local law firm in Inverurie. He reckons I'm pretty screwed."

"Listen, you're going to probably end up doing a wee bit of time, no doubt there, but my lawyer's a fuckin' class act, mate. Got me off with a few things over the years. If there's a loophole, he'll find it, no doubt about it. Here's his card, give him a call, tell him you know me."

"Nice one, mate. I'll call him first thing Monday." I needed somebody bent to get me out this mess, and lawyers were like cops, bent.

"When's the court date?"

"Well into August."

"What about Timmy?" Micky was the only guy to call Tim, Timmy.

"Tim never hit a fed, but they've pinned the same charges on him. The cops are giving statements saying he hit one of them. It's all bullshit, bent bastards."

Tim did nothing to any cop, they pinned him down the same way they pinned me down.

"Overwhelming police force." He was just drunk and interfering. Poor cunt, I didn't want this for him, but knowing Tim, there's an ace up his sleeve somewhere.

"Aye, wankers they are. Jail isn't that bad, depending on where you get sent. You'll get sent to a short-time nick. You don't want to be inside with any paedos. Cunts should be shot, full stop. You shouldn't, though. But, you're a big lad, you'll be able to handle yourself. Do the time and get on with life."

Yeah, get on with it, easy for him to say. He's spent most of his life doing time, right back to his juvenile years. My phone started to ring.

"Better no' be the wife." Pulling my phone out of my pocket, I didn't recognize the number. "Hello?"

"Joe Marks?" He asked bluntly.

"Aye, who's this?"

"Steve Dean. I have a problem and wondered if you could help me out?"

"Go on, Steve." I knew this call was trouble, more than likely unwanted trouble.

221

"There's a man of mine up your way. I need to keep tabs on him. Can't tell you the whole story, but I need him followed and not let out your sight for a split second. Understand, Joe?" Exactly to the point: he wanted perfect surveillance on his man.

"Perfectly, Mr Dean. What's he look like and where is he?" Mr Dean was a man of precise engineering. He operated on a 'Get things done properly' basis.

"Glad you asked, Joe. I'll send you a picture straight away. Right now, he has just walked into the petrol station at the bottom of the Haudagain roundabout. You have to move now, or this opportunity will be lost. I won't talk figures just now, but I'll see you alright."

"Alright 'en." The phone went down and instantly a picture came through. Having to move quickly, I turned to look at Micky. He anxiously waited for me to tell him what the fuck was going on. "Did you drive here?"

"Aye, ma' Aunt's motor's outside. Why?"

"Let's go, I'll tell you on the way."

Chapter 43

The Chase:

"Where the fuck's he going?" Taking the exit at the roundabout onto the A77. Prestwick airport approaching up on the sign posts, so automatically we presumed that's where he was heading, but we couldn't be sure.

We followed the blue 2012 v6 Golf out of Aberdeen and kept on his tail. Following him in Micky's Aunt's silver Volvo v60, we felt like we were in a movie chase.

The Golf regularly hitting speeds over a hundred miles per hour traveling down the dual carriageway. Trying to keep as far back as possible, but close enough so we didn't lose sight, was tricky. The 140 horse powered Volvo was fairly new, the only thing keeping us close. We were struggling and eventually he would notice us or we would run out of gas. The Golf was vastly more powerful.

"Fuck knows, Joe. But, I'm needing a piss, am busting." Having only stopped once since we left Aberdeen, with a few pints worth in our bladders from the afternoon, we both needed to go.

The Golf stopped earlier at the McDonald's in Dundee, so we took the opportunity to have a piss ourselves, behind a couple of trees, avoiding coming into sight of the target.

"Better give Steve a call, update him on where he's heading." Calling him for the third time since we left. My battery low, so was the fuel. We had to hope he was stopping soon, or else we would lose him. "Steve, we think he's on his way to Prestwick airport."

"Prestwick, are you sure?" Sounding confused, he didn't think getting on a flight was an option.

"Well no, I'm not. And where's the backup car? We're nearly out of fuel." Mr Dean sent a backup car once we passed Dundee, but there was no sight of it.

"He can't be getting on a flight. He wouldn't leave his car unattended for that long. He's got a boner for that thing. The backup car is north of Glasgow, it can't be far away, a blacked-out Range Rover, with black alloys. You can't miss it. I'll inform them of your position. Keep following him, he's heading for Troon to catch a ferry, if my instincts are correct."

"I think we're about twenty or thirty miles from Troon. Check the ferry times?"

"Stay on the phone. I'll put on the speaker. Lukas, get on that computer, find out what times the ferries are leaving Troon tonight."

"OK, Boss." Said in a deep, Eastern European accent. "Troon to Larne ferry... last sail, six o'clock, Boss."

"OK, it's almost eight so he's not getting on a ferry tonight, but I expect he's on it tomorrow morning. I'll need you to keep close to him overnight, then follow him if he gets on there tomorrow. I'm short of staff this weekend, that's why I need you to carry out this task for me. Trust this is OK with you?"

"Well, I came this far. Be as well to keep going." Micky could hear the conversation, shaking his head, concentrating on the road. He had gone as far as he liked to. Tired from the long chase and hungry from the pints wearing off. We both were.

"Aye, that's fine, but what about getting on the ferry? I have no ID." I didn't carry any, no driver's licence and nobody carries their passport with them. Was only supposed to be going for a couple of pints. May was probably at home wondering where I was, but I wasn't concerned about her.

"Don't worry about that. Micky will have his driver's licence."

"Have you, Micky?" I asked.

"Aye, I've got it." Answered reluctantly, glancing round at me from the wheel. Unwilling to get involved further, but he already was, we both were.

"My men will bring something for you to hide under in the back of the Range Rover. You can swap cars. I have men working for me on this ferry. I take deliveries through this port on a regular basis. They will be paid and will let you through. I'll inform them of the Range Rover and it won't be touched by anyone. I'll pay Micky's ticket and send him the confirmation e-mail. He can show the email to get onto the ferry. Job done."

He had it all planned, the Don Corleone of the Scottish criminal world. Everything calculated to perfection, his men as loyal as a Mafia stable. He was a man that had no need to get his hands dirty, his fingers in every criminal pie around the country, from prostitution to guns. The police gave him a wide berth, and were in his pocket.

"Anything you need before you get on that ferry, my boys will fetch for you."

"Shit! Battery's died. Give me your phone, Micky."

Chapter 44

Northern Ireland:

This was the fifth day we were stuck in Northern Ireland. The wife kept trying to contact me, phoning and texting every hour of the day, I told her I had to go away for a few days, never told her why, or what I was doing. She must have been doing cartwheels, cursing me with all the names under the sun.

I called work to inform them I had a bug at the start of the week, couldn't come in. They didn't ask questions, but I didn't care.

This was more amusing. Staking out this house in a Protestant area of East Belfast that belonged to 'Roy the Rover' as he was called. A passionate Northern Irish Protestant. Complete stoner with a bony build. Wore baggy jeans hanging down his hips, long t-shirts with a baseball cap, puffing joints like fags.

Mr Dean's boys sorted us out with everything, from phone-chargers to spare clothes, before we boarded the ferry, without a glitch. His boys brought suitcases. Micky stacked the luggage on top of me, as I hid in the boot.

Micky drove in without a hitch, clueless to which members of staff were on Mr Dean's take. Once docking in Northern Ireland, we followed the Rover home.

Micky received an email from Lukas explaining one of us had to keep an eye on the target at all times. The following email was a check into the Hilton hotel in the centre of Belfast.

Nothing but the best for us. A four-star hotel with all the luxuries we needed, room service, free food, laundry and a ton left at the desk for us each day to keep us afloat.

We had instructions to keep an eye on the Rover, monitor any unusual activity. Splitting up, myself taking the day-shift and Micky, the man that needs no sleep, taking the night-shifts. Steve was constantly on the phone during the day which was good, it passed the time. It was Hellishly boring. God knows how the pigs do stakeouts.

Across from the Rover's house was an abandoned terraced housing scheme. We broke into the top floor and made ourselves at home, ripping off a small hole in the side of a boarded-up window. It left a view looking directly into Roy's bottom floor flat living-room. We picked up some stakeout essentials, candles, binoculars, a padded folding chair and a notepad to document any cars that came and went. It wasn't perfect, no electricity or comforts in the place, but we did the best we could. Before clocking in for shift, we would gather the day's food, drink, reading material or fags. Micky would chain smoke twenty a night and me ten a day, due to boredom.

One thing we both noticed, was patrols of the Northern Irish police force. Most of the time panda cars, but from time to time you'd see an armed truck appear. We figured it wasn't to watch the Rover, just routine. Roy and his car was constantly on the go. We had to follow him sprinting to the street behind us, to jump into our own motor.

Not having much driving experience, Micky sorted me out with an automatic Vauxhall Vectra giving me a crash course on how to drive. I had to,

228

it was that simple. Following the Rover was nothing exciting. Stopping off at his customer's houses and locals keeping them stocked with cannabis. Times we weren't fast enough getting round the corner to the car and lost him, then we would just have to drive around a little, trying to spot him, if not we just returned to the terrace.

Mr Dean's instinct told him there was some double-crossing in his outfit regarding his next shipment from Ireland. He had a firm operation running, but knew something was going down behind his back.

'Pitbull' Marijuana was created in 2003. A blend of two seed strains, it was extremely aggressive and in high demand. Roy, a dedicated professional, was a stickler for fine details and researched how it was to be grown down to a T. Never a drop of resin or buds wasted in Mr Dean's weed farm. The street value of the next shipment was a colossal two million pounds.

The location of the weed farm was unknown, but thought to be a vacated farmyard. Hundreds of thousands went into the operation. Roy was left to his own devices, and very rarely did he receive a visit from Mr Dean. Every couple of months, Lukas was sent to oversee things. It was him that became suspicious about Roy's intentions and Mr Dean had someone monitor his whereabouts. That's why his scent was picked in Aberdeen.

The load was scheduled to travel across sea on the Larne to Troon ferry in five or six months, the date not yet set in stone. A couple of staff members on the ferry were getting paid very handsomely to get the stuff on and off without a hitch.

This operation had been running for a couple years now and any problems ironed out. Mr Dean knew growing that much marijuana in Scotland was a dangerous move and set up this operation miles away from his own soil. If he paid someone to grow and ship it over, his hands weren't in the dirt.

The transportation was frighteningly easy. A truck was bought and styled to copy an Argos one. Mountains of bags packed with potent grass, vacuum-packed and hidden inside various boxes stacked into the van. On top of that, this time Mr Dean was transporting a large quantity of nine bars, a 9oz block of hashish made from cannabis resin. The driver of the truck was also on the take. That part of the operation was flawless and operated smoothly for the past two years. Not once had the truck been searched.

Approaching six o'clock on Thursday night, it was almost time for shift change as Micky walked in.
"Micky, you seen what Roy uses to fill his joints?"
"Aye, a fuckin' half-smoked nine bar."
"How the fuck does he manage to run Steve's weed farm? The cunt's wasted 24/7." Roy was a major manufacturer of cannabis and had an abundance of supplies at his disposal. The smoke piled out his window like a chimney-stack

A car parked up the road near a junction. Some big burly guy in a black leather coat lumped out and walked toward Roy's. We both imminently took notice, he looked shifty.

"Who's this geezer?" Micky uttered as he got closer to the hole in the boarded-up window.

"I'm no' sure mate." As he got closer, I spotted who it was. "Fuckin' hell. That's Mike Jenkins."

"Aye, fuck me, so it is. What the fuck is he doing here?"

I pondered for minute and stood up from my seat. "He's doin' over Steve."

"Sneaky bastard." Micky said.

Mike was an appallingly bitter man, didn't want to see anyone do well in life. This kind of thing, you wouldn't put past him. A double-cross, that would suit his personality. He tried to set me up against Skinner, and now he thinks he's going to do over Mr Dean. This was only going to end up in trouble for Mike.

"Better get on the blower to the Boss, Joe."

I called right away. "Mr Dean, I have news."

"Go ahead, Joe."

"Mike Jenkins has just strolled into 'Roy the Rover's' house."

"OK. Good news, good job." He was as cool as a block of ice. No hostility in his voice, just calmness. A tactically violent man, capable of disposing of Mike in a variety of wrathful ways. Mr Dean was experienced in encountering similar situations, and probably had a plan already in mind to deal with this predicament. "Joe, you and Micky make your way home and head straight to mine."

Chapter 45

The Meeting With Mr Dean:

"Care for another whisky, Joe?" Mr Dean opened one of his glossed, walnut whisky cabinets in his impeccably expensive drinking lounge. Pulled out his twenty five year-old bottle of Talisker whisky, pouring a couple overly large tipples. All round the room, collectible whisky sat in his cabinets. He liked the best, the very best of malt, with a small montage oak round pedestal table in the middle of the room, surrounded by four shiny, brown leather arm chairs. This was where he planned hundreds of criminal activities.

"Aye, another one would be fine, Steve."

Standing with his thin, finger-length cigar hanging from his mouth, his scar prominent under the bright spotlight, you could see the evil glimmer in his eye. The whisky was superb. Tim would appreciate this more than me.

"Are we clear on what's happening in the upcoming months?" Steve said. We had been planning the consequences of Mike and Rover's actions for forty minutes. Micky waiting outside in the lobby, probably getting a bit stiff and losing patience. Mr Dean didn't require him to sit in on the meeting. Micky was just as eager to get up the road, as I was.

"Perfectly, Steve." I answered with certainty. "Just perfect."

"Good. Your first fight will be against Tommy Masson in five weeks, in the same venue as you fought Warsaw."

"No problem, I'll get back to Kilgours, start training and keep a closer eye on that grumpy cunt, Mike." I had no intention of returning back to work, I was getting paid a handsome fee by Mr Dean, a salary you might say. Agreed to keep me afloat with a couple of grand a month and five for each fight.

"OK. I'll arrange the necessities. You will be using Tim as your man, will you?"

"Aye, Tim will be my man. I'll pay him from my purse?" It was only courtesy that he should be paid.

"Yes, that's your department. He's not on my take. If the plan falls into place as we've discussed, you win your next two fights, then I'll arrange the fight with The Reaper later on in the year."

That was Mr Dean's condition. I had to fight under his name, then eventually take on The Reaper from Liverpool.

The Reaper: A complete Barbarian who had a fearsome reputation in the underworld of the bare knuckle. He'd already viciously taken two of his opponent's lives. One, already defeated, sank to the ground as The Reaper thundered a knee into his face, obliterating his nose and ramming it into his brain. He was a young guy, only twenty four, but a beast none the less, who must have had a brutal upbringing to turn him into the man he was.

Mr Dean longed to see the end to his reign and get one up on his rival Jack Gallagher, who looked after The Reaper. He also had a burning passion to have the best of men working under him.

My thought need not be on The Reaper, but on Tommy Masson. A local thug from Dundee easily dispatched, Mr Dean implied. Battle hardened, bald with a massive head, five foot eight as wide as a door, jacked up on more juice than the entire Gold's gym. Mr Dean told me he was brainless.

"Steve, if our business is concluded, I'd like to head up the road."

"Yes, no problem. I appreciate the work you've done for me this week." Opening a drawer on one of the whisky cabinets, he handed me a plump envelope. "Just a little token of my gratitude."

Me and Micky picked up the Volvo with a full tank of gas, heading away from Steve's 17th century mansion in the Dundee countryside, around the water-feature that was in the middle of the long, pebble-laid drive.

Opening the chunky A5 envelope inside the car, revealed a pile of £50 notes. "Holy fuck, Micky! Ten grand in here!"

"Woooo hoooo! Get the fuck in, ching's on me tonight, baby!" He yelled out.

Fuck that. I needed to get home to see May and the kids.

Chapter 46

Changing times:

I arrived home that Friday night to an empty house. Locks had been changed, and May wasn't answering her phone, letting it go straight to answer-service.

Micky sat in the car, watching me stomping around. "Fuckin' bitch! Where is she? Fuckin' bitch!" I snarled from the side of my mouth.

Where the fuck was she? And the kids? Mangling a couple plant pots by launching them against the door steps, then tried forcefully to yank the door open. All the whisky drank in Mr Dean's house fueling my outrage.

"Come on, pal, get back in the car, you can stay at mine." I don't think Micky saw me as a family man. Neither did I, anymore.

"Fancy that ching, 'en?" I asked.

"Fuck, aye. I'll nip round by my mate's on the way to The Fountain." Micky, itching to get on it, so was I now.

An 8-ball, 4 grams of the finest Aberdeen coke, was collected. Micky jumping into the car beside Seaton Park, opening the glove-box, pulling out an old worn CD case, pouring the chunky coke on top of it. Took a bank-card out his wallet, chopped it into two chunky white lines of Heaven.

"Roll up a note, bud." With a slice of style, I rolled up a crisp £50 note from Mr Dean's generous envelope. Waiting to lose my coke virginity, a new kind of rush started to flow.

Micky sank the first line. Passing the note over, my hands clammy with anticipation. Watching the granules of coke disappear up the fifty note, flooding my bloodstream, causing me to gasp with euphoria.

Two minutes later the urge to smoke arrived. Mickey fed me fags and I sucked the life out of every one until beefed.

Ten minutes later standing in The Fountain, I was sky fucking high. I couldn't stop talking, hyper as fuck, starting another sentence before finishing one. I realised why Micky was so hyper now. This stuff blew my head off. Full of bravado, I could take on the world.

"What you drinking?" Micky asked as he hovered over the bar, chatting to Margaret at a rate of knots, his chin wagging around and head bobbing in and out like a turkey. Margaret wore round glasses behind the bar and dolled-up as usual that night.

"Eh, whisky!" I was on a self-destructive mission now. Blended whisky rolled in one after another.

Bouncing around the bar, thousands in our pockets. I felt on top of the world, everyone showed their respect, buying us drinks all night and we repaid the favour. We regularly disappeared into the cubicles for line after line.

Three hours in, we were well into our third gram. I was paranoid, my arms locked out straight in my pockets, fingers curling around and my jaw struggled to stay straight, switching from side to side.

The anger left me, I had no interest in any kind of aggravation.

That's when I see her.

This seductive looking, twenty-something, sitting at the end of the bar with her luxurious midnight-blue hair cascading over her shoulders, down her backless top.

She was easy on the eye. Her rounded breasts fitting tightly into her top. Left arm painted with dark tattoos. The euphoric high I was on made her Pacific-blue eyes look like an exotic ocean. All I yearned for, was to grab her and fuck her until the sun came up.

The high from the ching gave me the confidence of a sports star, and I thought nothing about courageously coasting up to her. We shared a few drinks and both of us knew we would end up sharing a night of passion. She was well aware of what she had, knew every man held the same lust I did.

I was so fucked at this point, I bought rounds for all the punters in the bar, time after time. Thirty odd drinks a round. Micky passed out up against a wall, his head perched peacefully up against the bandit, a nip of untouched vodka and lemonade balancing in his hand.

Me and the girl, Katie, started to get very intimate at the back of The Fountain, almost fucking right there. My tongue so far down her throat, blocking her airwaves. Her hand slid down my jeans. Her sluttiness would easily rope guys to her. I couldn't get enough of her. Margaret came over from behind the bar.

"You guys need a room! Here, take this key to the bed-sit upstairs and get out of here." She was a good soul, was Margaret. I could see why Micky liked her so much.

"Cheers, Margaret." I slurred, while giving her a peck on the cheek, then stumbled upstairs, pulling Katie by the arm up to the disgusting bed-sit. Before I could get her through the door, I stripped her half-naked, tearing the top of her dress down to the waist, her body toned and tanned, squeezing her perfect breasts, pulling her into the room by her hair and chucking her forcefully onto the bed before I fucked her brains out. I was instantly addicted.

The Fountain was now my new home. The irony, my Father's old local.

Chapter 47

New Life:

Four weeks later, all settled into my bed-sit, I started to feel at home. I helped out behind the bar and drank for free. Gave Margaret more money than she wanted every week and kept an eye on the bar, keeping all the thunder-cats under control.

I met up with Tim daily and trained like a machine at the gym, pounding the bags and pads. Tim thundering punches into my gut for body conditioning.

Skipping, jogging, circuits, weights, I'd done it all. My now constant supply of steroids helped me push myself. I became obsessed.

Mr Dean payed me handsomely to fight for him, I had to be in top shape if I was going to tear apart my foes. Constantly thinking about finding Dad fueled my passion. My next fight was the following week in Dundee. Tim kept on my back, making sure I was training well. He turned a blind eye to the 'roids.

Kilgours was full of new faces, guess nobody lasts in this game. It's brutal and not for the faint-hearted. Toby and Chris were the only two guys in the gym that I remember. Toby, to everyone's surprise, beat the fancied hooligan from Watford.

Thursday night we sparred. The plan, do six rounds each with Toby and Chris, the only two boxers that could handle me, but it didn't quite work out like that.

Moving around with Chris that night, he upset me with a cracker of an inside left uppercut in the second round. I saw spots before the mist took over. Body pumped with 'roids, I turned into a walking, Barbaric animal, a man on a mission.

Wearing no head-guard, I propelled my head back as far as it could go, catapulting it forward, smashing it into his jaw, I continued my insane attack, hurling left and right-hooks, his head pinging from side to side like a conker on the end of a piece of string, until he fell hopelessly to the ground. Leaping on top of him, I continued my barrage.

"That's enough, boy." Mike jumped on my back and used his body weight to drag me from him. Tim entered the ring and gave Mike a hand to hold me down.

"Joe, calm down. There's no need." They held me until my rage calmed. I just flipped, fueled with 'roid rage. I could have killed him.

"Fuckin' hell, boy!" Mike screamed, sticking his nose right into my face, but I knew I could snap him in half if I wanted to. I listened though and as hard as it was to calm down, I did. The 'roids taking control of me like the full-moon takes control of the werewolf.

I didn't apologise, looked down at Chris's bruised face and walked out the ring.

Sitting on the weight bench, I had a word to myself. Calming down, I did the right thing and apologised. He wasn't knocked out, but badly confused and dazed. He walked right past me without acknowledgement on his way out.

The mood was sombre now, I could hear the whispers in the gym as they talked about me. I didn't know what they were saying, I was sure it wasn't good. Everyone left, another night everyone got sent home due to my lack of respect for my colleagues. That left Mike, Bull, Tim and me.

"You'll destroy Masson, Joe." Bull said, as he sat down next to me on the bench mumbling out his small mouth, softly spoken. He didn't seem the hurtful kind. He was just a business-man that looked the business.

"Hope so, Bull. That's the idea." Swiveling my head round.

"What you getting paid for this?" I didn't care for his nosey tone and never took him on.

"Enough Bull, enough." He knew I wasn't in the talkative mood and left.

Mike was leaning over the ropes talking to Tim. I didn't learn anything from their conversation about the drug-deal he was planning with the Rover, I never did. He was very sly like that. I could see his shiftiness, though.

There was something going on in his dishonest head and you could see it. He thought he was so smart with his obnoxious attitude, but little did he know he was going to get done over.

The gym was just a ten-minute walk from my new home, and I left saying goodbye to everyone.
My body still pumping with juice, I needed to come off this, but had to wait till after the fight. Masson was full of 'roids, so I would be too.

Bull sorted me out with the supply of 'Deca' and instructed me to take 600-800 mg a week. Getting more bulked and ripped by the day, my traps and triceps and back bulged, my whole body grew considerably, my biceps and inner forearms bursting with veins.

The fat disappeared from my gut, taking my weight down to ninety two kilos. My t-shirts were now skin-tight, obvious to the trained eye I was on the gear.

A few times a week, I would take fits of rage wherever, in the bar, out and about, or even with Katie who I spent most evenings with. I became totally obsessed with her.

Heading round to her flat in Woodside most nights, round the corner from The Fountain, it suited me fine when I craved her, which was most nights. I'd wait until her three kids went to bed before heading round.

I could feel myself getting more hooked on her. Because how unstable my life was at the time, my jealousy and insecurity bubbled to the surface, especially when she messaged or snapchatted other men. This drove me to unleash emotions I didn't know existed.

The steroids just cranked up the tension.

Sex with Katie was rough and wild, not like May who was more of a conventional lover. She knew how to please me in the bedroom and wind me up out of it. Her relaxed, promiscuous way was dangerous to any man who thought of settling down with her.

Three kids to different Fathers, tells her story. It was only a matter of time before I would lose my cool with her.

There was no contact with May and the kids. I spent a lot of my time thinking about the kids, but not her. Guess I had fallen out of love.

A couple nights before the fight with Masson, I stayed over at Katie's. Her kids were in bed and we sat on her sofa watching a movie. I nipped to the toilet and on returning, I caught her on Facebook messenger talking to some random guy.

"Who the fuck is that?"

"Just a pal of mine." Sounding like she was already guilty.

"What pal? Why you talking to him right in front of me?" Losing patience, my voice raised.

"Relax Joe, it's just a pal, nothing else." Her attitude enraged me.

"Give me that fuckin' phone!" Making a grab for her phone, she slipped it down the side of the sofa.

"Joe, get the fuck off. Get off me!" I planted my knees either side of hers, on the sofa, leaning my weight over so she couldn't move, gripped her throat with my left hand, taking a firm hold of both sides of her neck. She sunk into the seat trying to wriggle her way out.

With the force of the grip, in a choking panic, she released her hold on the phone. Her slender, five foot four frame had no strength.

Holding her firm, I retrieved the phone and scrolled through the conversation, while her blue eyes looked helplessly for some compassion. Scrolling up and down the screen, to see they were flirting like young teenagers.

I crunched my knuckles into her face, knocking her over to the side, unable to fall because my knees were either side of her. Opening the window, I launched the phone out, smashing onto the path below

One of her three kids, the youngest at three years old, blonde, came through after hearing the commotion, witnessing his mother slumped over, shaking frantically.

"Get back to your bed." I said, harshly. Her kid, with that innocent look in his eye, stood in fear. Who was this bad man? "NOW BOY!" Roaring out, as I took a half step forward, stamping my foot. He jumped off his feet, getting the point, running out the room and back to the comfort of his bed.

Katie was scared stiff. Afraid to move, jaw trembling, with her head crunched down into her chest and arms awkwardly by her side.

"Get up and go to your bed, woman. And don't come back through here the night." Getting to her feet, sheepishly tip-toeing to her room, legs buckling with shock. I spent the rest of that night on the sofa.

Chapter 48

Been Here Before:

Twenty minutes before clambering into the ring with Masson, Tim had wrapped my hands in his usual impeccable manner. Slipping the gloves on, I prepared to go to war again, top off, beefed up and wearing a pair of black shorts and black trainers. Now really cut, my frame bulging with the abuse of steroids.

The crowd inside the cauldron had doubled in size from last time, and so did the noise. The shed full of the raw breed of Dundonians.

Having my shot of steroids this morning, my chemically-filled bloodstream was now a ball of rage. All I wanted to do was inflict pain. The nerves were buried beneath my emotions. Seething and deep in thought all day, as I seemed to be every day now.

Tim, weary of my act, left me to my own thoughts. The creaky door opened to the changing room, inviting the noise of the audience waiting for my entrance. Mr Dean and Lukas entered. Lukas silent as always, dressed in his usual black, standing bolt upright, hands crossed over his waist at his boss's side.

"Joe, sorry I couldn't catch up with you before. How's things?" Swaggering in, Mr Dean carried a brass-topped, cherry-wood walking-stick, dressed impeccably, a tailor-cut Italian suit and his tinted shades, to dull the light in his eyes.

"Steve." Feeling comfortable being on first name terms with him. "I'm good."

"Good, it won't take long tonight, guarantee that, Joe. Everything else going well?"

"Aye." I gave him a knowing look, then back to the ground when finished, keeping my head in the right place. Understanding my vagueness, knowing this was not the time for chit-chat.

"Good. We need to have a word after the fight." Lukas opened the door for his boss.

We got down to business, Tim instructing me to take it easy in the warm-up, but take it easy I wouldn't. I hit my opponents with hate for my Father and love for Mom in my heart, bless her soul.

Muscles contracting from the 'roids, bulked up, I felt the real deal now.

When Dad was younger, he trained but didn't have any muscle bulk, just naturally huge, cold-hearted and savage. He was made for fighting. Time would bring my trained brutality out.

"Twist your body into it!" Tim instructed. "Come on!" Carrying out countless hours of training together, our pad-work was flawless. I always had an advantage over anyone I fought because of my boxing history, the technique and sharpness my rivals didn't have.

With that power, mixed with the cocktail of juice and rage, I was deadly inside the ropes. Drenched in sweat, the heat combined with the humid night made it uncomfortable. There wasn't anybody going to defeat me tonight.

Leaping up and down, lager spilling bodies tried to engage with me on the way to the worn-out ring and blood-stained canvas. The heat intense and irritating, as more sweat poured off.

Blacking everything out, I could only see blood, only hear my heart beat. Once at ringside, I climbed up the three steps and slid between the ropes, with an itch to get this done. Walking straight to the centre of the ring and stood idle, 8oz gloves by my side, eyes in a trance, sweat pouring down my Vaseline-coated body, fists clenched, ogling Masson.

I could tell he shat a brick, right then. His big, bald, ugly head attached to his bloated, five foot eight height. He meant nothing to me.

The short, fat ref in dress trousers, shirt and bow tie, reluctantly pulled Masson to the middle of the ring, where we exchanged deep stares of warriors, the ref saying his piece.

Masson's eyes showed fear. First mistake.

Turning his back, walking away from me. Second mistake. That showed disrespect.

His third mistake? Wasn't his fault the bell went.

Chapter 49

Restraining Order:

At the end of July, an unusually hot month for the seaside city of Aberdeen, I tried constantly to contact May, having no joy. I missed my kids and longed to see them. Countless times I turned up at the house, most of the time out of my tits on whisky or coke, or both most times. She now had a restraining order, I couldn't go within half a mile of her, or my kids.

One Saturday night, wasted on coke, around eleven thirty, I ordered Micky to drive out to Inverurie from The Fountain, stopping for a couple extra lines on the way.

"May, open the fuckin' door! I want to see the kids!" Pounding the door viciously with the outside of my fist, trying desperately to get inside, fag hanging out my mouth.

I could hear the kids in tears and probably May too, but I didn't care. Snorting a couple of grams that night with Micky, I wasn't in a fit state to be in the company of my kids. It was so quiet at that time of night, I'm sure I woke the whole neighbourhood.

"FUCK OFF JOE! YOU'RE NOT WANTED HERE! I've called the police!" She screamed from the window above.

"Come on May! Just open the door, MAY! Ten minutes, max!" Desperate, drunk, and out of control, I started to thump down the door with the sole of my boot.

Bang! Bang! Bang! The door weakened, splints of wood came loose from the Yale lock. Thundering the door with both feet, it caved in.

Micky sprinted out the Volvo, through the gate, up the steps leading to the door.

"Joe, stop! FUCKIN' STOP!" Micky crashed to the floor, tripping over the front step.

May waited, agitated at the top of the landing outside Junior's bedroom. Pushing my palms onto her chest, I catapulted her through our bedroom door. Bursting into Junior's room, I found him and Jess perched on the edge of the bed, petrified and holding each other in their arms.

"Kids!, How are you?" My arms held out open, then leaning in to cuddle them. Trembling, they didn't respond, their bodies tried to wriggle away. I squeezed them tight, terrifying them even more.

"Daddy, what are you doing to Mommy?" Jess asked, completely confused to what was going on. Junior sat with his head between his legs. May had risen, then hysterically burst into the room, punching my back and kicking the back of my legs.

"GET FUCKING OUT, YOU! GET OUT!!!" Turning round, using my weight, I shoulder-charged her into a chest of drawers.

Mickey entered. "Joe, what the fuck you doing? Get out of here, the pigs will be on their way!" As he spoke, the sirens sounded. They were already here. Four uniformed filth came storming in the door, truncheons in hand.

"GET OUT THE WAY!" They shouted, running up the stairs.

May pulled Jess into the lobby, Junior followed them out. They tossed Micky to the floor, his skinny frame thundering down outside Junior's door, two pigs on top.

That left the other two for me. Handling both, flooring the first one, smashing a bedside-lamp across his face. I wrestled the other, holding him in a headlock, repeatedly punching him in the face.

The rest of the squad arrived right behind them, striking the back of my legs with their truncheons, gripping me in a choke-hold before pinning me to the floor. My head buried into the carpet from the weight of a copper's knee. My hands and feet tie-wrapped. Picking me up, they carried me out like a log.

Screaming to the top of my lungs "Fuckin' pig fucks! I'll find out where you fuckin' stay and fuck your wives!"

Needless to say this is when the restraining order came out. Spending the rest of the weekend in the cells until Monday, having yet another interview with detective sergeant Barry Magill, who was not very pleased to see me. Having to come in on his weekend off didn't please him in the slightest.

My lifestyle dramatically changed since beating Masson. For the worse. Drinking, smoking and snorting powder every day, I was out of control.

Getting paid handsomely for my victory against Masson and taking in a salary from Mr Dean each month, couriered up to Aberdeen from a member of his staff, made me reckless, free-spending on whatever high I wanted. Spending hundreds on gear each week.

With another fight in the middle of August, I wasn't in a good place, mentally. I was on a self-destruct mission of sex, drugs, alcohol, rage and violence.

The fight was close to home this time, in the top floor of Bon-Accord centre parking complex, against ex-professional boxer, Matt MacGregor from Glasgow. All being set up by Mike Jenkins with Mr Dean's permission. Bare-knuckle for ten rounds, this would be very different from the unlicensed scraps. I wasn't training, I was taking coke every day, thinking I was invincible.

Me and Micky spent almost every day together, wherever it was, inside The Fountain, round at his place, or at his dealer's flat on Hayton road. We were kept well-stocked by Kenny Mackie's limitless supply of gear. Spending nights unwelcomed at Katie's, coming in coked out my box. Bloodshot eyes with an unpredictable personality filled with tins of lager, I was bad news. Disappearing regularly to the toilet, murdering line after line. She knew exactly what I was. Terrified of me, she had to let me in. Making her feel trapped in her own home, probably fearing for her kids' lives.

Was this how my mother felt all those years?

The endless supply of coke left me with a short fuse and Katie wound me up, sitting on her phone all night WhatsApping and Snapchatting. Testing my patience. My insecurities about myself and a bucket load of jealousy flooded out. Katie started to hide her second life from me , knowing it would annoy me.

Her kids were starting to get to know me more, as I came in more often when they weren't in bed. They didn't like me, and I didn't like them. Little fucking pests. One night we were switching channels on the telly.

"Joe, put East Enders on." Katie shouted trying to grab the remote, I kept it out of her reach.

"No, woman. I'm watching the football." Aberdeen were playing in a Europa league qualifying match.

"Listen, it's my TV. Put it on." I didn't like it when she made demands. It wound me up more than her phone.

"Put it fuckin' on!" Yelling in my ear. Taking the butt of my right elbow, I jacked it through her temple as we sat side by side. Clenching my teeth together.

"Keep that fuckin' shut, woman."

Lying motionless on the sofa, a sudden flashback of my Mother's corpse came into my mind. Freaking out, I legged it out the door. I had hit an all-time low, disgusted at the person I was turning into.

Chapter 50

Pre - McGregor Fight:

Nine days before the 27th August. The McGregor fight in sight. I'd spent the past seven weeks with a note on the end of my nose and a bottle in my hand. Me and Micky went out every night and got home early. We drank through the day and perked our hangovers up with a line. Eating wasn't important and neither was training. I had lost May. I kept calling, but there was still no contact between us.

My damaged past and troubles of the present, took a grip on me. Thinking I'd be able to walk in and out of the scrap without care, was a serious mistake. That morning in the gym, told the story.

Pounding at the bag for ten minutes, getting past the initial break of sticky sweat, I didn't feel right. Tim held the bag as I went through the motions, seeing my struggle. Three, two minute rounds later my chest tightened. Carrying on, my heart ached, similar to a tight cramp. I couldn't breathe, coming over lightheaded, gripping my chest as it felt I was entering a spasm.

I passed out.

Coming to, Tim was holding me, his arms around my chest, shaking me from side to side. Confused, I took my time to register what happened. Hoisting me to my feet, he led me over to the weight-bench.

"Fuck me, Joe. What happened?" Looking as stunned as I felt.

"Fuck knows, just got some chest pain an' passed out." Coming to terms with the fall, I knew my body had been pushed too far in the past weeks. "Give me a couple of minutes."

"Joe, you're a fuckin' coke-head, look at the state of you. You're blowing out your arse after a few rounds. How the fuck are you dealing with McGregor? You need to buck-up here, this guy's an ex-boxer."

"Aye, I know mate." As usual, he was straight to the point.

"You've got to cancel this fight."

"No chance. We can't cancel, not an option." I was very definite. It wasn't an option to pull away from this.

"Just train me until the fight and I'll worry about the rest." Tim was right, I was a coke-head, hooked on the rush and it was about time I admitted it. Every day I craved line after line, making me sweat uncontrollably, shake violently and take hot-flashes. I was in serious trouble, but had to grind it out the same as I've always dealt with my difficulties.

With my coordination coming back, I wobbled through to the changing-room to splash my face with water. Turning the tap on, I gazed into the mirror, not recognizing the eyes staring back. My flattened nose red raw, skin peeling off the sides of my nostrils, my once bright eyes had lost colour, greasy skin with wrinkles gathering under my eyelids. Hair out of shape and needing a cut. My face worn out with the recent abuse and family grief. Looking a different man to the one I knew. What had happened?

I had little recollection of the past couple of months. Tim appeared as my drained face reflected in the mirror. Now thirty three, looking fifty three.

"You need to sort yourself out, lad."

"I know mate, I know." I understood his concern, I was out of control.

"Get out for a jog, sweat it out, I'll wait here. We can start fresh, Thursday night when the rest of the lads are here."

Flicking my hood over my aging face, I jogged through the Tilly streets for twenty minutes, finding it hard to battle through. Struggling for breath, legs feeling like they were dragging the weight of the world, my chest so tight. My body wanted to shut down. I used the time to reflect on what was happening to me.

After a while, I changed thoughts to Matt McGregor. Had to make the most of the short nine days left, do what I could. A retired boxer and fit as fuck, two advantages I'd be giving up straight away.

Tim was waiting outside Kilgours when I got back.

"My ticker's going to pack in." My face bright red.

"Aye, it looks it. Let's get some grub, then I'll take you back to The Fountain. I've got some work to do this afternoon, for Mike and Bull."

"Good man. Cheers." Scraping the bottom of the barrel, I needed someone like Tim looking out for me. "What work?"

"There's a big cash order going into Skinner in a month or so, heading down the road to Glasgow, somewhere. We need to shift his equipment to a new location. The feds are on to him. The next order's massive. Four million in twenties, so he doesn't want to take chances. Doing it tonight, we just need to meet in Montrose, beforehand."

"Four fuckin' million?! Fuck me!" That's a lot o' ink cartridges."

"Aye, that's the size o' the orders now. His paper's in major demand." Tim took me back to The Fountain via Pizza Hut for a good feed. I did the sensible thing for a change, stayed in my room and tried to relax, fatigued from the drama earlier in the day. Margaret was in the kitchen cooking the supper for later on, when my phone rang.

"Mr Marks, how are you?"

"Just fine, Steve. Yourself?"

"Good, good. I have some news for you." Sounding overeager.

"I've got something I need to run by you, as well."

"I'm setting up the fight with The Reaper at the start of November, at Glasgow docks, you'll get your chance."

"No problem, Steve."

"McGregor will be difficult for you and you have to win. But, The Reaper will dismember you, rip you limb from limb if you're not ready. There's no one that will fight him now, he's too dangerous. However, I have faith in you." His confidence in me was unquestionable, but the confidence in myself was the non-existent. Quite frankly, I was lost on this road but the end was in sight. All I had to do was get past McGregor.

"I know who he is Steve, I won't let you down." Seeming sure of myself but in reality, I'd never been so sceptical about what I was doing.

"What did you want to tell me?" Mr Dean asked.

Chapter 51

Ball Point:

Three nights before the McGregor fight, I tended the bar for Margaret who wasn't feeling well. A discreet Thursday night. Micky mixing at the bar with the locals. The juke-box volume kept low. I stayed off the powder and ale for the past week, feeling human again. Micky looked anguished sipping his pint, staring into space from time to time. Thinking he was having a bad come-down, or maybe paranoid.

"Joe, want a dram?" Micky asked.

"No mate, orange-juice for me the night. No drinking behind the bar." The unlicensed boxing was rarely talked about in public. Certain people knew about it and when anyone asked, I would conveniently change the subject. Similar to the football-hooligan scene, everyone knew but nobody spoke about it, unless you were all involved. You never knew who couldn't be trusted.

"Fuckin' orange juice, always knew you were a poof." Nodding me out the way of the punters, wanting a moment in private.

"What is it?"

Leaning his weight over the oak surface. "I have a wee problem." He sounded seriously concerned, something I'd never seen. Anxious and jumpy, rather than his usual quirky and hyper.

"Remember that cunt Billy I kicked the fuck out of?"

"Aye, we ended up in the nick, remember."

"Don't be a clever dick. His old man's getting out soon, and word is, he's going to be on the look-out for me."

"What's his name?" This was going to end in trouble, I just knew it straight away.

"Harry 'Ball Point' Duncan earned his name because he tried to murder his own brother by beating him senseless with the ball-point end of a hammer. "He's coming for me, I know it." Micky said with concern.

This was a big problem. A man being released from jail after an eighteen-year stretch for the attempted murder of his brother and probably wanted to blow- off steam, Micky MacDonald was right in the firing line.

"We'll just have to put the word out, be ready for him. I'll tell Tim to spread the word, too. Don't worry mate, it'll be fine. He might even be a reformed character, you never know. When's he getting out?"

"Aye, right. Piss off! You and me both know that won't be the case". Relaxing back into his stool. "I'm no' sure when, I'm trying to find out." Micky could handle himself, that was for sure, but when there's a man on a revenge mission, they will stop at nothing for redemption.

I setup a WhatsApp group, adding Micky, Bull, Tim, and some locals I could trust. Everyone loved Micky despite his aggressive side after a few drinks. He disappeared to the toilet, probably to sedate his worried state. His paranoid head was about to get much worse in the coming weeks. Having my face buried into my phone, Katie appeared.

"Hi, Joe." An inviting smile.

"How are you?" I gave her a smile back, happy to see her lovely face. She came in wearing a tight pair of jeans, her plump ass squeezed perfectly into them, and a t-shirt showing her inked arm. Looking casual, but so fucking hot at the same time. Her freshly dyed midnight-blue hair glowing under the bar lights.

"Aye, I'm good. What's new with you?" We hadn't seen each other since I elbowed her in the face. I got the feeling she was as hooked on me, as I was on her. She craved the need for attention, and I was certainty willing to give her some, in private.

"No much, chick. You're looking amazing the night. Coming up to see me after am finished?"

"Mmm, feed me drink all night and I probably will, Joe." Her eyes dropped their guard, whisking me back under her spell. I had a deep love for her, which was obvious by the way I lost myself in her company. I loved everything about her and enjoyed sharing conversations. When I spoke to her, I forgot about all my troubles. If I got to spend the rest of my life with this woman, I'd count myself a blessed man.

"Look, I'm really sorry about what happened. I was out of control." The hurt that I felt after my action really tore me up inside, and I had to let her know that.

"Yeah, I know Joe. Now give me some shots, baby." I fed her shots and drink all night, hauling her upstairs after closing time to have another amazing night of passion, screwing her roughly up against the wall, throwing her around the room like a rag doll, both moaning with lust until the early hours.

Chapter 52

Matt McGregor:

With major doubt racing through my mind, I wasn't prepared for that night's events. The recovery from the binge going well, but the training sessions not. I couldn't keep up with the pace, my brain on a downer from the constant high, it couldn't operate as normal.

Spending a couple nights in Katie's company did relax me a touch. Adding to my worry that week, was fighting bare-knuckle against an ex-boxer and a good one at that. Having his boxing licence removed for too many assaults, he naturally moved into illegal boxing. My advantage of having a career in boxing wasn't there now, the advantage of being rage driven by 'roids against Masson wasn't there, either. There were even less rules in bare-knuckle fighting than there were in unlicenced rings. You could pretty much get away with anything, and that terrified me.

No gloves, no ring. Just a bare-knuckle scrap between two men, one of them walking away with five grand. I was just preparing to leave The Fountain, when Margaret caught me.

"Joe, listen son. Make sure you come home tonight?" We grew close over time. Not having any sons, Margaret felt the need to watch over me like a fairy godmother. I welcomed her love.

"Course I'll be back, Mags." Reassuring her I would, but honestly, who knew?

"Well, if you're not coming back 'til the early hours, text me, cos I'll have to go home." She stayed a few streets away from the pub.

"Sure Mags. I will, definitely."

"OK honey, good luck." She gave me a tight hug before I headed outside, Tim waiting for me in the car.

The journey to the high-rise parking complex was too short. I hadn't had much time to myself before leaving. Entering through an emergency exit door, guarded by one of Mike's henchmen, I walked to the fourth level. I couldn't slow time, my head was in a panic, worried about not being prepared for this.

Opening the door to the top floor, the evening sun shone through the gaps in the wall. A gathering of about a hundred people stood in the north-east corner. Tim dressed ragged in a farmer's shirt, carrying a plastic bag with water and a towel. My untidy hair, heavy stubble and loose dress made us both look ragged.

We stepped towards the fight area, hearing the patter of every step and every beat of my heart, taking a stance opposite McGregor. Spotting him straight away dressed as if it was a pro-fight, boxing boots and long shorts, hoodie hung over his eyes, hands in the waist pockets. His shoulders loose, cool, calm and collected. No sign of nervous tension. He had done this many times. He was focused, totally mute while sizing me up me.

The mood in the room was bleak, shuffling feet of the congregation and conversation heard behind the noise of traffic. Taking off my t-shirt, I tried to loosen up, swinging my arms around and having a shadow-box. No warm-up necessary in this type of fight, just meet in the middle and get on with it. Tim wet my gum-shield, placing it in my mouth.

A few of the crowd could be recognized, Micky, Bull, Mike and members from the gym and other local faces from Tilly and The Fountain. People gossiped together while we caught stares and walked out to butt heads awaiting the beginning.

Stepping back, McGregor removed his hoodie, baring abs that looked like an oil-painting, and a clean-shaven chest. Short, inky black hair with long sideburns cut down his jaw. His smooth face wasn't one of a bare-knuckle fighter, except for his bumpy nose.

McGregor stood next to me, flexing his pecs, eager to get stuck in. I gave off the impression I was ready, but far from it. I wondered if he could see the weakness in my eyes.

"Right, men. Fight until the other can no longer continue, three minute rounds. One minute to go." An accomplice of Mike barked the orders and it wasn't ten rounds as I was told. The rules the way I saw them: Three minute rounds, knocked down, you had an unlimited time to stand before the round ended and fight until your foe couldn't continue. Ignoring the original rules was expected here, after all, Mike was running this operation.

Voices raised and comments exchanged, anticipating the beginning.

"Come on Joe! Do him!" Micky shouted and turned his body in the direction of MacGregor. The traffic noise drowned out the usual eerie silence these events brought, and helped the crowd give more voice. For the first time, cheers and shouts for my name sang out, being the local Granite City boy, it was expected.

"Time, gentlemen."

McGregor fixed to the spot, waiting for me. I hovered around him throwing a couple feints, looking to make him flinch, but nothing. He was unruffled. He had that arrogant air of confidence in his ability that talented boxers had.

A cagey affair, a minute in, no punch had been thrown. Gawking at him, he returned. I wasn't about to break stare, or fall for his tactics. He waited. The tension sharp, aggression building in the crowd. They wanted entertainment. They wanted blood.

Two minutes in, he watched my movement. His way similar to mine. Analyse your opponents, look for weakness in their eyes. Did he see mine?

Out of nowhere, he started to bounce on his toes, edging around me, his right hand by his chin and left hovering in front of him.

Moving with him, he floated, looking light on his feet as I expected from his boxing past. Only showing me his left side, there wasn't much target. Bobbing and weaving, he edged closer.

"Come on, then." I spoke, taunting him, trying to wind him up. It didn't go as planned. Smirking at me, both of us in punching distance, a lightning left-jab and right hand snapped into my face, hands so fast I never seen it coming.

"Time." Fucking cunt planned that to perfection.

"He's a smart one this, watch yourself, don't get suckered in." I wasn't in the right frame of mind for this, spending the past couple weeks getting over my coke binge, training was shit. And, I worried about not seeing my kids. "Keep your wits about you, Joe."

Sipping water, I cocked my head at McGregor. Standing by his trainer, taking in water and advice. Here he had the beating of me. Had I lost the heart for this? Maybe I had, right at this moment.

"Time, gentlemen."

Lacking confidence, I crept out, trying a little bounce in my toes.

Nervously I went in for an assault. Throwing a jab, he swiftly dipped his sculpted frame to the right, countering with a right-hook, then back-handed his forearm, chopping it through my throat.

Grasping my throat with both hands, slumping in panic, my trachea blocked. Trying to breath, taking deep gasps, but I couldn't inhale. Sounding like an asthmatic having an attack, slobbering down my chin. I took my time, I had until the end of the round to stand.

He stood smugly, glowering at my state. Close to surrendering, I could stay down and this could end now. The look on MacGregor's face was one of satisfaction, counting on an early night, I seen he wanted me to stay down.

"Joe, get up. Come on!" Micky's words did nothing to inspire me. What did, was the thought of my Father. I didn't want him to know I gave up like this, gave up knowing I could stand. Pulling myself off the ground, less than a minute to go in the round, still fighting for a proper breath.

The look of satisfaction was wiped from McGregor's face and his smile turned to a frown. I was no mug, he had to learn that. The crowd cheered as I stood. Coming straight at me again, filled with annoyance, a left-jab then a right hand, slipping them by swaying my waist from side to side, a left fist impacted into my ribs. Not yet recovered from the throat punch, the blow took my breath away again. His fists were too fast, his bare-knuckle thrown upward into my rib with a bouldering blow. Usually pain wasn't a problem, but in this this scrap, I lacked adrenaline. I wasn't up for it.

"Time."

"Jesus man, hold your hands up, take deep breaths." Tim shouted. Looking and feeling like a wimp, I lifted my arms above my head, inhaling deep breaths.

"Can you not hear me out there?"

"No, I can't hear fuck all!" On the ground in panic, I could hear nothing. My brain cared for nothing more but to breathe. Letting my lungs fill with air was a relief.

"Only been two rounds. You better switch on here, Joe." Tim took it upon himself to pour the entire bottle of water over my head.

"Fuck! What the fuck you doing man?!" It had the desired effect.

"Just get out there and wake the fuck up." Drying me off with my t-shirt, it was time again.

I heard whispers from the crowd. "Joe's done here, he'll be gone in this next round."

"Time, gentlemen."

I came out for the next round with a fast stride, deciding to give this fuck a fight. Anticipating his evasiveness this time. Throwing caution out the window, wasting no time, taking him by surprise, I thundered in with a right hand, left-hook combo landing both. He felt the pain, replying rapidly with two successive left-hooks, a right uppercut, and then a straight right.

Now able to absorb the pain, letting go of my fear, I planted my feet and tried to rally. He wouldn't stand still, bobbed around on his toes, his sharp jab in my face making me look stupid, but I wouldn't stop till I got close. Leaping into him was the only way I could close the gap.

Standing toe-to-toe, clinching for the advantage, interlocking elbows in a wrestle, a sickening uppercut sent my head pinging to the roof as I went into a haze. I was in trouble again. Not stopping, he kept the pressure on, my legs weakened, and the next thing I knew, I was lying flat down in a parking space.

He sniggered arrogantly, looking down his nose at me.

That changed things. I decided to play a game of my own. Taking my time again, coming round, and pretending I was suffering more than he thought.

I crouched onto one knee, then slowly rose to my two feet, slouching over my waist, hands on my knees, appearing done in. He seen his opportunity to finish me, the audience rose with anticipation.

The emerging Joe Marks, son of the great Davie Rhodes, about to fall.

I looked at McGregor. Appearing broken, only wanting him to fall into my trap, come into my range and seal his fate. I could see his face tighten, in his eye a glint of victory. He stepped closer, then a little closer, he pulled his leg behind his body, ready to volley my head all the way to Pittodrie.

There he was, right in front of me. His foot travelled in the direction of my skull. Clenching my fist tight, opening my body, I pivoted with a right uppercut from the floor, thundering the punch straight through the base of his chin, lifting him from his feet and sending him onto his back. He tried to pull his upper body up, but his hands were useless, like elastic.

In the struggle to rise, he rolled over, his tongue hanging out, licking the tarred surface.

There was still time to stand before the round ended. The crowd didn't want to see that, neither did I. Time still not up, he flapped about like a fish out of water, his arms almost paralyzed from the shoulder down, his brain only knowing he had to rise, but couldn't relate that message to his body. Determined, he tried again and failed, crashing back down onto the tarmac.

"Time."

After the shout, Matt McGregor's crew ran to his aid. As soon as they did, it confirmed it was over. Gratified, I ambled cock-sure over to Mike, who stood with his arms crossed. Holding my palm out, he knew what I craved. His eyes dropped, annoyed at me once more. Slipping his hand into the inside pocket of his leather jacket, prodding around for too long, he was reluctant to hand it over.

Swiping the envelope from his greedy paw, I picked up my wet t-shirt from the ground, throwing it over my shoulder and swaggered out the door. Five grand richer.

Chapter 53

Date With Destiny:

Early November, my date with destiny was set in stone. Becoming a reformed character after Matt McGregor took me apart mentally. I didn't drink, stayed off the coke, worked in the bar, trained, and treated Katie with the respect she deserved, falling deeper in love with her. May was now a memory. Beginning to see the end to this journey of destruction, I hoped for a non-violent future, with peace and happiness. Not finished yet though, the path still had to be cleared before I could settle.

Plans were in motion.

The rules of the fight were simple, last-man-standing. Once you hit the deck, you've got a minute to stand, if not, you lose. Winner taking home serious money: twenty grand. Taking place down in the dock-yards of Glasgow.

Any name worth mentioning in the criminal world intended on making an appearance. Important illegal activities would take place that night. The Eidolon would be conducting a massive arms-deal with a dangerous list of clients.

The Eidolon was a phantom, appearing and disappearing at will. Some say he was Irish, some say English. The main arms-dealer pulling in crates of weapons supplied from the active IRA, into the country, by plane or boat, changing his route from deal to deal. Every corner of Britain, every outfit worth their name, from Aberdeen to London, got distribution from The Eidolon. He could get you any weapon you wanted, from a

Second World War standard, USA issue M1 Garand rifle, to the most powerful hand-gun in the world, the fifty calibre Magnum 500. Smoke-bombs to poison-darts, you name it, he'd get it. Scotland Yard, MI5 and the G2, the Southern Ireland Intelligence Agency, were constantly pursuing him. Their search useless, they had leads on The Eidolon, but find him, they wouldn't. Being top of the wish-list on every authority's desk around Britain, it would be a huge achievement for any member of law enforcement to catch him.

A boss of his crew, his loyal four, The Stable.

Bred from the streets of Belfast, experts in guerrilla-warfare, they could conduct deals for their boss with enviable skills. They would be unknown. Their appearance hidden. All of them furiously dedicated to The Eidolon, they stayed off-grid, no fingerprints and no medical records. Men who lived in the darkness. An effortless relationship built on their fear and unquestionable respect for their boss. Anyone that crossed this five, were dealt with in a calculated, inhumane manner. They had no compassion for life. The scar on Mr Dean's face, the result of a miscommunication between him and two of The Stable. He himself was fearful of them, and that from a man of ruthless reputation.

The Govan Gang and The West London's Ghetto Gang were stocking their supply of automatic weapons, Mr Dean himself taking a handful of Glock pistols. Skinner's four million pound counterfeit deal, going down with Glasgow's independent gangster Bobby Munroe. A vile man who grew up with death, though not initially in a murderous way. His father was a mortician with a succcessful business. Bobby gained a fascination for the dead, killing innocent people for fun, then hacked them up for his own pleasure. He went from being a serial-killer to a hitman and now he was assisting the Govan gang in moving upmarket. He was rotten, greedy and idolised being Glasgow's new Godfather. It wasn't the cash, it was the opportunity to dabble in even more criminal activity. The men he had working for him back in the city were brainless, but brave to mix with such a man. A small disagreement would land them in his private morgue. All the deals going down that night were just an excuse to witness what would be a violent, bloody affair between two warriors fighting for different reasons. Or, so I kept telling myself. The real truth is, it became part of who I am, I just had to separate it from who I would become. I trained like a professional bare-knuckle fucking demon for this. Rising in the mornings, injecting a hit of juice followed by a four-mile jog. Trained every afternoon. Hit bags with bare hands, toughening my knuckles and I sparred twice a week.

Boxing at the gym, I told my training partners to leave their gloves off. I wanted to feel the impact of raw knuckles. I wore mine, so when I fought The Reaper without them, there'd be no weight, my hands faster, looking for any advantage over him. Matt McGregor was too quick for me and too smart, a valuable lesson learned from him.

Underestimating my talents for this game was an error, one I won't make again, especially up against this Barbaric man. He was famous in his own right. Bitter, angry and no care for his wellbeing, he would come at you blind with broken bones or lost limbs. He didn't drink, didn't take drugs, didn't socialise and had no friends. His sole purpose in life was to inflict pain. Jacked up on daily injections of steroids made him even more dangerous.

When I become victorious, my name will always be remembered, mentioned in the same sentence as the infamous Davie Rhodes. He wasn't proud of me as a youth, but I'm sure he'd be appreciative of me now. Ironic that. It humbled me inside, knowing he would be honoured to be my Father. A son will always look for his Father's praise. Maybe that's why I did this, maybe deep down inside, all I wanted was for him to love me and accept me. And when I turn over The Reaper, I can say 'Look Dad, look at your boy now.'

Chapter 54

Pumped Up:

Mid-September. Before heading down Kilgours for a night's sparring, I joined Margaret behind the bar. Micky MacDonald, now my good pal, had come in for a few jars.

"Did you get your stew, love? I left it in the kitchen for you."

"Aye, cheers Mags." I gave her a peck on the cheek to say thanks. "It was great, by the way." She was a gem, old Margaret. She had seen my soft side, just as she had seen Micky's. Gentle and stubborn, with a cheeky sense of humour, the perfect landlady. I became increasingly worried about her though, on nights I wasn't here, in case anything happened in this bar.

"You're spoiled here, Joe. Think I'll start nipping round for supper every night." Micky was acting odd that night, one minute quiet, in a trance and next cracking jokes as normal.

"You're welcome any night, Micky. You know that." Her mothering instinct was always there. She would bend an ear to any man's problems at the bar.

"No chance you're coming for supper, that'll make my portion smaller. Besides, you don't look like you've had a meal in your life." He was a skinny radge, Micky.

Margaret walked away to serve a punter. I leaned over the bar and spoke quietly. "You seem off the night, Micky?"

"Aye, I'm off the gear. Canny handle it any more. I'm too old for it now."

"Away and fuck, mate. How old are you?"

"Forty one. I've been taking panic attacks all week. Just need to chill out for a while".

"Fuck, I know how that feels, just calm down for a while, you'll be fine".

"Aye, I'll just play it cool for a few weeks." He took a little bow closer to me and spoke from the side of his mouth. "That fuckin' Harry Duncan's on the loose. He's out."

"How long's he been out for?"

"Twenty days apparently, and I've no idea where the cunt is." His fingernails took a chewing that night. Probably the reason he's off the coke.

"You've maybe dodged a bullet here. If he was that keen to find you, he would've caught up wi' you by now." I tried to reassure him, but I didn't know what else to say.

"Anyway, how many days you been off the ching?"

He looked down at his pint, head tilting side to side, mouth mumbling numbers. "Eh… twenty hours now."

I burst out laughing, complete joker this cunt. "What a fud! Twenty hours! You've not even reached a day yet, you bam!"

"Aye, you're right. No point making it twenty-four. I'm away for a line. Catch you later."

That was Micky down to a T. Complete lunatic and just on the planet to have a good time. Micky sent me out the door in a good mood, but that didn't last long

Walking into Kilgours around that time, my mood would automatically transform, sending my mind to a cold place, a dark place I had to go to. I needed to sink into the same mental state as The Reaper.

I spoke little to anyone except Tim, but lately, he just left me to my own devices. He could see the task on my hands. That night, the bags got a pounding as usual, cuts from knuckles were constantly opening from scrapping the leather. I moved rapidly through the circuit, chin sunk into my chest, getting on with it. Still sitting at ninety-two kilos, I was ripped and confident. Every sit-up, every pull-up, every punch was all about becoming the victor. Sweating like Hell, my furious pace leaving the rest of the gym behind.

My pure dedication to this was frightening. Tim told me to slow down at times, I just kept on, didn't care for life, didn't want to stop and think.

Every day I thought of the kids, May and what I had done to her. Once The Reaper was done, I had to make amends to see my kids again. There was no hope with May, I knew that, I could see my future with Katie and her kids, if she'd have me.

This must have been my best night's training to date. I sparred with all four guys in there, one after another, three minutes a time. Gloves on to save hurting them, but I preferred them to wear wraps only, get my reflexes up, get used to feel of hard knuckle on my flesh. Twelve rounds in the ring I completed that night, not at full pace, but hard enough. Well aware The Reaper done no sparring. No one was stupid enough to step in between the ropes with him, unless they were paid a decent amount, even then they would fall to save the pain. Any advantage I could gain, would be badly needed.

Seven weeks to go, I was solidly psyched and longed for the notoriety of being the hardest man in the country.

Chapter 55

Micky:

Waking the following morning at 6.45, cuddled into Katie's luscious body, I struggled to pull myself out of bed. Sleepily making it to the kitchen for some tea and on for a seat in front of the telly. Turning on the local news. 'A man was found dead on the streets of Torry, in the early hours of the morning, thought to be murdered. No further information can be disclosed at this time.'

Thinking nothing of it, I continued to channel-hop, wondering what to have for breakfast. Then, I jumped up and ran to grab my phone from my jeans pocket. In a panic, I dialed Micky's number. 'Welcome to the Orange answer phone...' I had a bad feeling, that squirrel in your belly when you know something's not right. Anxious to find out what was going on, I called Tim.

"Tim, you heard about the body found in Torry?"

"What? Jesus Joe, it's seven in the morning, lad." Half asleep he wasn't cracking on to what I was saying.

"There's been a body found in Torry. Is it Micky?"

"What you on about? Can't be, surely."

"HARRY DUNCAN, TIM!" Yelling down the phone to him, I needed him to wake the fuck up.

"I'll phone you back. I know who to get a hold of." Straight off the phone, I dressed then legged it out the flat door, sprinting to Bucksburn Police

Station, hoping I could find out the information I needed.

The panic continued on the way. Almost certain it was him, knowing in my gut it was him, I wasn't ready for the reality. Storming through the door, straight to the reception-desk where a young female constable worked.

"The murder last night. Who was it?" Alarm in my voice, preparing myself for the news.

"Calm down, sir. We can't release that information." She had that arrogant charm any copper had, and didn't like my hostility.

"WHO IS IT?!" Shouting, she flinched, petrified at my tone.

"Look sir, calm down. Take a seat." This bitch was pushing it. Close to jumping over the counter, Mr Magill's ogre-like body strolled past, holding his polystyrene cup of coffee by his chest, looking weary like he had no sleep. I knew he had the answer I needed.

"MAGILL!" Yelling in his direction to get his attention. "Was it Micky last night?"

"I'm sorry Joe…it was Micky." My heart missed a couple of beats, then took five or six thumps to catch up with absorbing the shock, instantly forgetting about my own worries.

Taking four steps backwards, falling onto the waiting area seats, my insides felt empty. Staring into space, I didn't know how to take this, even though I'd experienced it before, you're never ready.

.The same horrific pain when I saw Mom, stone dead, on Dad's seat. That same gut-wrenching horror of someone taken from you, knowing you could have done something to stop it. Instant feelings of regret.

"Joe, you OK?" No, I fucking wasn't, fucking idiot.

"How was he murdered?" Knowing it was Harry Duncan, I wanted to know how he did it.

"We found him on the street, close to his Aunt's, a kitchen-knife in his back, must have been jumped, probably full of a night's coke and alcohol. Do you know anything?" Wrenching my head round to Magill as he gave me that evil stare of suspicion. He needn't bother asking.

"Not a clue." He knew I was speaking shit, but he entertained me.

"OK, Joe, OK." He was more compassionate than I expected.

Leaving the police station, I walked back to The Fountain to break the news to Margaret. Dreading telling her, to be the one to broke the terrible news.

I called Tim, he couldn't take it in. He would need time.

Eight o'clock, Margaret wouldn't appear until 10.30am to ready the bar. I would sit in the pub and wait. I couldn't tell her over the phone.

Soon as I entered the bar, I headed straight for a bottle from the storeroom, grabbing a glass on the way back, propping up the bar on the last stool Micky sat on. Dull and silent like a morgue, left with only my thoughts, only the pool-table light shining, casting dark shadows across the room. I opened the bottle and watched the golden liquid fall willingly right to the brim of my glass. Picking it up holding it above my head, I toasted. "Here's to you, Micky."

The back door burst open at 10.00am, Tim walked in, anxiety plastered all over his face. A bottle of whisky now lay in my stomach. I couldn't take it, didn't know how to take the pain. All I wanted was for someone to take it away.

With no nourishment in my guts, the liquor flowed straight to my head. I couldn't see straight, couldn't stand or barely talk.

"What the fuck, Joe? I can't believe it." He still struggled to process the truth.

"Better believe it, mate. Micky's gone." Completely plastered, I slurred my words.

"Look at the state of you!" Tim sounded concerned as I swayed my head back and forth, stretching my hand out, trying to find one of the three glasses in my blurred vision. Downing the rest of the alcohol.

Tim collected his own glass, filling it to the brim with Grouse from the optic, taking a pew with me at the bar. As I tried to stand to head to the bog for a piss, I fell over in a heap.

"Fuck me, Joe get up." I couldn't stand on my own, Tim helped me back onto the seat, slumping my head over my arms at the bar, my head spinning around, I passed out.

Tim shook me vigorously, as piss soaked my jeans.

So drunk I didn't care, and didn't move.

Right then, Margaret walked through the front door, finding me slumped on the bar-stool. As she discovered the pool of piss by our feet, she looked into my half-shut, bladdered eyes. The first tears of grief rolled down my cheek.

"JOE? What's wrong?" The tears started flowing helplessly, I couldn't hold them back. Telling her would make it a reality. "What's happened? Tim?"

"I don't know how to say this, Margaret." I managed to stutter but couldn't continue as my body started sobbing uncontrollably. I could no longer talk, it was up to Tim. My hands covered my eyes, my chin sank to my chest.

"Tell me what? You're scaring me now." Margaret lifted her trembling palm to her mouth. She could tell the news she was about to hear would to be devastating. Tim was awkwardly silent, only prolonging what he had to say. It was out of my hands. I didn't have it in me.

"Fuckin' tell me, Tim!"

"It's Micky, he was…found murdered in Torry this morning." Margaret stared, trying hard to take it in. "What?"

"It's true. I'm so sorry, Margaret."

Her knees buckled, using the bar to hold her up. Tim helped her to sit.

"He was here last night, sat where Joe is. It can't be right."

We were all in complete shock and denial. I wasn't able to stand, couldn't console her as she fell apart. Tim put an arm round her shoulder. Fuck knows how he stayed so calm, but he was good at that, nothing in life fazed him.

"Joe, get upstairs lad, clean yourself up."

"Aye, help me." Picking me up, still weeping, trousers stinking and soaked in piss, Tim carried me up to my bed-sit, sitting me on my bed. I wrestled with taking my trousers off, bumped my way into the toilet, my head fell into the pan and I spewed out the contents of my whisky-filled guts.

Chapter 56

Grief:

The next few weeks sent me deep into grief. It seemed people I cared about, left me. A lone soul, only accompanied by my demons, I couldn't cope with people, and drank myself into destruction. Lost in depression, thinking there was no way out. Hounded with regret I wasn't there for my pal. I could've done something about Harry Duncan, I could've found him and dealt with him before he got to Micky. I kept asking myself why I didn't? Harry Duncan had disappeared from the radar.

That week, I relived the time I'd spent with Micky, but that wouldn't bring him back, nothing would.

Alcohol and an abundance of coke became my coping mechanism, again. It became a hundred pound a day habit, Micky's dealer Kenny Mackie dropping off gear at the pub whenever needed. Margaret's store frequently raided, even when she changed the padlock, I found a way to break in. When the whisky ran out, I drank vodka, when there was no vodka, I would drink anything. Smells of stale booze, stinking feet and smoking twenty a day filled my bed-sit. I didn't wash or clean my teeth, wore the same clothes, only changing after vomiting.

Tim took it upon himself to visit daily, trying to pull me out of the hole. Worrying more than anyone, aware of my imminent date with The Reaper. That man didn't have a soft side, didn't care for life nor anyone's well-being. His job, simple. Turn up, take his foe's head off, collect his money, and go home.

Katie made attempts to help me in the first week, shouting at her in bouts of rage every time she got close. It's possible I hit her a few times as well, I can't honestly remember. Margaret dealt with her grief in her own way, by just getting on with things. She helped Micky's Auntie prepare for the funeral arrangements, once his body was released by the police. Making an effort to look after me, she would bring up plates of food, leaving them on my bedside-table. Sometimes I ate them, most times I didn't. Opening my door each morning, picking up empty bottles and wraps of cocaine. Also to check I was still alive. Attempting to speak to me about the situation, I wouldn't take her on, knowing we all have our way of coping with grief. Locked up in my room for three weeks, built up a level of aggravated tension I'd never felt before. Holding it in, trapping it, to be used another day.

The day before the funeral, in the first week of October, Margaret held a gathering in the pub in remembrance of Micky MacDonald.

It was the first day I left my room, showered and stopped drinking. The Fountain bar mobbed out the door. Jukebox kept to a low volume, echoing stories admiring the main man. Tim, Katie, Bull, Mike and all locals of Woodside and Tilly turned up. The grief in the air could be felt, friends and relatives breaking down in tears.

Margaret was particularly pleased I surfaced from the bed-sit. Probably thinking I was beyond help. Not sure what changed that day, maybe I just got through the first stage of grief. Probably the thought that one day, my life might end like poor Micky's.

"Joe! You've showered! You OK?" Hearing the relief in her voice, beckoning to me, an instant smile on her sad face. Leaning in, giving me a tight hug. "So glad you're up, love." Affectionately rubbing my shoulder up and down.

"Thought I better get on with it." Reassuring her I was OK, but I wouldn't be until my path was cleared. Having a few matters to deal with, before I could leave this life behind.

"So nice to see you up. You want a drink?" Standing behind the bar, the lure of alcohol not taking my fancy now. My head needed screwing on, starting…now.

"No, I'll give you a hand, it's busy the night." Needing to keep occupied, I helped her behind the bar.

Locked in a room, minced for three weeks, made socialising difficult. Hot flushes making me sweat uncontrollably, with a constant panicky feeling stuck in my gut. Struggling to function behind the bar, my attention span at a minimum and hands shaking, uncontrollably making pouring drink and operating the till frustrating. Trying to count change in my head especially difficult. I had to disappear into the kitchen often to have a moment, before I needed a paper bag to breathe into. The background noise from the punters ran through my head like a rebounding echo. My body had been violently abused, turning me into a desperate case.

My mind wanted to explode. That's when I knew, attending the wake the next day was out of question. I might regret it, but I'd done my grieving, needed to re-tune and get the fuck on with what I had to do.

"Joe…you're white as a ghost." Katie came for a word with me, seen me struggling to function. I was glad to see her, once again it seemed like she had forgiven me.

"Aye, I'm OK. Honest, I'm fine." Obviously I wasn't. Ready to pass out at any time, sticking it out to help Margaret.

"You don't look it, Joe. You want to go to the service with me tomorrow?" She had a lot of affection for me, I had no idea why, treating her like shit all the time. Guess she needed loved, too.

"I'm not going, Katie. Can't face it."

"That's not right, you have to."

"Look, I don't want to argue about it. Micky will understand my reasons."

"Ooh Joe, you'll regret it. What if I come see you after the service? It's not good sitting on your own at a time like this. I'll get a babysitter for the kids." For the first time in weeks, I could handle company, especially hers.

"Aye, that'll be good. Give me a text before you come round."

Tim was in constant conversation with me all night. I told him I needed his presence at the gym every day. He handled the whole situation better than I ever could. Dealing with my Mother's death will always have a knock on effect. Never getting over it, it spilled out after Micky's murder.

Chapter 57

In The zone:

Alarm struck at 7am, time to get up, time to run. Every morning I rose, there was a procedure. Take a shot of 'Deca', eat two bananas, drink water, wrap up warm and pound the Aberdeen streets.

Four miles every morning, no matter how painful, boring or cold it was.

The distance left me time to ponder my date with destiny, my life and how it's spiraled out of my control. Feeling like I was on a journey that had already been laid out in stone. It drove me to complete this massive task on my hands. Sending all emotional baggage to hate, the only way I'd get through this.

I didn't talk to anyone, except Tim or Margaret. Releasing Katie from my grip, I didn't want her in my life for this, too addictive, too much of a distraction. I loved her too much to bring my life of destruction down her road any more. Causing her too much pain already, she deserved better. Maybe after this is all over, there might be a future for us, maybe?

Margaret was well aware of what was taking place on November 7th. She lived in a man's world, knew my reasons for throwing myself into this. Taking it upon herself to look after me even more after Micky passed, I felt the duty to repay her a favour. Seemed like she was recovering from the ordeal quite well. Telling her my story of why I had to do this stunned her, leaving her worrying that I too might be murdered. Reassuring her I wouldn't, was a lie, there was every possibility that could be the outcome.

Two weeks to go. Tim sent me through Hell every training session. Two hours every day, including the weekends, at 11am.

"Come on, get on wi' it! Fifty more push-ups!" The morning warm-up consisted of two hundred reps of every exercise. Sit-ups, squat-thrusts, pull-ups and press-ups. Fifty each at a time, repeating the process four times. After that was done, fifteen minutes skipping, then shadow-boxing for five rounds with 4kg weights to speed up my hands, then onto the bag for ten rounds of torture, then pad-work.

Three days a week, the bag being punished without gloves. The skin on my knuckles now never broke. Hardened by the grueling training. The hard bag so solid when hit, it hardly swung unless I released, let go. It was frightening, able to turn instantly into a boiling beast, leaving a dent when done.

A heavy weight-training program was introduced. Tim brought in an Olympic Bar, a stand and stacks of heavy weights. Using the bar every day became religious. Squatting 240kg, dead-lifting 280kg, bench-pressing 180kg, turning my body stronger than ever before. Combined with the flow of rage from the steroids, my boxing ability, years of pain and motivation, I was a formidable force. He pushed me further past my point of retiring, every session. It was welcomed, I needed it more than ever.

Tim saw the fury in my eyes erupt on a daily basis. Blanking out from time to time. The 'Deca' taking effect, adding to my deep well of anger. Words were few in that time. In a deep mental trance, I cared for nobody and nothing, fixated on the end of the journey, end to the burning torment.

"Thirty seconds left! Come on, let's get it out!"

"Agggh! Agggh! Aghhh! Aaaaahhgg!" With every punch, I howled and hissed. I breathed like a possessed vampire at the sight of blood, inhaling and exhaling heavily unable to calm, feeling the terrifying urge to disembowel The Reaper, rip him apart, end him.

The terror in Tim's eyes. What had he got me into, he asked himself. Too late for that Tim, here and in the moment.

The 'roids helped send me the furthest along the road of destruction I had ever been on. Pumping the blood to my muscles, feeling like some days I could go on and on. It added to my level of aggression, but I learned to hold it in for when it counts.

Thirty minutes of pad-work continued with little breaks exhausting me, then the 'roids would kick in, give me more energy. Gave me so much, it took two hours each day to drain the tank.

There was no sparring leading up to the bout, Tim instructing that it was too dangerous, I was too dangerous and didn't need it. Holding my temper was difficult, another reason I cut Katie loose. The damage I could inflict on her, I didn't want to think about.

"Right, outside and flip the tyre." Bringing in a used tractor-tyre weighing a hundred and forty kilos, spending a few rounds at the end of every session flipping it up and down the small parking area in any weather, rain or shine. Doing this exercise at the end of each session, was designed to physically and mentally break me. Four, three minute rounds of flipping the tyre drove me to breaking point each day, exhausting me, running out of kick from the steroids.

The training made me ravenous, I ate constantly, cooked my own food during the day and Margaret made me supper every night. I helped in the bar only when required, normally I would offer help for the room, but I didn't care for company, I wanted the solitude of my bedsit. Didn't want to make small-talk, or laugh at bad jokes.

Only wanted The Reaper's reign to end.

Chapter 58

Mags:

The morning of the fight was a cold one, the first of this year's frost layered on top of the cars. Margaret came round early to cook me up some breakfast and send me a farewell. Sitting in one of the bar-booths, we ate and enjoyed a lovely feed. Full Scottish breakfast with plenty of extras. I grew so close to her over the past six months. She was worried I wouldn't return. And, so was I.

"This breakfast is brilliant, Mags. Thanks." Nobody called her by that except me, but it felt like I should be saying Mom.

"Joe, you don't have to say thanks, it's my pleasure, honey." With no idea where I was headed after today, there was a chance I'd never see Mags again, so I needed her to know I was grateful.

"I just want to say something." Her face was blank, thinking she knew I was saying a last goodbye in case I never returned. "I want to say thanks for everything. I didn't deserve any help and you gave me a roof when I had nowhere to go."

"You can thank me when you're back. I want to see you come back, honey." Her jaw fluttered, holding in a tear. She wasn't willing to accept there was a chance I wouldn't be able to walk into The Fountain Bar again.

Accept it, I had to. But, I had to say thanks to her, give her some closure, just in case.

"Joe, do you have to do this? It's madness!" Placing her hand over mine at the table.

"Mags, I've told you, this has to be finished so I can move on with life." I explained this a few times, the only person I could open up to, because I trusted her.

"Joe, this is crazy." Her eyes teared up.

"This will be all over by tomorrow morning, then it'll be forgotten." No words from her would change my decision. This path had been set out for me since the day I was born, and ends tonight.

While waiting for Tim to pick me up, we chatted about Micky, reminiscing about his crazy personality and the mischief he got up to in The Fountain. Right there, that morning, I felt a profound happiness sharing time with Mags, content this part of my life would end tonight, even if I had to walk through the gates of Hell to get there.

Tim turned up at 10.50 and it was time to say goodbye.

"Joe, take care down there." Mags giving me a hug, squeezing the life from me, passing tears, I feared it would kill her if I didn't come back. "You make sure and text me. OK, Joe?"

Cupping her cheeks with my hands, I reassured her. "Of course I'll text you. See you later, OK?" I kissed her on the forehead, hugged her, and then left with Tim.

"Well. Ready?"

"Aye, I'll be ready when the time comes. After this, I'm out."

"I'm doing the same, like." He surprised me, he seemed very at home in this world, maybe he was too comfortable.

"Shite! You won't get out this game."

"No seriously, that's it. I've seen enough." Everything he'd seen me go through, pushed him to the edge. Besides he had a family, eventually they'd be pulled in somewhere down the line.

"What you going to do, 'en?"

"My scrap business. Gonna make a go of it. Want a job?" Fuck me! All I wanted was a job in the first place, now he's offering me one.

"Aye, I'll have a job!" That was it settled, after today was over, I would work for Tim, suited me fine. Get me back on the straight and narrow.

Taking off my jacket, I slouched down in the passenger seat for what I hoped would be the last time I'd have to, shutting my eyes and ignoring the world. My body by this point had been pushed to its limits, the past month in the gym. My brain drained, but in the right space, my body fatigued, but more ready than ever. I only had one more workout to complete. That would push me mentally and physically to the edge of life itself.

Stories surfacing. The Reaper was like a man possessed, hearing a nobody from the Granite City being lined up as his replacement. As far as I knew, he'd only ever had bare-knuckle fights. I didn't know much about his past, only what Mr Dean told, which wasn't much. The money wasn't important to me here.

Living out my demons and having a future, was everything.

Chapter 59

The Docks:

Arriving near the venue too early after Tim grabbed some supper, I had no appetite. We pulled into the banks of the neglected shipyard on the edge of the Clyde. The traffic noise of Glasgow buzzing in the background, but the sound of water trickling downstream made it feel peaceful, the river adding to the cold chill in my body that night. We parked outside a large, brown-cladded fabrication shed, still operating. This must be it, I said to myself.

"That's it over there, see it?" Tim pointed over to a derelict square building, hundreds of metres away to the east.

"Why the fuck we parked over here?"

"See this huge welding shop. There's a tunnel stretching from here to that building over there."

This obviously happened before. Tim's knowledge of the place no coincidence.

"How the fuck do you know that?"

"I've been here before, lad. Many years ago." Tunnels were common around the shipyards, mainly used for running electrical mains cables under the river and across the huge expanse of land. Tonight, the tunnels would be used as a gateway into the venue, as they had been, time and time before. Parking the cars beside the massive fabrication shed was a good disguise, misleading snoopers and the filth from the trail.

"It's too early to head over."

"Aye, I know. Come on, we'll find a pub an' chill out for an hour-ish." Fucking sick of pubs. Usually by this time, I'd be tortured by anxiety and nerves. Something else pre-occupied me, something I had to know was done, before concentrating on my reason for being here.

"You hear that?" My phone rang from inside the Merc.

Call from Steve Dean:

"Steve."

"Joe, you in Glasgow yet?"

"Aye, we're here."

"I hear the truck's in London as we speak. It's your call." It wasn't my call, it was in another man's hands, a man that I would be delighted to see the back of.

"Sorry, Mr Dean. It's not in my hands at all. I'm waiting on confirmation."

"And what about your friend, Skinner?"

"No word yet, I'll keep you posted."

"Remember Mr Rhodes, this stays between us. Understand?" The reference to the family name I disowned, telling me I was still in his pocket, and how much information he held over my head.

"Perfectly, Steve." Not one for goodbyes, he hung up. I searched for a number I didn't care to have in my contacts list. Bewildered by the conversation, Tim tilted his head and screwed up his face. "What the fuck's going on?"

Call to Detective Magill:

"Where's the truck?" I asked.

"It's just pulled up in a lorry depot. We're waiting for the switch, before we jump in."

"And Skinner?"

"Just preparing the road-block, shouldn't be long. Are you at the venue?"

"Aye, I'm here. There's nobody here yet. Stick to the plan. I'll text you the address later on." My plan was coming together, not long now.

"Joe, you're doing the right thing here." Magill tried to reassure me being a snitch was creditable. It wasn't, but what choice did I have? I had a burning need for something. Willing to do anything for that one chance I needed.

"What the fuck's going on?" Utterly bamboozled, Tim couldn't understand. His first thought I was a snitch, working with the filth, playing Mr Dean.

"You're on a 'need to know basis' and you don't need to know, my friend." I had to return the call to Mr Dean, update him on the progress.

Call back to Steve Dean:

"Steve, both arrests are close to completion."

"Excellent, Joe. The gun deal will be proceeding as planned." Once again, he hung up. His conversations short and sweet, preferring conducting business face-to-face, analysing body language.

"Look! Will you tell me what the fuck's happening here." Tim's brain ticked over, trying to find the answer. "Are you working for the filth?"

In a way yes, I was. But, working with them to trap Magill in my web.

"No Tim, this is retribution."

Chapter 60

Back To The Interview:

Back to the weekend of Micky's unprovoked assault on Billy Duncan, and the second half of the police interview with detective Magill. Magill got my attention the second he muttered my Father's name.

"Well, he's hovering around somewhere. Where is he?" Magill began to see he made a breakthrough. Unaware of my undying need to locate my Father, he was about to find out how much I craved that Father and son catch-up.

"Yes, he's definitely about somewhere, Joe. We just need to know where."

"Aye...where, then?" I didn't intend on leaving this grotty interview room until the information was laid on the table.

"We're kind of hoping you can enlighten us to where he is." A professional in his trade. He caught on to my desperate need to locate my Father. Fuck knows why he figured I knew, I continued to dig.

"Not a fuckin' clue. But, you obviously know something!" His body language changed, became tense and shoulders tightened, trying to squeeze what information I had. Desperate for information, both of us were.

"He's a wanted man, Mr Marks. Or should I say, Mr Rhodes. Have you heard from him at all the past few years?"

"No, not a peep."

Hadn't seen or heard from the callous cunt since that day in The Fountain, where he left my broken body lying under the shadow of the slot-machine in shards of glass.

"Wanted for what?" He needn't bother with the chit-chat. This was the nearest I'd got to his throat in years.

"Aberdeen Police have been trying to locate him for some years, Mr Marks. We made the connection between you two, through your juvenile records, and his old Tilly address."

"Fuckin' Hell, took you long enough." I started to act disgusted at his amateur police skills. It annoyed him and his silent colleague.

"We've been looking for a Mr Rhodes. That's why we've had no luck finding you."

"Well, you've found me. What do you want?" He was surprised at my forwardness.

"What?" Detective Magill maybe wasn't the professional I'd thought.

"Let's not play any more games, Magill. Both of us want his head on a plate. What do you want from me?" My desperate need to find my Father, made me go against my morals about dealing with the cops.

Magill switched off the interview recording. This was the first signal from him that he needed my help. "Glad you asked. Let's say you feed me information now and again...I could keep you informed of his whereabouts, if we get any leads." His colleague sat silent, awkwardly gazing at me, he wasn't surprised at Magill's behaviour. Pausing, the effect it would have on my name on the streets if it leaked out. "And the charges you've picked up this weekend will be thrown out before the court date." That proposal sealed the deal for me.

"Tim's charges?" I felt responsible for his arrest outside The Fountain, only trying to help me with the squad of filth. Here, Magill turning to his trainee, Munroe, who wore goofy designer rectangle glasses, nodded in agreement. Tim would just have to live with the charges until I could tell him. Magill thought I would be sown into the inside of his pocket, but I managed to reverse the roles.

"What kind of information do you want?"

"Micky MacDonald, Mike Jenkins, Kenny Mackie and Skinner." Soon as I heard the first name, there was no chance I'd ever give him up. "We know they're all crooks, I want them off the streets of Aberdeen." Kenny Mackie was Micky's dealer, and a loyal friend of mine.

"Aye, I could do that, on the condition I get information on ma' Dad, regular as possible, no bullshit, Magill." I'd keep him happy with whatever I could give him.

Chapter 61

The first half of the meeting with Mr Dean after returning from Northern Ireland.

"So, Mr Jenkins is planning on cutting my feet on my next delivery?"

"Looks like it, Steve. Can't see no other reason to why he would visit The Rover."

"Well, I'll have to cut his throat before he cuts my feet."

"I have another option." Preparing to tell Mr Dean I was in Magill's pocket could result in serious repercussions and a painful afternoon for me. Gangsters like Mr Dean slashed the throats of people like me with no second thought, no mercy. We were cast aside.

"I usually don't care for other people's ideas but, go on." Crossing over his legs, placing his whisky glass on the round montage table, taking a more comfortable place in his seat.

"I'm about to tell you something that will shock you, but hear me out until I'm finished." Ogling me, waiting to hear my proposal. "I've gone and got myself into a little hole with the filth. Detective Magill knows my Father's whereabouts." Pausing, he didn't speak, waiting for me to finish, an impassive look. "I've agreed to feed him info, on local faces, in return for that information. One of those locals, is Mike Jenkins. We could set him up, hand him over to the filth." Finishing that part of the story, Mr Dean allowed things to run around his cunning mind.

"I know your Father, Joe. We met on a couple of occasions, years ago. Why you so desperate to find him?" He knew I wasn't a back-stabber at heart, gathered that by the way I conducted myself and spoke with honesty. Plus, the job I had completed in the past week, helped my cause.

"It's a long story, short version. He caused my Mom's suicide." His face stayed stone cold.

"You don't have to say any more." He understood straight away. "So you want to set Mike up, and that's because of the Skinner fight?"

"Aye, that and that only. I've got to give the filth something. That gets my own back, then you can do whatever you please with him."

The genius that was his mind ticked over, wandering over to his bottle of Talisker whisky, pouring another large one, then opening his humidor, lighting one of his finger-long cigars. Stood with his back to me, taking slow drags, creating a plan with little thought. The experience he'd gained over the years worked it all out. Dealt with problems and snitches all too often, he knew the way.

"The delivery will enter the ferry as planned with Roy and the driver. I'll send an empty van on with two men, two men not known to them. Overnight, they can empty the stash from the Argos truck, swap it over to our van. Paying the men on my take a little more, I can make sure the two vehicles sit back to front." He made it sound like a flawless plan and he could make it happen. With a collection of loyal men on his take, it would be easy.

"And what happens when the truck gets to this side of the border?" But, I underestimated him and his planning expertise.

"That's where you come in. The filth can hijack the truck at the finish line. I would wait until it reaches its destination, catch everyone involved."

"Will they not check the goods during the ferry ride, or after they're off?"

"That's a gamble. Obviously the weed will be in the other van by the time they're off the ferry. Usually the back door stays padlocked, not opened until it reaches my hideout. The lock can be cut, then replaced." Sucking in another long drag, the plan developed. "What we'll do, we'll replace the contents of the boxes with a little present." Thinking outside the box was a natural skill for him. The present would be a fitting shock to everyone at the scene.

"It sounds good. I trust this conversation will stay between us." That question answered itself. Knew he wouldn't want anyone outwith his inner sanctum knowing anything about this. What made him so keen to help me, was his need to outsmart anyone trying to meddle, or double-cross him in a trade he'd been operating in for the past thirty years.

"Of course, Joe. I won't tell anyone you're a snitch." The answer meant I was now in his pocket. Now on his take. He could use me as he pleased, having a hold on me.

"What you going to do with the three of them, once this is over?" There was little chance Mr Dean would let any of them off Scot free. Let them return to their normal lives without punishment.

"Have them killed, Joe." Calm, peaceful and frightening, his attitude towards ending a life. "One more thing, if I'm prepared to give myself all this stress, there's something you can do for me." There it was. The condition, the demand he required from me. Lounging back on his brown leather side-chair, slightly tipsy. I was relaxed, and satisfied with his acceptance of my idea.

"And that is?"

"You, Joe, can fight for me." At the time, that's the last thing I wanted. But, his condition was non-negotiable. I needn't argue or complain. After all, he agreed to work with me, agreed to my request. People agreed to his demands, not the other way round. Assigning me onto his take, keeping me afloat with two grand a month, and five for the next two fights. It took the money worry away. The two grand a month was virtually a gift. All I had to do, was keep him informed of Magill's schedule. The rest of the money was for my fighting services.

Chapter 62

Lousy Bastard:

Magill called while we sat sharing a juice in a local bar. By this point, I had to explain the whole story to Tim, taking time for it to sink in. He was stunned that I was capable of such a thing, while spending much of the time in a drug-fueled rage.

During my two-month binge after the Masson fight, the grief-ridden spell after Micky's death reminding me of Mom, it was obvious to him now. This was a massive build-up of pressure, causing me to erupt in alcohol and coke binges.

The charges on the night of Billy Duncan's slaughter were dropped by the police, in exchange for my inside knowledge of Mike Jenkins and Skinner. I relayed that information to Tim, and he was grateful I thought of him in the middle of everything. Reassuring him his name wouldn't be dragged down with mine, reassured him I was close to coming out the other side, close to a promising future.

Call Back From An Upset Magill:

"Magill." The simple word indicating I expected the call.

"JOE! You lousy bastard, you knew there was no weed in those boxes!"

"What boxes?" Playing dumb to piss him off.

"Fucking child-porn, you sick bastard!" Replacing the weed with kiddie-porn was Mr Dean's touch of class. Knowing they'd get put on the paedo list amused him. The weed driven to his warehouse in a white transit van, arriving early afternoon, leaving the driver and The Rover with the truck-load of child-porn traveling down the motorway toward West London, where Mike rendezvoused with them.

They planned on conducting a private deal with an acquaintance of The Rover. After concluding the deal, they all planned on flying off to live a new life in the Costa del Sol. Tickets booked to leave Monday afternoon from Heathrow. During the ferry ride, in the early hours of the morning, the padlocked truck was broken into. Getting away with this con for years, the boxes were lackadaisically taped shut. So easily sliced open and replaced with explicit images of child-porn on DVDs, USB sticks and laptops. Once the exchange was made, the padlock was replaced with an identical one. Mr Magill himself followed the truck to London, working in connection with English police forces. Once all parties were on the scene and Mike broke the lock, they were flooded by a raiding squad, to the great surprise of Mike, The Rover, the driver and the other party involved. Their faces once the boxes were opened, priceless, and all arrested.

"Really?! Child-porn? That's fuckin' disgusting. What about Skinner?" I really wanted to rub his nose in it.

"We got him and his two side-kicks with four million." Skinner's arrest was just cream on the cake for me. Just what the bully deserved in my eyes. Informing Magill of the counterfeit deal particularly pleased him. Skinner was a hard man to track down. Lived off-grid in his own anti-social bubble. After moving their operation to a location in the fishing district in Torry, Aberdeen, I gave the location of their previous counterfeit operation in Montrose over to Magill, knowing full well it was abandoned. Did this only to keep him off my back, ticking over an idea I had at the time.

That idea I ran past Mr Dean. Hijacking him and his two side-kicks on the way to Glasgow, four million of fake paper inside his motor. He didn't question my request, Skinner's set-up had no effect on his dealings and he didn't care for him.

"What have you got to complain about, Magill? I've held my bargain and you've held yours." I don't know what his problem was, he got his two arrests, took a few crooks off the streets of Aberdeen. OK, the weed wasn't in the truck, but he underestimated me and his lesson wasn't over yet. I was due to text Magill the address of the venue later that night before the fight took place. The Eidolon due to appear, conducting that massive arms-deal. The filth longed to get their hands on him. They had a specialist squad put together, members of Scotland Yard, MI5 and G2 grouped together, in their desperation to land his capture. That was the final part of the deal.

With this part of the plan concluded, I could concentrate on what mattered now.

"I'll see you later, Mr Magill."

"Wait a minute..." I stuffed the phone in my pocket.

"Right, that's that done. What time's kick off the night?"

"Nine o'clock, lad. You sure you want to go through wi' this?"

"Tim, you know I have to. Have faith, mate." He looked more worried than I've ever seen him. Because, anything could happen tonight.

Time to send my mind into that darkened corner, re-live my memories of my past, picture my violent Father, my Mom's face, the abuse we received, think of Micky, think of the chance to make amends with my kids. Let my pain and anger flow to the surface, spill over and take control.

Chapter 63

Pre-Fight:

Bitterly cold, alone in Tim's car facing the river, I used the next hour to channel my fear, control the flow of nerves flooding through me. The idea of my own death unwilling to leave my thoughts. Even the music in my ears couldn't control it.

Tim left me in the car as he travelled down the tunnel, reassuring him I'd make my own way. Cars came, parked and punters entered the shed. Every face on the island came to witness history.

Reclined back in the seat, I felt a tingle in me, a presence. Hearing a door close, I shifted in my seat and gazed over my shoulder, catching the sight of an enormous man, ripped jeans and a long, plain black t-shirt hanging loose due to his heavily-muscled upper body. As he ducked his head under the door he paused, waited for a few seconds and turning lazily around, catching my stare from the rear window. There, I felt an indescribable connection to him. His accomplice also took a glance. The loathsome, inhuman look from the giant burned into my core.

We both knew we were destined to meet on this cold November night.

Thirty minutes left, before I would take the walk of death. Ignoring the events of that day and remembering my reasons to complete this journey. Removing the stab of doubt. Reminiscing everything in life that turned me into the monstrous man I'd become. Every ounce of pain from my childhood. The eternal feeling of grief, loss and regret from my Mother's suicide. The knife in my friend's back, the need to reunite with my kids, my need to feel the touch of Katie's addictive skin.

One more piece of the puzzle to complete before taking the walk down the tunnel.

A text informing Magill of the venue.

Sinking deeper in thought, I filled my thoughts with demons, letting that other part of me make it way to the surface

I was ready, time to take the walk. Getting out the car, gulping a large swill of water, I removed my jumper and t-shirt in the freezing night. Beefed up, body filled with rage, I no longer felt the cold.

Racks of redundant electrical cables stretched down the left side of the long, grim passageway, the fluorescing lights casting a shadow on my 'roided bulk, muscles pumped full of the blood. A fearless walk, with breath filling my lungs, expanding my chest up and down in a bottled anger. The echo of each step in the two-metre wide tunnel, heightened. My eyes fixed ahead, burning with passion, focusing on what's in front of me, in a trance, snarling. With no idea what would happen, I could only hope fate had a plan. Hearing the clatter of voices, I was almost there.

A glare of white light entered the tunnel in the distance, a gateway to my future. Turning into an alcove passageway, boring into a well-lit basement, purpose in my stride. Ambling to the middle of the room, bare-chested, the chatter phased out, my presence duly noted.

Eight round concrete towers, designed to hold up the old, abandoned office building, situated around the rectangular basement perfectly. The crowd scattered around the outside, leaving the stage in the middle, the area dirty and grey, light shining down onto the canvas. I walked straight to the left side where Tim and Mr Dean stood, The Reaper at the other side of the room. I didn't have to look, I knew he was there, I could feel him.

"Joe." Mr Dean uttered, his way of saying hello. I only had one question.

"Has the gun deal gone down, yet?"

"No, midnight." He walked away from me, tinted-glasses on, nodding to me in good luck.

"You look pumped, mate. Drink some water." Tim handed me the water and I gulped it down, dry from the dusty atmosphere and anticipation. I avoided looking in his eyes, he'd have the same concerned look, as always.

The audience moved to the sides of the room in line with the pillars, leaving The Reaper and me standing opposite. I kept my back to him.

Personal bets around the crypt in progress, with thousands soaring from pockets of the criminals. The room filled with thugs and gangsters.

The Govan Gang, wearing the usual ned uniform of expensive shell-suits and trainers that will never see inside a gym, grouped with the dangerous independent gangster, Bobby Munroe.

The coloured West London Ghetto Gang stood opposite the Liverpool Rouge Riders. Jack Gallagher stood with his son Jimmy in the shadow of The Reaper.

Bull made the journey with Toby, and kept the company of Mr Dean and Lukas. Sixty other spectators rounded a room full of talent Magill would be pleased to lock up.

I couldn't allow the nerves, or the uncontrollable fear lurking under the surface, get hold. I would keep it there for just a little longer. The build-up of rage from the past month, all too noticeable in my face. Trying to keep the anxiety at bay wasn't easy, like an itch you couldn't scratch. Taking in some more water.

"Joe, whatever happens here…I just want you to know I'll do right by your kids." His words didn't help me, changed my thought pattern for a minute.

"Let's not speak about that." Knowing it was getting closer, I felt the need to turn, catch the proper sight of my foe on a seat, his square head sunk into his chest, going through the same ritual as me, zoning out everyday life. His head lifted and his six foot three frame with it, off the seat. A heavy-lidded stare at me, he slipped his t-shirt off and removed his jeans, chucking them on the ground, leaving him standing with black shorts.

Joe Gallagher and his crew watched as the rest of the room sized him up. His massive stature was threatening, but I just smiled grimly, my eyes staring. Shaved head at the sides, with a short layer on the top, wide cheek bones combined with his frame, added to the look of a wild Barbarian.

I saw nothing in his eyes, nothing but a rotten hatred.

Have I made a mistake? Would this be the end of me? Running out of time. "You're a fucking warrior, Joe. Rip this fucking cunt's head off." Those words were my own, no pep-talks needed from anyone else tonight. The rage resurfaced to the top, as the pain of my past resurfaced.

That past dies tonight…

Chapter 64

The Beginning Of The End:

Standing in this run-down, retired shipyard building on the banks of the Clyde, a desolate part of Glasgow, staring down at the palms of my shaking hands, wondering what my fists had turned me into. Wondering how I let things escalate so far.

Across from me, was a beast like no other I had seen before, a modern day Barbarian, only interested in seeing me defeated, lying in a puddle of my own blood and piss. A man that had no mercy and had destroyed everyone he stood across from. That gave him the reputation of being the hardest man with two fists in the country.

The nonchalant look from his eye to mine as he stared me down across the circle of thugs and gangsters was one I had never seen, no sign of weakness. Instead, a fire of hatred for life hidden beneath his intimidating eyes. The doubts were racing around my head like never before, where will I be after this is all over? Will I get through this?

But there was no time to dwell, I had to stay focused on the task at hand, or I'd be lifted off this cold, concrete floor in a body-bag.

It was the money, or so I kept telling myself, but to be truthful, I was hooked on the game. The buzz of the crowd, the feeling of tearing your opponent apart, the pure adrenaline you get when you start exchanging blows, the sight of your foe lying on the floor in front of you, partially paralyzed. The cash that's handed to you after you are victorious.

The countdown was on. Five minutes to go.

There was going to be a duel between two warriors that no one in this crowd of peasants had seen before, and a battle no one in this room will forget. My hands began to feel clammy with sweat and my legs started to shake with a temporary fear. All this was hidden on the inside, but, on the outside, the only feeling that was projected from my face and pumped-up frame, was the need to see The Reaper broken down. In pain. Bloodied and bruised and begging for his life.

I was the main man. The top dog. He was just some cunt in the way of me becoming the hardest in the country. I had come too far, gave up everything. Lost the love of my life and my two kids, to let this degenerate Liverpool faggot beat me.

Time was ticking and I could smell his blood already, picturing it, me smashing his head off the cold concrete floor. He gave me another stare from across the room. He looked as pumped as I did, standing a few inches taller than me, every bit of his body had muscle rippling out. His arms were bulging, his stomach, body and back were ripped to shreds, with a set of traps on him that made seeing his neck difficult.

That physique and look of hatred in his eyes made him look spine chillingly evil. His two sidekicks looked like they were giving him his last pep talk. That wouldn't help him, no pep-talk was going to stop me fucking him up and sending him in a taxi to the morgue.

I took my eyes off his and turned my back on him to give myself a final word, as I pondered the memory of my recently dead mate.

It went quiet as a morgue, like they were waiting for the start of a hundred metre race. Everybody knew what they were about to witness, they knew history in the underworld was about to happen. I briefly felt a shiver up my spine and the strangest feeling like I'd been here before. Or, was this my destiny?

A shout of a minute to go. This was it. The time had come to dethrone this cunt and separate his head from his body. My heart beating like a mad man. The adrenaline kicked into overdrive. The blood pumping through my veins. The fear racing through me, making my breath heavier in anger and in anticipation of the first exchange of fists.

Tim, one of a few friends I had left that didn't fear me, turned and fixed his stare on me. "You fucking ready for this, Joe?"

"Born ready, friend."

"Last-man-standing, no fucking mercy, or you'll be a dead man."

"There will be none!" I replied with no sign of remorse in my voice.

"No guts! No glory!" Tim shouted.

"Let's get the show on the road." The so-called ref between me and The Reaper shouted.

Tim took a step back, still looking me in the eye with terrible anxiety written all over his face, as if this could be the last time we exchange words.

I turned around, started to walk towards The Reaper, leaving all doubt behind, ready to fight for everything. The Reaper locked eyes with me, both

watching each other like a couple of wounded warriors.
We met in the middle.

Chapter 65

The Reaper:

There wasn't the usual facing-out process. His Goliath frame towered over me, his weight around 115kg. His hands hovered under his chin like bare-knuckle boxers do, left hand lower and hung out. Standing square-on wasn't the best boxing tactic, but his size more than made up for it, and he knew his deadly trade. His biceps bulged as his arms squashed together.

No bobbing up and down on his toes, he just plodded his hulking frame around, casting his shadow over me. Leaning most of his weight over his front foot, a left-jab from his bare knuckles struck my jaw. Taking it without flinching, I replied with my own jab that he parried down with his left, exposing my face to his right hand counter, with his twisted knuckle protruding down, planting one on the top of my lips.

The fear was gripping a hold of me more than ever, admitting to myself I was apprehensive for the first time in this game.

Shaking the last attack off, he shadowed my evasive movements, patient and obviously loving every second of hunting me down. It's what he lived for, that bullish nature made losing not an option for him.

I moved around on the balls of my feet, racking my brain to devise a strategy to overcome this brute.

With the next opportunity, I threw a four-punch combo, ending in a left-hook flashing across his face. He felt it for sure, as I returned to the back foot. Fear still gripping me, not willing to stand toe-to-toe.

He came back in seconds, closed the gap, cutting off my movement, forcing me back against a concrete pillar. Without hesitation, his shovel-like left hand pinned my forehead to the concrete, elbowing me across the face in a hook-like style.

With nowhere to go but down, the first round was over.

Rising with a stunned look, I could hear the sick, baying crowd cheer at the first sight of my destruction.

The Reaper waited in the middle.

"What the fuck was that?" Tim removed my gum-shield and handed me some water. "Fuck sake man, get under his skin, rough him up, punch him in the fuckin' throat, use your brain, and don't play his game. Make your own rules." He was right, I had to change the rules, fight my own fight.

"Time, gentlemen."

The glare of the floodlights set up at height around the room, shone down on his vast shoulder caps, making the daunting task of facing fists harder. He only knew how to take a man apart, that was his life, whatever he went through as a child made him this way.

Soon as I walked out he was on my case, dropping me made him envisage the end closer than expected.

Starting the next round with more ferocity, he now had his business-head on. Approached me with more purpose, letting punches fly across my eye-line. Trying to grab me at any opportunity to restrict my shuffling around. Using my upper-body to bob and weave into empty space, where I could avoid his fists, hearing him hiss in annoyance and disgust as I refused to play his game.

After a few minutes of this, I needed to keep The Reaper thinking. Remembering Tim's words, not to fight his fight.

While shuffling around the dusty ground, I decided to keep him confused, change tactics. Planting my feet in front of his towering frame, I let the punches go, head and body in coordination, knuckle clattering against his heavily-muscled torso, fists rebounding from the bone of his chin, as he took impact after impact.

We stood together exchanging heavy combos. It was no use for me, he reverted to his dirty tactics. Push-kicking me in my guts, catapulting me back three metres.

Aggravated, I waited for him to approach with his next move. In the middle of the floor, we came to blows again. Now square-on, the frustration starting to build. A punch flew toward my nose, I jerked back my head, avoiding the connection by a hairline, whiplashed a head-butt onto his chin, skull to bone, and it stunned him. A rapid low-kick behind his knee made him dip, followed by a right-hook across his chin that made his knee buckle.

Round over. I returned to Tim leaving The Reaper groveling on the floor. The air of shock whispered through the basement. Once again he rose and stood under the light.

"That's fuckin' better, now you're awake! He's going to be pissed off now." He was right, I had to bend or break the rules.

Jack Gallagher sat still, cocksure, legs crossed, admiring his man in action. Mr Dean looked on coolly, like he knew something Gallagher didn't.

"Time."

My enraged state replaced some of the fear. Reaper was human, after all. His eyes had the same narrow squint, seeming like he didn't have emotions, didn't suffer pain. His workmanlike style came plodding across, before I got two metres away from Tim.

Straight away, heated blows were exchanged. Aiming punches at his head, popping my knuckles off his forehead and jaw, while keeping my body compact to avoid his assault, looking for that goodnight punch.

A brief pause found me with Reaper's hands clenching my traps, his knee dug four rapid thuds into my gut, and then he tossed me to the ground like a rag-doll. Winded, I gasped for breath, sprung to my feet, wary of his ground-attack and returned to my man Tim. This man had no concept of a fair fight.

"Fuck me Joe! Don't stand still man, don't give him a fuckin' inch, mate." His finger tapped my forehead, hard.

The next round started as quick as the last

Coming to blows again right in front of Mr Dean, in the middle of the room. Reaper's hands the size of slabs of steaks, my head an easy target. Following each other's combos around the floor. Breathing heavier, I struggled to deal with his size and constant pressure.

Standard left-jab, then his right hand thudded into my eye-sockets, temporarily blinding me. A blow to my left rib, sickening me, my head dipped to hip level, the last place I needed to be with this killer looming over me. Wildly throwing a downward hook across my temple, his four knuckles like a hammer blow, temporarily losing the use of my legs, hitting the floor, rapidly rolling across the dirt ridden ground, my body collecting pieces of stone and dirt as he kicked me with his boot.

Enraged with myself, I stood.

"Ribs?" Tim asked in concern.

I nodded my head, signaling for water. My mouth dried up, the pace of the battle draining.

"You can have this cunt, you've dropped him once, do it again." Filled with a fresh determination, I returned to eyeball the beast as he stood waiting for me, the same impassive stare.

"Time, gentlemen."

My temper began to unravel, I wanted this cunt decapitated in the quickest way possible. Now we both had the same brutal mind-set.

Approaching him with my hands down, he threw the same, vicious stiff jab. Me slipping it, then coiling a right-hook across his head, switched my left leg across the front of his body, thudding an uppercut into the base of his chin, pinging his head into the air, then sunk my knuckles into his lips, tearing them open.

The first flow of blood. I didn't stop there, clenching my fist tight, a left then a right-hook slammed across his jaw, loud slaps rebounded through the room as I made contact. He was hurt, I now had to punish him before he recovered.

Stunned, a full-power, low kick bent his knee, bringing his head down level. I head-butted him again, this time into his teeth, then stabbed my knee into his solar plexus. Slumped to the floor, it should have meant the round was over.

Taking a deep gasp of air made him choke, spitting out a mixture of blood and teeth at my feet. Lifting his Barbarian head up to me, a new found fury lurked in his eyeballs.

The hesitation of glaring at his collection of broken teeth, could've been spent pounding his face in. Re-screwing my boxing brain on, swinging my right-hook from my ear, The Reaper knew what was on the way, ducking under, evading my hook and using his right leg to stand. Three right hands rebounded off my nose, falling over onto my forearm, then kicked in the ribs by his size fourteen boot.

Looking up at his black shorts, muscle sculpted around his calves and thighs, I felt like a midget. He hacked up the blood in his airways, then spat it over my body, bringing with it fragments of teeth.

Standing over me, he sneered in disrespect as if I was nobody. The Reaper took his usual stance in the middle, leaking from his lips and mouth. The crowd exchanging bets on each round, noise reaching a crescendo as they cheered The Reaper. He didn't care, though.

"Time."

My face ached with bone-to-bone impact, stomach and ribs in agony, the reality of the fight taking hold of me, rather than the adrenaline. The 'roids were helping, flooding my muscles with the blood and needed rage. The Reaper, full of the same drug, knew how much men like us needed it.

He wouldn't stop until I was dead, or he could no longer breathe, simple as that. My face oozed with pent-up fury. Blood from our lips ran down our chins, eyes bruised and bodies drenched in sweat. Tim rehydrating me, while I burned stares across the room, showing I wasn't to be intimidated.

By the time the next round started, I was in the place I needed to be. The place that feels no pain, the place where demons lie, awaiting their wakening. I could now blank the crowd, tunnel-vision like, I had to show this cunt who the real beast was.

He waited for me on his spot, this time head-first into the assault, but I was gathering anger, fueled by thoughts in putting this fucker down.

Sticking my head in front of him, mauling punches from side-to-side on his face, the thud of each impact reverberating up my arms. Then, it happened. For the first time, I saw his body language change. A look dawned of frustration. That was a turning-point.

After pounding on his head, I bolted body-shots into his ribs, all my body-weight twisting into each strike, howling in blind rage from the depths of my soul with each blow. Dipping his weight down with the force of my attack, leaning into my body to stop the onslaught.

Stepping back willingly, his weight falling, pouncing a right uppercut into his already fat, burst lip. An unrelenting thirty second surge of savageness. Filled with fury, my heart beating fast with the impact of a church bell, the cold night forgotten, as the sweat ran off my hair, merging with my own flow of blood.

Looking shaken, continuing my assault, a massive right-hook ricocheted against his chin. This was it. Swaying from his shoulders down, I saw my opportunity. Using my left hand to hold the back of his monstrous traps, gripping tight, stabbing the pointed knuckles of my right hand into his windpipe.

Collapsing onto both knees, he dropped to his side in panic. Holding his throat with both shovel hands, gasping for that intake of breath. With less than a minute to rise, roles reversed, I chose to stand over him, admiring my own work. Thirty seconds left, the strength flowed from his body. The alarm in his face unrecognizable.

I noticed disbelief on Gallagher's face as he rose from his seat, never having witnessed The Reaper suffer so much. Mr Dean's body language only changed as his hands came out his duffle-coat pockets. Ten seconds left to stand, the relief evident, Reaper was able to suck in air. Devastated, he raised from the ground. What do I have to do to stop this monster?

"Time."

This was my chance to finish it. Still recovering, his body and brain registering the lack of oxygen. His eyes still held the look of surprise and shock. Ignoring all caution, swiftly moving back into the depths of Hell, my right hand tensed, winding up to end it. The Reaper coming to life, or maybe surviving on instinct, used the momentum of my stride to crash his fist into my face, like a wrecking-ball smashing into a building.

I could barely stand, strength drained, stuttering to the left like a drunk searching for a perch to lean on, I ended up on the ground in the shadow of the London Ghetto Gang. All senses abandoned me, crawling on the floor like a child, searching for an exit, a gate to the other side. Forty seconds passed before my vision returned, when I glimpsed Tim mouthing words, gesturing for me to stand. The Reaper came into sight then I knew, knew I had to stand. Couldn't let myself down, my Dad down. "On your feet, Joe". A shout of ten seconds from the timekeeper. Somehow my brain got a message to my legs to stand.

"Time."

Rising, I saw the colossal force of the Barbarian charge right at me. I only had instinct left, my brain unable to relay messages to my body. Still confused, almost concussed, The Reaper saw me weak again, saw his money and his glory there for the taking.

My mouth dry, legs unsettled, head battered and beaten with blood flowing from my freshly cut left eye, the next assault on the way. His every stride forward pounded in my ears, almost seeing him in slow-motion. Quietened, the audience could smell the end. Fate was about to be sealed, he suspected I was finished.

Remembering what my Father said. "You could be the best boy, but you're too weak!" Roaring in a horrific rage, The Reaper threw punches like a pinball machine. Tucking my elbows into my ribs, folding my arms over my head, I took his barrage of violence. Trying to strike anywhere he could, still grunting like an animal with every blow. With my wrists touching my temples, leaving a gap between my guard exposed, again he used his right elbow, in an upwards motion to the base of my nose, the impact cracking and crunching the cartilage and bone.

Taking a step back, I momentarily dropped my hands, seeing fragments of my nose hover under my eye, letting the blood leak into my mouth, I ran my tongue across my bottom lip. His facial features squinted, dumbfounded that what stood before him couldn't be broken like a nose. Wanting only victory, willing to die before this beast got my name on his CV.

The quiet tension in the air changed, spectators grudgingly admiring the show.

Again he came, with more bombs. I absorbed it all, tucking into my shell. It hurt making me step back, grunting when struck, winching with pain. Kicking me in the legs, pulling my head down, planting his knee into my gut. Trying to head-butt and use his elbows.

He tried it all, nothing I could do. Keeping out of the way and protected, letting him tire out. My body ached from head to toe, bleeding out and legs heavy, taking it all.

The Reaper breathed too much, sweating heavily from his activity, and warmth from the lights over-heated him. It was near. My mouth dry, I only needed time. After the constant onslaught of attack for several minutes without my response, he tired.

Mentally stunned, never having been in a duel this long, or confronted by a man willing to die before him, he arrived at his breaking-point. His building anger mixed with frustration, causing him to cease his attack, he prowled around my shell, analysing his prey like an animal in battle. Angered, dishonoured, confused, his emotions were now on show.

I had waited long enough, suffered too much pain in my life. His workman-like style now wilted. Dropping my hands, I smiled cheekily into his surprised face. Part of his lip hung to the side from my earlier blow, covered in crusty blood. His right eye burst, like his mental state.

Feinting a punch with my left hand, he flinched, leaving himself open to a storm of unreturned punishment. Still standing but weakened, his ribs and solar plexus were next. Burying my head into his chest, rattling his ribs from side-to-side, planting my feet, twisting my whole body into every punch. Kneeing into his ribs and guts, the impact breaking a couple of them in the process. I growled, I roared. He still stood. Legs begging to give way, I wasn't finished.

His busted body slumped, signaling the end was close. The sneaky fucker coiled from his right side, bringing with it a right hand, clattering it across my jaw. The power of the punch, sickening, hanging me on the edge again, and a high-pitched whine silenced my ear-drums.

Facing Gallagher and his men, dots of yellow and purple floated. My mind playing tricks, catching a glimpse of my Father of how he would look now, perched up against the wall.

The force of the punch left Reaper bent over in exhaustion. Some ten seconds passed, Reaper wrecked, on both knees. He looked up, lip hanging off the side of his mouth, eyes battered, half-closed, showing no self-pity and no beg for mercy.

Cupping his chin, gore from my nose dripping onto his cheeks, blood from his split-lip glistened under the light and flowed down my left hand. I lifted my right hand in the air, bent at the elbow and unleashed every last drop of hatred from my entire soul, delivering with only death in my mind. The beaten Barbarian's body plunged to the

326

ground, still breathing. Lifting my right boot, I stamped on his face, until the demon was dead.

Chapter 66

Remorseful:

Reaper's body still lay on the ground, covered over with a bloody coat. Sitting upright against the manky wall, Tim by my side, directly opposite the corpse. A collection of bodies still lingered in the basement. Holding the cash filled me with no joy. There was no feeling of achievement. Bringing a man to his death with my bare hands, beating him until his pulse ceased. I was remorseful, full of self-pity, the guilt of my actions. Taking a life I could never take back. Crouched up against the wall for the past hour, left me shaking uncontrollably from the impact of the event. Sitting there the realisation of what I'd turned into, sunk in. My Father, the one man I loathed to the depths of my soul, and I'd turned into him. The endless hunt for his throat and bitterness over the past spiraled out of control, turning me into the callous, horrible man. The vision of him at the end of the fight was an ironic reality.

"Tim, get me a smoke and a drink." Tim sprung up, dealing with my request. He was in shock, too. He saw this as his doing, his vision of me back in the ring. Did he regret it? I think we both did.

Reaper's body lay untouched for more than an hour. Gallagher's squad argued what to do with the corpse. No one took time to speak to me, except Tim and Bull.

Mr Dean left after a heavy argument with Gallagher. Gallagher had a piece in his coat, willing to use it. Mr Dean probably saved my life that night, reassuring Gallagher if he shot me, an all-out war between the two camps would begin. The Reaper knew the risks in this game all too well, taking the lives of two men before.

"Here's your smoke mate, lit it for you, a hip flask as well." Tim had a habit of continuing with life no matter what happened in front of him. In distress as I was, but it didn't show in his act.

"Cheers." No taste for conversation. The oval, stainless-steel hip flask full to the brim. Opening it, downing the lot, sensing every drop burn down my throat, an instant calm, it steadied my nerves.

I needed to get out of here, couldn't stay in the same room as the corpse of a man I killed. Not possible to leave, until I spoke to Mr Dean. The smoke was sucked dry, looking for that extra something to take the edge off. Agony in my body was forgotten for that hour, the fact that I just killed someone took precedence.

"We need to get out of here, can't sit here forever." Tim said.

"Can't...I've got one more thing to do."

"Like what?"

"Get Steve over here." Never informed Tim of the last matter at hand. The room now emptying, leaving only the criminals conducting the arms-deal.

Mr Dean came walking over. Feeling the need to stand to talk to him. From my bruised calves to my bruised forehead, everywhere ached as I had sat down for over an hour. "Well done Joe, well done. Pity about The Reaper." A cold response to his death, but a normal thing in his everyday life. Mr Dean got his wish, one of his men ended the reign of The Reaper

I thought about responding to his comment about the Reaper, but coldly as it sounds, I had other things on my mind. "Midnight? Where?" I had no time to mess around.

"Inside the fabrication shed." Mr Dean replied.

"And you'll be there? You need to give me that piece."

"Aye, I'll be there. I left it under Tim's passenger seat." Once again Tim looking confused about what we were talking about. Mr Dean walked away, I'd see him later.

"OK, what's going on now?" Getting annoyed I was holding something from him.

"Nothing you need to know. When this deal's going down, wait in the car, alright?"

"Why?"

"Don't ask questions Tim, just wait in the fuckin' car." Telling by the firmness of my voice I was deadly serious, he complied.

"Aye, alright 'en. I'll wait in the car when the time comes." He looked miffed, but I couldn't tell him anything for his own safety.

"Right, I'm heading out for some air."

Walking out the alcove archway, Tim spoke. "There's drink in the boot, mate." The long aching walk up the tunnel made me contemplate what I was prepared to do next. The pain in my body felt like I'd been in a head on collision with a tank.

Chapter 67

The Eidolon:

Steve Dean, Lukas, Bobby Munroe, The Govan Gang and six members of the London Ghetto Gang and myself all waited patiently in the open space of the dimly-lit fabrication-shed for The Eidolon and his weapons.

They were known for their punctuality and precision when conducting deals, there was little doubt The Eidolon and his stable would be a no-show. I glanced at my phone, seven missed calls and three unreturned text messages from Magill. The Eidolon's appearances at exchanges were scarce, but his presence was expected this evening. The meeting set up by Jack Gallagher who was still attending to the corpse. I stood behind Bobby Munroe, a short, fat, ruthless bastard from Glasgow. Been causing trouble since he was able to walk. In the game for the simple fact he loved to break rules, cause hardship and kill people for fun. A complete psycho who couldn't be argued with. Years of psychological damage, there was no hope for him. Looking at him, and hearing the stories, was enough to send me further to changing my ways. I didn't want to end up like him, and there was every possibility I could.

The only man here that would interrupt my plan.

A vehicle approaching. Bobby Munroe, opened the wide roller-door, lifting it just high enough for the Sprinter van to reverse in, closing the door behind him.

The driver reversed ten metres into the shed, switched off the ignition, and then killed the lights. The front of the van sat in the dark, too hard to see the men inside. The gathering of crooks stepped round to the rear of the rusty van, awaiting the back doors to be opened. Situated behind the pack, just to the right, looking onto the driver's door, waiting for a body to a step out.

Sliding the front of my t-shirt up, grabbing my Glock 35 pistol. The anticipation of pulling the trigger, sent my legs into a trauma-like shake. Mr Dean kept an eye on me, one of two men aware of my plan. Flicking the safety off as I slid it out, hiding it behind my back, one step closer.

My face pure white and nose looking like someone walking off a battle-ground, hardly able to stand on my own feet. My body ached from the impact of The Reaper's wrath, but I had to, this was my chance.

Only seconds away from witnessing the sight of my Father, sat inside the van, The Eidolon, my finger ready to send a bullet into his brain. The van-doors opened simultaneously, two men stepped out into the poorly-lit area. The light shone brighter behind the van. The driver stepped out, dressed all in black with a shoulder patched jumper and combat trousers, a full-face balaclava on, too short to be Dad, must be the passenger.

Rounding the pack of men for a better view of the passenger arriving at the rear. My hand took a tighter the grip of the Glock, prepared to pull the trigger. Wearing a balaclava as well, it wasn't him. Again, too short. Disappointment swirled through my head. I was told by Mr Dean he would be here. Still, the back doors hadn't been opened, he could be inside with the shipment. I prepared myself for the bullet again.

Mr Dean keeping a close eye on me, as loyal to me as I was to him, he was prepared to back me up if need be. The passenger and driver blocked the view inside the van after opening the doors. They moved to the side, the hand behind my back came round to my hip. Only the custom-built crates of arms lay in the back stacked two high, three back. The gun retracted, then slide down my back, out of view. I was devastated, I was informed that he'd be here. The longing, the desperation I had to kill the bastard wouldn't be fulfilled.

The intensity of the situation made even Mr Dean take a deep breath of relief. The plan we discussed was for me to fire the gun, with him and Lukas on standby, to counteract any responses made by The Stable, or Bobby Munroe. Once killing him, I had no idea what the next move would be. The aching longing to end his life, outplayed anything else.

The deal went through without problems, and I stood, watching closely. Guns unloaded and cash exchanged. The men spoke with a deep Irish tongue. Making any kind of approach for information regarding The Eidolon stupid and suicidal.

Desperate but not foolish, if able to escape the shed with my life, they'd find me and then kill, without hesitation. By this time, The Reaper's body was carried out the tunnel by Jack Gallagher, his son and two other men. Exhausted with carrying the colossal carcass, they dropped him as they entered the shed from the electrical mains room.

This caught the attention of The Stable, who were preparing to enter the van and leave.

The driver opened the van door, heard the commotion and a loud thud from the north-west corner, paused, ambled ten metres away from the van, the passenger joined him. Once they saw the body, standing side-by-side, they turned to each other through their balaclava eyeholes for a few seconds, as if they knew who it was. Uttering no words, turning around entering the van again, they were off. Bobby opened the door and away they went.

Chapter 68

Lukas:

Mike Jenkins, Roy the Rover and the truck driver's fate were sealed in the following two weeks. Lukas, Mr Dean's loyal employee, spent his previous life in a special unit of the Hungarian Police, where you need the same unforgiving ruthlessness as the men he hunted. His last years specialising in taking down the worst possible criminals, those involved with the trafficking of young women, forced into the sex-trade, and his biggest hate, paedophiles. The repulsive images he witnessed, left a permanent scar. He personally carried out the killing of each man, complying with Mr Dean's requests.

The first to meet his unforeseen death, was the truck driver. A wife and family of four, he was prepared to abandon them all for the sun of the Costa del Sol. After getting placed on the paedophile register, outcast by his family and sacked from his job. Left homeless, skint and marked out as kiddie-fiddler, you'd think that was punishment enough.

Flying to Northern Ireland, Lukas shadowed him one day, the man totally oblivious to his presence, until he joined him at a bar for a few drinks later on at night. Mr Dean asked for his death to be quick, by bullet. Being outcast by his friends and neighbours in Belfast, he turned to drink.

Pulling up a stool at the bar, Lukas took it upon himself to accompany the man for the evening, giving him hope he found a new friend. They drank all night, sharing stories of whatever. Closing time, leaving together, Lukas offering to give the man a bed for a night in his fictional flat. Relieving his bladder full of Guinness behind one of those big recycle bins. Lukas pulled out his Makarov 9mm pistol, a gun given to him by his Father before he entered the force, and his preferred weapon for killing. Screwing the silencer on, waiting for his victim to turn round.

Fixing up his buttons, lifting his drunk head, Lukas placed a bullet through the centre of the truck-driver's forehead.

The second to meet his end, stoner Roy the Rover. He knew he couldn't stay in east Belfast. Stoned but not stupid, he fled to Cork, Southern Ireland. Taking up residence in a seedy B&B. Taking three days to track him down, Mr Dean requested his death to be one of slight struggle. The Rover left the solitude of his room every morning 9am precisely, buying the daily paper. Returning to his room that day, a Hungarian hitman waited, lying on his bed, the Makarov 9mm pointed at the door. The Rover strolled in, laid-back as ever, reading the back page at the same time, he walked into his room unaware of the Hungarian's presence. The momentary feeling of 'This can't be happening to me, I got away' went sailing through his stoned skull.

The silencer wasn't attached, so he had no intention of shooting The Rover at that moment, unless he felt it necessary.

"Hello Mr Rover, I think you will never come." His English lacked the odd word.

"What the fuck?" The Rover looked round the room for an exit, he had nowhere to hide.

"Stay quiet, do what I say, and you live, OK?"

"OK…OK." Instructing the man to sit on the bed and attach a handcuff to each limb. He obliged, the gun still pointed in his direction. Handcuffing his limbs round the corners of the bed, then filling his gob with scrunched up duct-tape and then a slice over his mouth. He was now helpless and in the hands of death.

Because he got greedy, and tried to dip his hands into Mr Dean's pockets, Lukas had a special torture device for him. A ratchet cable-cutter usually used in the electrical trade. Two round, thick blades of this device closed together creating a gate, then ratcheted together till they met.

Placing the round gate of the cable-cutter around two of his fingers until a tight grip squashed his fingers together. Lukas began to ratchet gently, so Rover felt the most pain. Slicing through his skin before the initial crunch of the bone was meet with a silenced howl. The slow grinding of the bone as it cracked like a slow bite of a brazil-nut brought a rare, pleasant smile to Lukas. He counted the motions to The Rover like a primary pupil. Fifteen more ratchets before he had to stretch the device away from the skin like a melted piece of cheese, two unattached fingers lay on the reddened white sheets.

His call for mercy could not be heard, his screams muffled inside his mouth. The rest of the digits were removed in the same brutal manner, awake through it all, gave Lukas a tingle of respect for the man. The ten fingers lay on the bed. Blood went from gushing out, spraying around the room, to trickling out onto the sheets. Rover choked on his vomit. His arms were able to slip out the handcuffs as he sat upright, in complete panic. Terrified tears and groans like a wounded animal that needed put down came out his mouth. He flapped his fingerless hands in the air and tried to remove the restraints from his legs, his brain in shock, not registering that his fingers were no longer there. On top of his pain, came a splatter over the head from the butt of Lukas's pistol.

Lukas set the timer on his phone for an hour, read The Rover's paper, then shot him through the forehead with his silencer attached.

Mike Jenkins never returned to Aberdeen, instead taking his flight to Costa del Sol. His death was the choice of Mr Dean. Taking Lukas more than a week to track the grumpy bastard down, only added to his fulfilment.

Mike hired a lovely holiday-home under the plain name of John Smith. How Lukas managed to track him down was a mystery, but that was his specialty. Booking under such an ordinary name probably gave the game away, too obvious. Stalking him for a couple days, following his daily routine. Never off the phone, fearful of his predicament. Attempting to sell his belongings, car and house to gather funds for his new life.

His choice of cocktail, a tall glass of Planter's Punch. Consisting of dark rum, lime and lemon, grenadine syrup with a couple of local herbs resembling small leaves. Late Thursday afternoon, waited-on by a young local man from his beach sun-lounger, his delivery of the cocktail was a tap on the shoulder, then his hand grabbing the glass without so much as a thank you.

Lukas was unrecognisable to Mike wearing surfer-shorts, a weight-lifter's vest, shades and a Summery straw hat. Staying inside the beach-bar out of the sight of the heavy-set, arrogant man.

Inside his pocket, a selection of leaves from Gelsemium Elegans. Known to Russian and Chinese contract killers as 'heartbreak grass', inflicting a painfully slow death, if combined in the appropriate amount. Mike called the waiter, asking for another beverage. Lukas took it upon himself to have a Planter's Punch standing by, replacing the local herb with his own special ingredient. With the coolest of confidence, strolled to the beach, tapped Mike on the shoulder, his right arm stretched over his left shoulder, grabbing the glass, gulping greedily.

Not so much of a word was muttered as Lukas returned to his seat to admire his work. There are five stages that flood your body.

The first stage landed after ten minutes, Lukas watched and laughed at his misfortune. Mike was disorientated, his head shifted around looking lost as he rolled off his seat. Dizziness was the first stage.

Rolling around on the sand, clutching his guts for a few minutes, before leaning over his lounger and started vomiting uncontrollably over his seat. Lukas was enjoying the act and his own Planter's Punch cocktail from the comfort of the bar. Nausea was the second stage.

Some tourists tried to aid Mike and called for an ambulance. The constant vomit eased and then his body started contracting in timed formations of every twenty seconds like electric shocks, leaving him mimicking a zombie. Convulsions are the third stage.

There was no pill, no medication or miracles that could stop the process. After an hour, at this stage, inside the hospital, the poison shows its intended effects. Paralysis of the spinal cord and a loss of muscular function keeping you alive for some time, before asphyxia robs you of breath, resulting in choking to death.

Mike suffered immense pain for three hours.

I had one more favour to ask of Mr Dean, which meant I still owed him and I hoped it never had to be re-paid. In the small town of Turriff, thirty seven miles from Aberdeen. Harry 'Ball Point' Duncan took residence in The Royal Oak, a friendly bar where everyone knew everybody. The police had no leads to who left Micky with a knife in his back, which suited me. That meant he could be dealt with by my own wishes. Harry had taken a short-term labouring job with a loft-insulating firm, local to Turriff. Every night he chugged pints in the bar before returning to his room. Lukas, also an IT wizard, had gained access through a side-door leading to the upstairs rooms. A computer-virus was downloaded onto the computer, erasing the recording of his approach. In Harry's room, Lukas waited behind a door from a built-in wardrobe, a hammer gripped at the bottom of the shaft. Chubby Harry stuttered into the room, stripped down to his birthday-suit and climbed into bed. Lukas waited to hear the snores before jumping on the bed and used the ball-point of the hammer to leave an indented hole in his temple.

The murder of Harry 'Ball Point' was carried out to my request.

Chapter 69

Fate:

Returning to normal existence was so difficult. The torture of my life over that time, will forever cast an unwelcome shadow and define the man I'd become. The reason why I had to complete my journey, was to find the man that ruined my life, the so called Eidolon. My Father.

Ever since Magill informed me about his new address inside the interview room, I took notice, willing to do whatever necessary to come within his sight. A phantom who couldn't be found. Since leaving Aberdeen, he became number one on the wanted list by the Scotland Yard, MI5 and G2. Lived off the grid, away from civilisation. The address I sent Magill on the evening of the fight, was the venue in Dundee.

He had a massive riot-squad on standby, while he got a chopper escort from London. Needless to say, he was rather pissed-off after realising I'd played him.

When informing Mr Dean in our meeting that Davie Rhodes was The Eidolon, he was only too happy to help with his capture. Having previous history with The Stable who disfigured him, he felt it fitting he should help me. Now, having to face the reality my Father would never be found, I only had to get on with life.

I'd killed a man and prepared to kill another on the same night. My face had become unrecognizable in the mirror. Afraid of the reflection that gazed back at me, afraid of the company of my own kids. Terrified of their vision of me. Was it the same as I thought about my Father at that age?

It's a funny thing, life. Has a habit of repeating itself. If your childhood was spent growing up in front of junkies or drunks, there's a good chance it'll be passed down to the next generation. In my case, growing up with a beast turned me into one. The reality is, no matter what route through life I'd choose, I was always destined to walk my Father's path. Doesn't matter if it happened now or in twenty years, the end-result would be the same. We shared the same blood and with it the same demons. I had to change the path, lay a new one for my kids.

Spending the following months making amends with May, hiring a lawyer, countless letters were exchanged for eight months. Trying to convince her I'd become a reformed character, but May knew what lurked beneath the surface, lingered around for the next outburst.

After all I'd done to keep her away from the A&E and nursing, she returned to a role in the cancer unit in Aberdeen. Her Mother took the role as childminder.

Eventually, time earned me enough respect to be blessed with my kid's company on weekends. Wasn't until eight long, agonising months I'd get the sight of my two children, Jess and Joe Marks, Junior. The happiest I'd been for as long as I can remember. Overrun by pent-up emotion and heartache, tears streamed down my face, cuddling both of them with all the love I held.

After putting them through a rollercoaster of mental damage, I'd promised no more pain in their lives. They needed a decent upbringing to end this recurring nightmare in our family.

The regret at my family's suffering, added to the regret I had for Mom's suicide, and Micky's murder. Nevertheless, I got on with things as you have to in life. Using the blood-money, I paid off all outstanding debts on the house and moved back in.

Three months before, without my knowledge, May moved out, accepting a temporary home in Stonehaven. Despite how much love I had for Katie, I broke all contact. Even though the sight of her lovely face forever swirled around in my imagination, I had to break her loose. Couldn't let her get involved with me, because that man will always lurk beneath. After all, she was a good person at heart, she didn't deserve a beast like me. I would always think about her and the life I could have had with her.

Me and Tim did what we said, got out the game, entering a partnership together, working in the scrap trade, combined with house-removals. Work was tough going at times, the money decent and the hours were flexible. It suited us both.

Two years later, past my mid-thirties, all relationships were healed. Choosing to stay off the booze, scared of what might happen once the nectar hit my lips. But, I had a heavy smoking habit of twenty a day.

Boxing was put behind, never to surface, or so I thought. The gym equipment in my garage sold-off and replaced with a five-door family saloon, finally gaining my licence legally.

One Sunday afternoon, the back-garden filled with Dawn, Tim, their twin boys, Margaret, my kids and me. The barbeque smoked while we exchanged stories and laughed while playing with the kids. Me and Tim shared our own story, although most days we wished it could be forgotten. Managing to accept a lot of my past by now, moving on, being genuinely happy for the first time in years. Able to wake with a smile and sleep with a weightless conscience.

"Joe, there's somebody at the door." Dawn yelled out the kitchen window as she washed some dishes in the sink.

"Aye, I'll get it." Who the fuck was coming round at this time on a Sunday? Maybe it was May. Closing the kitchen door, I took a look out the living-room window, seeing a tall man stand with his back to me, hands by his side and a comb edging out his back pocket. A long, grey ponytail in a bobble hanging down the back of his vintage, denim jacket. Who the fuck is this? Opening the door, an arm flew in, gripping my neck, along with a couple of clunky steps inside my house, forcing me back.

"Alright, boy?" It couldn't be? His big-boned, wrinkled, callous face right in front of me, for the first time in fifteen years. That same effect on me again: fear. That same impassive look of pure evil. Stood up on my tip-toes, my back up against the bannister.

The blood-vessels in my eyes burned, face turned bright purple. Attempting to scream out for Tim's help, only made his hold tighter. My desperation causing my hands to grab his wrist was pointless. "What's wrong, nothing to say?" He tipped his head sideways in a sarcastic motion. Playing with me, as he always had. My inner rage longed to be realised, I'd waited all these years for a glimpse, and now couldn't mutter a word, leaving me gargling as I struggled to speak.

"Whcht' I fukkc' you doooin' here?" Managed to mutter out a question.

"Came to say hello, son!" How fucking dare he call me his son. Struggling with his grip, longing for release, so I could inflict my revenge.

"Seen your last fight, boy." I immediately took notice, stopped struggling.

"What?" He loosened his hold, just enough for me to speak.

"I was there, watching." The glimpse of my Father in the basement that spurred me to finish off The Reaper, had been real.

"Fuckin' prick." His hold on me was impossible to get out of.

"That's no way to speak to your old man! I never got the chance to tell you about your brother?"

"Who?"

"He used to be a fighter, like you. We called him The Reaper."

THE END.

Published in 2015 by FeedARead.com Publishing

A CIP catalogue record for this title is available from the British Library.